He traced the curve of her jaw with his finger

"Claire..." Lucas's voice was barely above a whisper.

But Claire couldn't bring herself to look at him. She wasn't ready for this. He was so...present... in the way his energy wrapped around her, in the way his body seemed solid and real, in the way he focused completely on her and her alone, as if no one else existed.

She shook her head, but couldn't complete a sentence in her mind, let alone form one with her mouth. Her lips lived with the memory of the feel of his lips caressing hers. She should just turn away, but instead her hand somehow found its way to his chest. His heart beat at her fingertips....

Dear Reader,

I'm delighted to announce exciting news: beginning in January 2013, Harlequin Superromance books will be longer! That means more romance with more of the characters you love and expect from Harlequin Superromance.

We'll also be unveiling a brand-new look for our covers. These fresh, beautiful covers will showcase the six wonderful contemporary stories we publish each month. Turn to the back of this book for a sneak peek.

So don't miss out on your favorite series—Harlequin Superromance. Look for longer stories and exciting new covers starting December 18, 2012, wherever you buy books.

In the meantime, check out this month's reads:

#1818 THE SPIRIT OF CHRISTMAS
Liz Talley

#1819 THE TIME OF HER LIFE
Jeanie London

#1820 THE LONG WAY HOME

Cathryn Parry

#1821 CROSSING NEVADA

Jeannie Watt

#1822 WISH UPON A CHRISTMAS STAR

Darlene Gardner

#1823 ESPRESSO IN THE MORNING

Dorie Graham

Happy reading!

Wanda Ottewell,

Senior Editor, Harlequin Superromance

Espresso in the Morning

DORIE GRAHAM

ISBN-13: 978-0-373-60747-1

ESPRESSO IN THE MORNING

This edition published by arrangement with Harlequin Books S.A.

For questions and comments about the quality of this book, please contact us at CustomerService@Harlequin.com.

www.Harlequin.com

Printed in U.S.A.

ABOUT THE AUTHOR

Dorie was initially struck by the writing muse at the tender age of nine, when she stayed up past her bedtime for the first time ever to finish a short story. That attempt resulted in her teacher reading her work aloud to the class, then submitting her story to *Highlights* magazine. Unfortunately, Dorie took the magazine's request to shorten the story as a flat rejection.

Over the years she followed the muse from time to time, but didn't get serious about writing until after the birth of her third child. Even then it took about five years of juggling husband, children, nonprofit work and her writing before she finally mastered the art of rejection and landed her first sale in September 2001.

Currently she resides in Roswell, Georgia, a suburb of metro Atlanta, with her two supportive daughters. A full-time working, single mom, she spends her free time hanging with her daughters and friends, watching movies, running and of course writing. You can stop by and visit her at www.doriegraham.com.

Books by Dorie Graham

HARLEQUIN BLAZE

39—THE LAST VIRGIN
58—TEMPTING ADAM
130—EYE CANDY
196—THE MORNING AFTER
202—SO MANY MEN...
208—FAKING IT

Other titles by this author available in ebook format.

To all those souls suffering with PTSD and the ones who've conquered it, your strength and courage are an inspiration to so many of us.

To my dear friend who opened my eyes to how a soul can keep going, no matter how weary, and still bring happiness to others, know that you will always hold a special place in my heart.

A special thanks to Berta Platas, Michelle Roper, Sandra Chastain, Nancy Knight and Haywood Smith for helping me brainstorm this story way back before it became a romance.

CHAPTER ONE

THE TV WEATHERMAN'S smooth, loud tones predicted rain for metropolitan Atlanta, while the computer speakers in the home office blared Iron Maiden and the old DVD player in the kitchen cranked Judas Priest. Claire Murphy pounded again on her ten-year-old son's door. The ever-present thudding of her heart sounded in her ears.

They had to leave.

"Grey, honey, step it up. We're out of here in twenty minutes," she said.

Shuffling sounded through the door, along with a couple of muffled expletives. Claire frowned. "I heard that, mister."

The door cracked open and Grey peered at her, his auburn hair sticking out at odd angles. Dark circles ringed his eyes. "I'm up."

Concern quickened Claire's pulse. She lifted his chin. "Honey, you look exhausted. Didn't you sleep well?"

He rolled his sweet brown eyes. "*You* didn't sleep well."

She'd tried, but the night had pressed in around

her. She hated that her troubles had such an effect on Grey. She shook her head, fighting the chronic fatigue she'd learned to live with over the past year. She could never explain to him how sleeping only made her feel smothered.

And gave her nightmares. She didn't always remember the specifics, but the terror often clung to her well into her waking hours. The nightmares made living without sleep a welcome alternative.

"I'm so sorry," she said.

"I don't get why you have to always crank your music. Even with your earphones on, I can tell it's cranked. How can you do that? *Normal* people sleep in the middle of the night."

"Well, normal's overrated." She ruffled his hair. "You'd better get in the shower. You're a mess."

"Mom?" He stepped out of his room, looking so grown-up in his too-small pajamas.

Her gaze fell on a wrinkled image of Abe Lincoln on his left knee. Various presidents dotted the rest of the fabric and Grey could not only name each one, but he could also recite each man's years in office, as well as highest accomplishments. They'd bought those pajamas on their trip to D.C. almost two years ago, but Grey refused to give them up, even though the sleeves and legs were now far too short. He'd been so thrilled to see the capital, they'd spent an entire day on the Mount Vernon estate alone.

"Mom?" he asked again.

Her gaze met his and her throat tightened. The

worry in his eyes these days was just one part of what haunted her sleepless nights. He was too young to bear the weight of that concern. "What is it, little man?"

He sighed in frustration over the pet name, but his expression didn't change. "Why can't you sleep?"

She waved her hand in dismissal, her gaze dropping. Why couldn't he remain an innocent child, unconcerned for her welfare? "I sleep. Besides, sleep is overrated."

"No, it isn't." Anger replaced the worry. "That's what you say about everything you don't want to talk about."

Claire tamped down her own frustration. She had to give him his anger. She'd be angry, too, in his position. She gave him her sternest mom frown. "Are you going to get into the shower?"

He shook his head, but said, "I'm going." He shuffled a few steps toward the bathroom, before turning to her. "You think I look bad this morning, you should check out a mirror."

She groaned silently. Grey could be brutally honest. She loved that and hated it about him. "I'll take your word for it. Hurry up. I need my espresso. And don't forget to keep the curtain in the tub and point the showerhead away from that spot I showed you, where the caulk is peeling."

"If we stuck around home more, maybe we could fix stuff like that."

"Maybe I'll get some caulk and we'll fix it this

weekend," she said, though the thought of hanging around the house sent a shiver through her.

His only response was another shake of his head as he continued toward the bathroom, his shoulders stooped as if he carried the weight of the world. Claire pressed her lips together as her unease spiked into fear.

Had she bolted the door last night?

Though she clearly remembered turning the bolt, she hurried to check, to twist the knob to be sure the door held fast. She pulled aside the curtain in one of the long windows bordering the heavy door. A cat lounged on the hood of her neighbor's car. Claire scanned the cars in the other driveways, her stomach tight with anticipation, though nothing seemed out of place. A door slammed up the street and she heard the muffled sound of an engine roaring to life.

She inhaled slowly, trying to stem the racing of her heart as she hurried to the back door to check that bolt, as well. Satisfied that dead bolt remained drawn, she paused to pick up one of the cabinet drawer fronts that had fallen off in the night. The builders of this house hadn't cared for quality when they'd installed the wooden fronts on the plastic drawers back in the early seventies

She tucked the drawer front into the gap between her refrigerator and the wall, along with the other two that had previously broken away from the cracking plastic. The missing fronts made her bottom cabinets resemble a child's toothless grin, with the gaping holes revealing the contents of her junk drawer, her silverware and now all her cooking utensils. Grey would have one more thing to complain about. She'd have to figure out how to repair them or work new cabinets into their budget.

As she headed to the living room to check the sliding glass doors, she grabbed her phone from her purse on the entry table. She made a quick note about shopping for new cabinets on her to-do list. Swiping her thumb along the screen, she scanned the long list of notes.

Confirm Sunday with Becca.
Add oil.
Call car place about noise.
Research winter break programs.

She frowned as she checked the bar that secured the sliding glass doors. What did *add oil* mean? To a recipe? To the car? Her memory wasn't what it used to be. If she didn't write everything down, she'd lose half the thoughts in her head, but sometimes she couldn't interpret her own notes.

While the splash of the shower echoed in the bathroom and the music and TV blared, Claire methodically continued her check of each room, each window and each point of entry. Then she rechecked each room, behind each door, inside each closet. Not until she'd completed the circuit did she breathe a sigh of relief.

They were fine. They were safe, and that was all that mattered. She forced herself to take slow, deep breaths, silently repeating her mantra.

I am safe. I am strong. No one can hurt me.

Still, the thudding of her heart contradicted her as she turned to finish getting ready.

LUCAS WILLIAMS, OWNER of The Coffee Stop, frowned as he reviewed the employee schedule spread across his monitor and his gaze fixed on Friday's date. September twenty-eighth. Had it been two years already?

Ken, a retiree who worked most mornings, leaned through his open office door. "Do we have any more coffee sleeves?"

"I have some on order. They should come in this afternoon, but there should be one more case." He moved past the older man. "Here, I can grab them faster than I can tell you where they are."

A few moments later, as Lucas headed toward the front, box in hand, Ken spoke up. "I can take those. You've got better things to do, boss."

"I've got it." Lucas nodded toward the counter. "You've got customers."

As Ken hurried away, Lucas smiled at the kid trailing behind the petite brunette who stopped in every morning. She and her son shared the same wide brown eyes. Double-shot Americano, two pumps of vanilla, room for cream and the kid always had a banana-strawberry smoothie.

“Hey, mister,” the kid whispered and motioned Lucas over, while he glanced nervously at his mother, who was placing their order at the other end of the counter.

Lucas was curious as he set down the carton of sleeves and turned toward the boy. Curious, and a little cautious. Kids weren’t his thing. “Can I help you, little man?”

The boy scrunched his face. “I hate when my mom calls me that.”

Lucas shrugged. “Okay, how about just young man?”

“Grey,” the kid said. “That’s my name. You can call me that.”

“Grey it is. I’m Lucas. What can I get for you? Your usual smoothie?”

“How much is that?” The kid pointed to a wall display of espresso machines. “The one on the right. In the green box.”

“Ah, good choice.” Lucas reached for the machine.

“Don’t. She’ll see.” The youngster glanced again at his mother, who’d moved along to the pickup area.

She stood with her arms tightly crossed, her gaze darting over her shoulder at intervals. Ken dropped a metal filter and she jumped, hands splayed, eyes wide. Lucas had seen that look and that reaction before—in Iraq and Afghanistan, and later with Toby. He hoped this woman wasn’t like Toby, harboring some horrible trauma.

"It's a surprise." The boy drew Lucas's attention back to the espresso machine.

"You want to get that for your mom?"

"Maybe if we have one at home, we won't have to rush out every morning. Not that we don't enjoy frequenting your shop…" The boy grinned, nervously. "But maybe sometimes we could have breakfast at home, instead. Just the two of us."

His wistful tone tugged at something deep inside Lucas, called to the part of him he'd retired when he'd finished his last tour with the marines and walked from his medevac days. The boy's eyes were almost pleading, as though he were grasping at a lifeline. Lucas glanced around for a reason to excuse himself, to retreat from that haunted look in the child's eyes. It reminded him too much of himself at that age—lost and looking for an anchor.

The boy shrugged. "It's worth a shot."

"Pun intended?" Lucas grinned, though he felt anything but lighthearted.

As if September twenty-eighth wasn't enough to deal with, the thought that this poor kid believed an espresso machine would solve his troubles added to his weariness. Lucas glanced again at the kid's mom. The kid wanted more time with her, a quiet breakfast, at least. That seemed a reasonable request. What kind of mother wouldn't give her kid that? Was she a workaholic or did she suffer from some other affliction?

She looked healthy enough. Even Lucas wasn't

so dead he didn't notice the shape of her body, the tone of her muscles. The woman was physically fit, if nothing else, but that in itself could be a symptom. His buddy Toby had been fanatical about working out. After Iraq, he'd stepped up his daredevil activities, jumping from planes, scaling impossible cliffs, diving from that seventy-foot rock. He'd needed the endorphins just to feel normal.

But even that hadn't helped in the end.

Was the kid's mother just going through the motions? She spent plenty of time in Lucas's coffee shop, always on the phone or her laptop, conducting her business from the comfort of his overstuffed chairs. Something in her overly vigilant attitude made it seem she wasn't ever at ease, though.

He'd gotten to know a good many of his customers, chatting with them on a regular basis, but Grey's mom always kept to herself. No matter how involved she was with whatever she was doing, she remained on edge, contained.

No, he guessed she wasn't comfortable, at least not here. Was she uptight at home, too?

The kid cleared his throat, drawing Lucas's attention again to the espresso machines. "How much?" he asked.

"Well, that's top-of-the-line." Lucas tilted his head to the left, indicating another machine. "That one isn't as pricey, but does the basics. It's eighty bucks."

"Eighty?" The boy bit his lip. "Do you have… some kind of…payment plan?"

"Not really, but I know the owner. I think we can work something out, probably even get you a discount," Lucas said. Though why he felt compelled to help the kid, he didn't know.

"Really?" Relief filled those brown eyes.

"Grey?" The kid's mother moved toward them, espresso and smoothie in hand. Her gaze skimmed over Lucas, than quickly away. "We've got to go, honey."

"Okay." Grey took his smoothie and turned to leave with his mom, but then he ran back to Lucas. He stuck out his hand, held Lucas's gaze and kept his voice low. "We'll take care of the details next time."

Lucas hesitated for half a second as his stomach tightened over the hope in the kid's eyes. He had no business getting into some secret deal with the boy. A stupid espresso machine wasn't going to do shit to solve the kid's problems.

As the boy's mother took a nervous step toward them, Lucas shook the small hand, feeling he was committing to so much more than helping Grey surprise her for her birthday or whatever, but knowing he couldn't turn back now. "Deal."

A smile split the boy's face, sending a sense of guilt spiraling through Lucas. Why did he feel like he was promising something he couldn't deliver?

GREY SIGHED AS Paul Cooper plopped into the seat beside him later that afternoon. He'd been stoked about the espresso machine for most of the day, but Paul had a way of bringing him down.

"So, what does your dad do?" Paul paused only long enough for Grey to frown. "Mine is an attorney. He goes to court. He helps people. Does your dad help people?" Again, the breath of a pause before he continued. "I don't get to see him as much as I'd like, but he brings me really cool stuff when he visits. Last week he took me to see the Falcons. It was so cool. Where do you go with your dad?"

Paul swatted at a stray fly that had found its way into the classroom. "He's coming to see me next weekend and I get to spend the summer with him," he said. "He has a place on the beach. Do you like the beach?"

Now he stopped and stared, waiting for Grey's response. Grey stared back, his stomach tightening. He used to like the beach, but Mom said she didn't believe in vacations anymore. Too much relaxing and peace and quiet.

He shrugged, saying, "The beach is cool."

"My dad said if I wanted I could live with him at the beach all the time, but my mom said no way. It's in Tybee, which is still Georgia, but Momma says it's too far. Does your dad live with you, or are your parents divorced?" Again, the stare, while Paul waited, his eyes round.

My dad's dead.

Grey gritted his teeth. He should just say it. It wasn't true, but it could be. For all he knew his dad *had* kicked the bucket in the years since they'd last heard from him. If he told Paul his dad was dead then Paul would quit asking all these stupid questions. Grey opened his mouth, but the words refused to form.

The bell rang over the intercom, dismissing them for the day and giving Grey a welcome excuse to escape. He rose to gather his books. "It's Wednesday. My aunt's coming to get me. She freaks if I'm not up front when she pulls up."

Paul nodded and said, "Tell your dad to take you to a Falcons game. Mine let me have a hot dog and popcorn and cotton candy and this ginormous soda. My mom never lets me have that stuff."

"Yeah." Turning quickly, Grey headed for the door.

Hurrying, he reached the front of the school in record time. Aunt Becca really did freak if she had to wait. As usual, she was one of the first cars in the pickup line. He slipped into the backseat beside his cousin, Amanda, who sat in her booster seat. Aunt Becca said he wasn't big enough yet to ride up front. She'd lectured his mom on the danger of air bags lots of times, but Grey preferred sitting up front when he was in his mom's car.

"Hi, honey," Aunt Becca said and glanced at him in the rearview mirror. "How was school?"

Grey shrugged. "It was school."

"Why is it dark under your eyes? You look like

a raccoon." Amanda peered at him through circles she made of her fingers.

"Amanda, that's not nice," his aunt said. Again, she glanced at him in the mirror. "You do look tired, Grey."

Grey shrugged and sank into the seat as they pulled away from the curb. "I'm fine."

"Can we go see Daddy at his work?" Amanda asked.

"Not today, sweetie. Daddy's busy. We'll go another time."

Frowning, Amanda turned to look out her window. After a while, Grey glanced up to find her staring at him again, her eyebrows furrowed. He straightened. "What?"

"Where's *your* daddy? How come I've never seen him?"

Crap. What was it with everyone today? "I don't have a dad. He's dead."

The words came out sharper than he'd intended. Amanda's eyes widened and her lip trembled. Grey glanced at his aunt, who'd turned in her seat to see him this time. Something like pity flashed in her eyes as she quickly shifted again when the light changed.

"He's not dead," she said. "He's just not around."

"He might as well be dead. He could be and we'd never know it." Grey stared at the back of his aunt's head.

She sat stiffly. "Honey, maybe we can talk about that later."

"How come he isn't around?" Amanda sounded scared, but she shouldn't have been. Her dad wasn't going anywhere.

"I don't know. I guess he just doesn't like us." Grey couldn't keep the bitterness from his tone.

His aunt shook her head. "The man's an idiot. Sweetie, what did Miss Penny say about your counting tree today?"

"Is Daddy going away?" Amanda's voice rose anxiously.

His aunt stopped at another red light and swiveled again in the seat, addressing her daughter. "No, Daddy's staying with us," she said. "We'll call him when we get home and you can say hi."

Amanda's chin quivered, but she nodded as she settled into her booster seat. Grey stared out the window. Why didn't his father want anything to do with him?

Sidewalks, driveways and manicured lawns flashed by, all part of the great suburb of Roswell, Georgia. Grey pressed his lips together. One thing was for sure. If his dad were a part of their life now, he'd hate it as much as Grey did.

The hum of the engine soon lulled Amanda into sleep. Grey relaxed as the classical music on the radio settled peacefully over him. Aunt Becca hummed softly. This is what his mom needed.

They'd had this before—normal—no rushing from place to place, cramming every activity they could into a day. Maybe Mom had never been a fan of classical music, but she'd at least listened to less acid rock and at a lower volume. They'd enjoyed periods of quiet. If she could experience this kind of peace again, there was no way she'd ever want to go back to running nonstop.

If only he could get her to slow down for a moment. A thrill of excitement ran through him. The espresso machine should do the trick. Why hadn't he thought of it sooner? He'd surprise her with the machine on her birthday. Instead of running out every morning, they could have breakfast at home, quiet breakfasts that could set the tone for the day.

What a plan, and the coffee-shop guy—Lucas—was going to let him pay over time. He might have to snag a few more chores at his aunt's and at home, but with his allowance, he should be able to do it. He settled back in the seat, content with his plan.

"I DID LIKE you said and I've been running nonstop all week." Peg, one of Claire's kickboxing students, puffed out a tired breath later that afternoon.

"Good, and you haven't thought about the divorce?" Claire asked.

Her heart thrummed to the beat of the music in the background. She'd been looking forward to this lesson all day. She could only sit and work for so long before she craved physical activity. She'd be able to get a run in, too, later, while Grey stayed with his friend.

She'd dropped her son at school that morning, and

then returned to the coffee shop. Her day had been filled with reviewing shipping bids and pulling together contracts. She rolled her shoulders, ready to get moving.

"Well, I haven't given myself the chance." The woman laughed, the sound like a nervous hiccup.

"Claire, want me to get them started with some warm-ups?" Bill, Claire's sparring assistant, shoved his hands into protective pads.

She nodded, and then joined in. Nervous energy cranked through her. Too much caffeine and too little sleep was never a good combination, but was all she ran on most days.

Her body loosened with the repetitive movements. She'd trained long and hard for the past year, earning her black belt in record time. Now, she taught kickboxing two days a week on top of her day job, while Grey had soccer practice after school, or went to her sister's.

After the warm-ups, Claire nodded to Peg. "Ready for some sparring?"

The group fell back slightly as Bill motioned Peg forward and the two circled each other. The rest paired off and followed suit, while Claire moved among them, correcting a stance here, giving a quick demonstration there.

Claire stopped beside Bill and Peg. Again, a nervous laugh escaped the woman. Peg threw a few punches, striking the big pads protecting Bill's hands and forearms.

"That's good, Peg, but you're holding back," Claire said. "Loosen up. Try some kicks. Remember to bring your knee up and twist from the hip."

The next few punches struck with astonishing force. Bill stepped back as Peg advanced with a kick to his left arm. With a cry, she advanced again, backing him toward Claire. Eyes wide, Peg threw two more kicks. A left hook. A right and a side kick.

Bill stumbled, knocking into Claire.

Claire threw her hands forward to break her fall as the side mirror rushed toward her. Her shoulder slammed into the mirror and glass shattered over the mat.

"Oh, my goodness." Peg gasped for breath. "I'm so sorry. I…I guess I lost control. Claire, are you okay?"

"Yeah." Claire pushed herself to her knees, staring in amazement at the shards of mirror. "Maybe we should take five."

Peg nodded, her face crimson as she dashed for the ladies' room. Claire bit her lip. Her fractured reflection peered back at her. It seemed Peg had too much pent-up anger. Maybe telling her to run from her problems hadn't been the best advice, after all.

CHAPTER TWO

CLAIRE SIGHED AN hour and a half later as she hung up the phone and turned to Bill, who'd been hovering over her since her fall. He meant well, but his closeness set her already taut nerves over the edge.

"The installers will be here with the new mirror on Friday," she said.

He nodded. "I taped over the broken part and cleaned up all the mess. You sure you're okay?"

"Not a scratch." She stood to move away from him, needing some distance.

She'd known him for years and thought having him around to help with the classes would be good therapy for her. Bill was safe. They'd played soccer together in middle school. He'd had her back on more than one occasion growing up.

During class, with the other students around, her fear had been under control. Now, with everyone else gone, her adrenaline spiked. "You can head out," she said. "I'm fine. I have an email to send, and then I'm out of here. I've got to leave to get Grey in a little bit."

Her cell phone chimed from the recesses of her

purse. She groaned. She'd programmed that tune for her mother.

Bill nodded and backed toward the door as she answered the call. Claire waved, the knot in her stomach intensifying. "Mother?"

"Claire, did I catch you at a good time? You're done with class, right?" her mother asked in her usual tone, her voice cold, polite.

"Yes, this is fine. What's up?"

"Well, I just wanted to see how you're doing. I never see you."

Claire rubbed her eyes. Her mother had made it abundantly clear she didn't *want* to see her, so what she was really saying was she never saw Grey. "You know how busy we are."

"I don't know why you have to cram so much into a day. Why don't you bring that grandson of mine by for a visit some weekend? He can spend the night and you can do something fun for yourself."

Subjecting Grey to an extended amount of time with her mother was one thing, but the thought of being home alone sent a chill through Claire. "I'm not sure that's a good idea."

Her mother grunted in disapproval. "You're stifling him."

She was doing anything but stifling him. She had him out and about as much as he could tolerate. The memory of Grey's exhausted expression that morning flashed through Claire's mind. She was the one interrupting his sleep at night.

Would he catch up on his rest at her mother's? Surely, she could stand one night alone. The thought sent a shiver of unease through her, but she stifled it. She could do it for Grey. He put up with so much from her.

"Maybe next weekend. Let me talk to Grey. I'll see if he's up for it," she said to her mother.

"That's wonderful, dear, thank you. Maybe you could go out, have fun. It's past time you started dating."

"I've got to run. I'll call you after I talk to Grey," Claire said and disconnected without waiting for a response.

Without a doubt, she was going to regret this. She glanced around the quiet office and studio. Her unease intensified as the silence buzzed around her. She had never gotten along with her mother....

"Why would you say such a thing? Becca would never make such wild accusations. Of course, she doesn't do anything to invite this kind of trouble." Her mother's words struck Claire as if they were blows. Why had she even come here? She should have known better.

*"*This *kind of trouble?" Claire stared at her mother, incredulous. "You think I* invited *this?" She stepped away in an effort to compose herself. She would not break down again in front of her mother. "This isn't a 'wild accusation.'" She yanked up her sleeve to reveal the bruises on her arm. "It hap-*

pened, whether you want to accept it or not. That man—that friend *of yours—"*

"Enough." Her mother drew up straight. "There's no need to involve the authorities when it will be your word against his."

"You're unbelievable," Claire said, turning to leave. She had plenty to show the police. She'd have her doctor document her condition first, then they'd see whose word the authorities believed.

"Claire, whatever physical evidence you may have, there's no way for you to prove you didn't consent and things just got a little rougher than you'd anticipated. These things happen all the time."

Tears pricked Claire's eyes. She refused to let her mother see. "How can you be so unsupportive?"

"I'm just trying to help you see this objectively. You have to think of Grey. How do you think this will affect him?"

Tears rolled down Claire's cheeks. She hadn't considered her son in all this. It would be hard to keep it from him if she pressed charges. Phil Adams was a public figure, at least on a city level. Would it be in the news? Would Grey hear about it at school? He might not understand, but he'd be devastated to learn she'd been hurt this badly....

Claire inhaled slowly now and straightened. The only thing she and her mother had ever agreed on was keeping the entire mess from Grey. Wanting to protect him from the horrific truth, Claire hadn't made a fuss.

As her heart thudded, she fumbled with her phone, breathing a sigh of relief once she had the music cranking from the device. Nodding, she lost herself to the ripping notes of an electric guitar.

ON FRIDAY AFTERNOON Lucas raised his beer in salute to the tombstone that barely showed the wear of the past two years. "Cheers to you, Toby," he said. "I'm still pissed at you, bud, but sometimes I think you got the better end of this deal."

A rough breeze whipped around him, making him shiver. September twenty-eighth had dawned unseasonably cold for Atlanta. He squinted into the clouds covering the sun. A sixteen-wheeler pounded along the highway hidden behind a thicket of Georgia pines and maples. He took a long drink from the bottle. The thudding of the tires echoed through his mind, as he thought back....

Lucas slammed his fist against the door. "Toby, open up. Open up or I'll break down the damn door."

Was he too late? The door swung open and Toby Platt stood, squinting into the haze of the day. His hair hung in an oily curtain around his gaunt face. He reeked, as though he hadn't showered in weeks. Rather than scowl, as would be his normal response to such an interruption, he stared at Lucas, his eyes blank.

Ignoring the fear curling through him, Lucas pushed his way inside. The stench of rotting food and unwashed clothes mixed with the rank odor emanating from his lifelong friend. Lucas fought the impulse to gag. Instead, he drew a steadying breath and opened all the windows, letting in as much fresh air as possible.

He turned to Toby, who still stood in the doorway, frowning at the passing day, as though he couldn't remember that the world existed, let alone what it was.

"When was the last time you ate?" Lucas didn't wait for an answer.

He moved to the kitchen, to examine the refrigerator. Half a rotten head of lettuce, an empty milk carton and a jar of mayonnaise sat on the shelves. He rummaged through the cabinets, but couldn't find anything to fuel a man who'd once given him hell on the football field.

He nudged Toby toward the bathroom. "I'm taking you out to eat, but you're definitely showering first."

He'd gotten his friend cleaned up, taken him to eat, and then made him an appointment with the V.A. Lucas had stayed with him that night, and then driven Toby to the appointment the following day. He'd stuck around for as long as he could, sleeping on the lumpy couch, cooking and cleaning up Toby's tiny efficiency. Therapy and antidepressants had seemed to do the job and Lucas had gone back to his life, thinking they were out of danger.

But they weren't.

"You've got some nerve coming here today." Contempt laced Louisa Platt's voice, drawing Lucas back to the present.

He turned to face Toby's sister. So, she hadn't softened toward him over the past couple of years. He couldn't blame her.

Her gaze darted over the beer in his hand. She said, "You think this is some kind of celebration?"

He shook his head. "You know he was my best friend, Louisa. No one misses him more than I do. If I'd known—"

"Well, you *should* have known. You're the one with the medical training. How could you not have seen what was happening? You should have been there for him. Then maybe we'd still have him. You owed him at least that after all the trouble you'd brought on him in the past." Her voice faltered. She nodded toward the tombstone. "He should never have followed you into the marines."

"We both needed to get away."

"Because of you. Because you dragged him into that gang in the first place."

Lucas gripped the neck of the beer bottle. "I never meant for him to get hurt."

"Hurt?" The accusation burned in her eyes. "He was literally broken, in both body and spirit. He didn't walk for months. If you had left him alone, maybe we could have avoided this."

Lucas stared at her, unable to dispute her claim. He'd gotten into some stupid stuff in high school and Toby had gone along with him, not always willingly. Sometimes he went just to keep Lucas out of worse trouble than he'd be in on his own. Neither of them had come out of that time unscathed. But Toby had been scarred in a way Lucas hadn't realized until it was too late.

Then, in the marines, Lucas had been an EMT and medevac pilot, not a shrink. Guilt still churned in his gut. He'd missed the signs. He'd gotten caught up in a stupid love affair during that last leave. Who was the woman? He couldn't remember her name or even picture her face.

"I'm sorry." No matter how many times he uttered them, the words fell flat. He left, fleeing the accusation in her eyes.

Nothing had changed in the past two years. Louisa was right. If anyone could have helped her brother, it should have been Lucas.

CHAPTER THREE

CLAIRE GAZED AT her sleeping son on Friday afternoon, overwhelmed with regret. Becca and Amanda's voices drifted to her from one of the back rooms. Claire brushed the hair from Grey's forehead. She hated to wake him. He'd been exhausted again that morning, but now his young face had softened. Surely, she'd known such peace once. It seemed so long ago.

What she wouldn't give to feel that again.

The quiet of her sister's house pressed in around her. "Grey? Grey, honey, time to go."

When he didn't respond, she gently shook his shoulder. He opened his eyes. She folded her arms as a floorboard in the hallway creaked.

It's only Becca.

She pressed her lips together as her son groaned in disappointment. Heaven knew he needed the rest, but they had to get out of there.

"Hurry up. We'll be late for soccer practice," she said and grabbed his backpack from the floor. "Did you finish your homework?"

"Yes, ma'am." Grey reached for his bag, but she threw it across her shoulder, and headed for the door.

He hurried after her, half running to keep up. She didn't breathe until they reached the car. He slipped into the passenger seat beside her as she cranked the engine and the radio exploded with the screeching of an electric guitar.

He winced, and then turned down the volume a notch. Claire frowned, but didn't turn it back up. At least they'd escaped Becca's tomblike home.

"Why don't you like quiet?" he asked, annoyance coloring his tone.

She shrugged and said, "Quiet is overrated."

"No, it isn't. It isn't normal to always crank your music, to have the TV and the DVD player and the computer going at the same time. You don't sleep. You don't like quiet. We're never home. It's soccer, or kickboxing or wall-climbing. It isn't normal. We didn't used to do all that. What happened? Why does it have to be so crazy now?"

She didn't answer, just bobbed her head along to the music, her attention on the road. The "normal" Grey wanted no longer existed for her, though she'd give anything to have it back again. Why couldn't he accept their life without all these questions? She didn't have answers, not ones she could share.

This wasn't easy for either of them. All Grey wanted was a normal life, a regular mom. Claire wasn't like other moms, though. Not anymore.

And she'd never been like Becca.

Becca would never make such wild accusations.

"I want to know about my father. Where is he? What's he doing?" Grey asked.

She strummed her fingers to the acid beat and sped through a yellow light. "You know as much as I do."

"Why don't I ever hear from him?"

Shit. Why now? "What difference does it make? He's gone and you don't need to worry about him."

"It makes a difference to me. Why won't you talk about him?"

She braked at a light and turned to him as the electric guitar squealed to a stop and the radio announcer came on. "There's nothing to talk about, Grey," she said. "I'm sorry you don't have a dad, but we're fine on our own. None of that matters. The past is past. Let's focus on today. Are you ready for this game? Who are you playing tonight? Oh, and we need to talk about this weekend."

"I don't care about the game," Grey said. "I want to know about my dad. Did I do something to make him leave? Did you?"

"Grey." The knot in her stomach tightened. "It's nothing like that. He left, but not because you did anything wrong. He just didn't deserve you."

"So he left because of you."

"Yes," she said. The light changed, so she accelerated through the intersection. "He left because of me."

Grey turned from her, fuming. She clenched the

steering wheel, hating the sick feeling in her gut, hating having her son mad at her, hating that she couldn't give him normal, hating that he missed his dad. Hadn't they been fine?

She provided adequately for them. Their house needed fixing up, but she gave Grey lots of attention. Why wasn't that enough? Did it matter so much that he didn't have a father?

ON MONDAY MORNING The Coffee Stop regulars lounged about as Lucas emerged from the back to fill his own mug. Ken talked quietly with an older gentleman at the end of the counter. Lucas stretched as he surveyed the seating area.

The sweet old couple, who'd talked him into expanding his tea assortment, sat focused on the cribbage board they'd donated to the growing stock of board games he kept under one of the big oak coffee tables. Whatever it took to keep people lingering and buying more coffee and the occasional panini was fine with Lucas. Comb-over guy slouched in the corner of the long leather sofa, his feet propped on the other table, his bony fingers curled around his pencil as he scribbled in the daily crossword.

The customer of most interest, as always, was the woman by the window, staring vacantly out, laptop keyboard silent—Grey's mom. The boy's bright smile flashed through Lucas's mind and he shook his head.

Lucas shouldn't let the kid get to him. Was he

reading too much into things, or was the kid unhappy? Surely if he were, his mom would do whatever was needed to address the situation. Maybe Lucas should talk to her, surreptitiously figure out if the espresso machine might help. Maybe he should just tell her about her son's plan.

He stirred sugar into his coffee and frowned as the woman jerked. Something in her expression, in the way she startled like that, brought back memories of Toby. Lucas's stomach clenched. Was she experiencing a flashback or did everything remind him of Toby these days?

He should pretend he hadn't noticed, walk back to his office and finish payroll, or maybe have a quick nap. He hadn't slept the past few nights, not since that visit to Toby's grave and the confrontation with his friend's sister. All the more reason to avoid Grey's mom.

The familiar heaviness filled his chest. He missed Toby.

He glanced again at Grey's mother. Absolutely, he should avoid her. He had no business butting in to her life, even if he felt for her son. Yet, the memory of the hope on Grey's face as he eyed the espresso machine carried Lucas between the tables to stand beside her. She blinked, then pressed the heels of her hands to her eyes, as if waking.

"Would you like a refill?" He nodded toward her empty cup and cursed himself for not having thought of a better excuse to approach her. Leading with

"Your kid thinks an espresso machine will fix things at home" didn't seem like the best way to go, though.

She'd had her usual espresso earlier, when she'd stopped in with Grey and he'd slipped Lucas a ten-dollar bill, with a conspiratorial nod. Lucas had hated taking the kid's money, but he would have hated himself more if he hadn't. Who was he to stomp on the kid's hopes?

"Actually, that…would be nice," she said, her brows knotted in uncertainty. She cleared her throat. "I…didn't realize…you offered refills…on the good stuff." Her words came out choppy, as though speaking drained her.

"This one's on me," he said. "A way of saying thank you for your frequent patronage."

"Oh," she said, a tentative smile curving her lips. "That's nice. I hadn't realized…do you own this place?"

"Yes." He stifled a laugh. She'd thought he was an employee. "I needed something to keep me out of trouble." He grabbed her cup. "I'll be right back."

Ken eyed him curiously as he cleaned the filter for her espresso, but when Lucas shrugged, his employee continued his conversation with one of the customers. A few moments later, Lucas delivered the brew as the woman shoved her phone into her bag.

She took the cup with both hands, her fingers trembling. "Thanks, I need this."

"Having a rough day?" he asked as he perched on the table beside her.

Nodding, she glanced at her monitor. "Freighter is late with a shipment."

"You're in shipping?" he asked.

"Strategic sourcing," she said. "I find the best sources, run analysis, act as a liaison between the customer and shipper and negotiate freights and terms. Only I can't always get everyone to do as they agreed. Then it gets rough."

"But you can do it all from the comfort of a coffee shop." He spread his hands to indicate their surroundings. "Beats working out of an office."

"Or home," she said, her voice a whisper as she raised her cup.

"Really? I guess I'd get tired of being cooped up in the house, too."

"It *is* nice to be able to work remotely and arrange my schedule around our other activities."

"You and your son?" he asked.

"Yes, my son, Grey. It's just the two of us," she said and cocked her head. "What was that the other morning?"

He frowned. Should he tell her about Grey's plan? What if he ruined the surprise for no reason? "What was what?"

"He ran back to shake your hand."

"Oh, that. He was introducing himself. I introduced myself, since the two of you are always in here. I like to get to know all my regulars." All of that was actually true.

"Oh." She stared at him a moment, frowning.

He stuck out his hand and said, "I'm Lucas Williams."

Somehow, she withdrew without moving. He stubbornly left his hand suspended between them. With a sigh, she took it and gave it a surprisingly strong shake. "I'm Claire Murphy."

"It's a pleasure, Claire."

She nodded, her gaze anchored on a spot beyond him, her smile stiff. He felt odd noticing, but she'd be gorgeous if she could just loosen up a little. Her nose was a bit small, her chin slightly crooked, but it worked for her.

He shifted. "That's a great son you have."

Her gaze found his. "Yes, Grey's an incredible kid."

Lucas stood for a moment as silence fell between them. She crossed her arms and said, "Well, thank you for the refill."

"You're welcome."

He should walk away. The kid and his mother were none of his business. His curiosity about Grey's reasons for buying the espresso machine again rose, though, and kept him in place.

"Just for the record, is it the robust flavor of our coffee that brings you here every morning, or do you just prefer your coffee on the run?" he asked.

"Both, I suppose." She raised her cup. "You brew great coffee, but we're most definitely on the run in the mornings."

"During the week, at least."

"Always," she said, then sipped her espresso.

"Even on the weekends?" He sometimes stopped in at The Coffee Stop Saturday mornings, but always stayed in the back.

"Oh, yes," she said. "We keep on the go."

"What about downtime?"

Her gaze drifted to her keyboard. "I don't believe in downtime."

"I see," he said. Poor Grey. No wonder the kid wanted an espresso machine. "Don't you get tired?"

A dry laugh worked its way from her throat. "I'm always tired."

"Why not slow things down then, catch up on some rest?"

She straightened in her seat, placing her fingers on the keys. "It wouldn't make a difference."

He should stop. She was obviously uncomfortable talking to him about this. He felt as if he'd just uncovered the tip of a very large iceberg, though. Should he tell her about Grey's surprise?

"So, how's the shipping business these days? Overall, I mean, other than today's late freighter," he asked, in spite of his uncertainty. Maybe she'd be more comfortable talking about her work.

Her eyebrows arched. "Not bad. Things are definitely picking up."

"I'd think that would be a good indicator for the state of the economy." He shrugged. "People shipping things means other people are buying them, right?"

"Yes, I suppose so."

"Do you do this full-time?" He indicated her laptop.

"I do," she said.

"And do you work regular hours, like a nine-to-five job?" he asked.

He had no idea what he was babbling about, or why he was grilling her. What he really wanted to ask her was if all their running around was good for Grey, because, obviously, Grey didn't think so. Lucas didn't know her well enough to go there, though. He still wasn't sure why he even cared, but the memory of the hope in her son's eyes kept him where he was.

"Some days. Not always," she said. She unfolded her arms, though her posture remained stiff. "I teach kickboxing a couple of afternoons a week, so I work around that. It depends on what's happening. I work on reports some evenings." She smiled tightly. "Depending on what time we get done with soccer or rock climbing."

"Wow, sounds like you two do keep pretty busy. And when do you sleep?"

She gestured with her hand. "Oh, sleep is overrated."

Bingo. She didn't sleep. Toby had slept all the time. Neither was a good scenario.

He said, "I think sleep is very important."

Her gaze again drifted out the window beside her. "Well, lots of things are important."

He nodded. He'd pressed her enough. "I should get back to work."

Her eyebrows arched again. She checked her laptop monitor then said, "I hadn't realized it was this late. I need to finish up so I can get to my class."

"Sure, I didn't mean to keep you. It was nice chatting with you, Claire. I guess I'll see you around."

"Yes…thanks…Lucas," she said and for a moment her gaze caught his.

He thought she might say more, but then her gaze flicked away. Her shoulders rounded as though a weight pressed down on her. An air of loneliness descended on her as she turned back to her laptop.

Lucas headed to his office. Why had he let the kid get to him? Was that really loneliness he sensed in Claire? Or was that loneliness a symptom of something more troubling? As much as he hated to interfere, he felt compelled to help in some way.

Did the kid even want him to? Well, maybe not him, specifically, but someone. Surely, on some level, Grey suspected something was up with his mother.

You could have prevented this.

Maybe Louisa hadn't been right about Toby. Lucas hadn't really understood what his friend had been going through then, but now he recognized the signs. He didn't know Grey and Claire, but he was drawn to them. Maybe it was Claire's isolation that called to him. Toby had pushed everyone away for weeks before he'd blown out his brains. Would there be any harm in Lucas befriending this woman and her son? What if Claire had isolated herself to the point of not having anyone to talk to? If he acted as a sounding board, she might eventually admit that keeping Grey constantly on the go wasn't the best for him.

Maybe sometimes we could have breakfast at home, instead.

Grey's haunted plea drifted to him again as he peered out of his open office door to where Claire was packing up her laptop. Maybe the problem wasn't complicated at all. Maybe all Claire needed was a friend.

CHAPTER FOUR

DUSK APPROACHED AS Grey pushed himself off the ground, feeling both exhausted and angry. Nate Patterson hooted his exultation over once again getting the ball past him. Hell, it was happening more and more these days. Grey should be used to it.

But he wasn't.

Nate trotted toward him. Grey brushed the dirt from his hand then extended it, though he couldn't bring himself to smile.

"Nice dive, Murphy," Nate said and pumped his hand with genuine enthusiasm.

Grey pressed his lips together, for fear the anger might spurt from him in a less-than-sportsmanlike manner. He nodded and Nate sped away, whooping with his teammates as the ending whistle shrilled.

At least the torment of this game was over. After a short pep talk from their coach, Grey headed across the soccer field toward the parking lot, scanning it for his mom. Too bad she'd missed another of his magnificent fails. If she'd seen how he'd sucked throughout that game, she'd understand his decision.

He was done.

The sun streamed down, glinting off metal and drawing his attention. His mom was standing on the far hill nearest the parking lot, something bulky slung across her shoulder. As she drew closer, he groaned. She was carrying a golf bag and clubs. She had to be kidding.

When she was within hearing distance, she smiled and waved. “Hi, honey!”

He shuffled toward her, shaking his head, refusing to ask the obvious.

She waved to his coach in the distance, and then ruffled his hair. He ducked away, hurrying toward the car.

“Hey, don’t I get a hello?” she asked. She caught him in a few quick strides. For a small woman, she moved quickly.

“Hello,” he said, keeping his attention on the parking lot. The sooner he got them to the car, the sooner they’d get home, where he could shut himself into his room and try to block out the noise.

“How was the game? I’m sorry I missed it. I had a lost shipment….”

Couldn’t she just drive them home for once and not expect him to talk?

“Look what I got,” she said. “Saw them at a yard sale earlier and had to stop. We can fit in a little golf on Sundays, before rock climbing.”

He shook his head and kept walking. What the hell did she expect him to say?

“Grey?” She touched his arm.

He twisted out of reach and increased his pace.

"Hey, what's up?" She stopped.

He stopped, without turning around, closed his eyes and said, "I'm done."

Mom moved in front of him, shifting the golf bag on her shoulder. "What do you mean, you're done? Did the game not go well?"

Grey was too tired to be polite. "What don't you get? I'm done, finished," he said and swept his arms wide. "I'm through with all of it."

Her mouth and eyebrows puckered like she was trying to understand. "You don't want to play soccer anymore?"

"No," he said. He had trouble keeping his voice level. His throat tightened. "I hate it."

She frowned. "But you love soccer."

"That was before—before rock climbing, before all the other stuff." He waved his hand toward the clubs. "Before golf. I..." He shook his head. Soccer was just part of the problem, but he'd settle for this one concession. "I'm not playing soccer anymore."

His mother met his gaze, her mouth quirked to the side. "I don't know, Grey," she said. "You know how I feel about idle time."

"I'll do stuff at home."

She glanced away, her jaw tense. "I don't want you to be unhappy, hon."

"Then say I can quit. I don't get why we have to always be doing something. We didn't used to be like that. We used to have downtime."

Her gaze dropped to the ground and she said, "Well, downtime is overrated."

The urge to hit something welled up inside him. Without responding, he turned and headed again toward the car.

He glanced over his shoulder. The light had gone from his mother's eyes. She seemed beaten down, defeated. The look struck him in the pit of his stomach.

When had that started? She'd always been tough, ever since he could remember.

Thinking back now, though, he had to admit she'd worn that defeated look on other occasions when she hadn't thought he'd noticed. At some point, somehow, she'd changed.

And it wasn't for the better.

A COLD WIND hit Lucas as he opened the back door of the coffee shop, trash bag in hand. Ramsey Carter, one of the high schoolers who worked part-time, pushed himself away from the wall and stubbed out a cigarette. He took the bag from Lucas.

"I was going to get that," he said.

Lucas nodded at the cigarette butt. "I thought you were quitting."

Ramsey grunted as he shoved the bag into the Dumpster. "I am. Maybe I should try a patch or something."

"You're pretty tough," Lucas said. "You can kick a little nicotine."

Ramsey *was* tough. Lucas had met him in this very spot nearly a year ago. The kid had taken a gang beat-down. Lucas had first befriended him, then eventually given him a job.

"I know," Ramsey said. "I'll do it. I'll quit. I've just been a little stressed. You know, senior year and all."

In spite of the cigarette breaks, Ramsey more than pulled his weight at The Coffee Stop. Lucas crossed his arms. "Have you figured out yet what you'll do when you graduate?"

"College for sure, if I can get in. It'll have to be in state. At least my grades should get me some Hope Scholarship money."

"That's a good move. Sometimes I wonder where I'd be if I'd gone that route," Lucas said.

Would Toby have gone with him to college? Would they have stayed out of the gangs, out of the military, and kept his friend alive?

Ramsey gestured toward the building behind them. "Looks like you managed okay."

Lucas let his gaze travel over the back of the shop. "I'm not exactly saving the world, but I am managing."

"You saved me," Ramsey said quietly.

"You're smarter than I was. You would've eventually figured things out on your own. I think you already knew you didn't want that life anymore."

"I just got kind of sucked into it."

"I know," Lucas said. "Happens to the best of us."

But Ramsey didn't smile. "I don't know if I ever said a proper thank-you for all you've done for me."

"Thank me by going to college and making something of yourself."

Ramsey nodded. "It's a lot to figure out, you know, who I am and what I want to be. You said you joined the marines to straighten yourself out, but what made you decide to become a medevac pilot?"

"I was an EMT first. I guess I did that because I liked being able to help people." And helping people had felt good, because he'd spent too much of his childhood feeling helpless—helpless in the face of the rage that consumed his father in the days he was still with them and drinking.

"So, why did you stop? I mean, couldn't you still be an EMT, even if you weren't in the marines?" Ramsey asked.

"I just wanted a change," Lucas said. "So, do we need to cut back your hours, so you can quit stressing about college?"

"No, I'm good. I want the hours. I'm saving all I can to help pay tuition. I don't want to put it all on my folks."

Lucas nodded.

"I'm going to head back. Ken probably thinks I ran off or something."

Lucas followed the boy inside, turning into his office, as Ramsey headed toward the front. Lucas settled into his chair.

So, why did you stop?

That question had haunted him for the past year and a half, since he'd bought The Coffee Stop. Helping people had made him feel useful, but when Toby died, Lucas stopped feeling anything for a while. He wasn't really sure why he'd walked away to buy this shop, but somewhere, somehow, he'd wanted a little peace after all the trauma.

Still, had that been enough to have him turn his back on a career he'd been proud of, one that had fulfilled him? He'd had his share of people die on his watch. Each one felt like a penance of sorts, his punishment for the violence of his past. But he'd also saved lives. It seemed that after Toby, all he could focus on were the losses, though. And then he couldn't take it anymore.

He glanced around the cluttered office. He might not be saving people here. Owning a coffee shop might not be the most rewarding occupation, but at least nobody died on his watch here. That had to count for something.

THE FOLLOWING MORNING, Claire frowned as Grey shuffled into the coffee shop beside her. He hadn't given up his plan to quit soccer. Why was he acting up now when she had so little energy to deal with him?

She stiffened as Lucas Williams stepped to the counter. As his green gaze met hers, her pulse raced and her stomach fluttered. That too-familiar fear stirred in her, warring with unwanted…curiosity. Why had he been so friendly with her the other day?

Not that she hadn't enjoyed meeting him. He had the broad shoulders and strong demeanor that made her nervous, but something in his eyes calmed her and drew her in.

"Good morning, Claire," he said, then nodded toward Grey. "Grey."

Grey simply waved.

"Good morning, Lucas," she said.

Even with the counter between them, his energy seemed to reach out and touch her. It wasn't an entirely unpleasant sensation. She focused on her wallet, pulling out her debit card.

Her nerves couldn't handle him this early. She said, "Large Americano, double shot, two pumps of vanilla, room for cream and a banana-strawberry sm—"

"Espresso," Grey said and crossed his arms. "No smoothie. I want an espresso."

Lucas grinned and asked, "Do you want just a shot, straight up, or in an Americano, like your mom, or do you prefer something else?"

Grey hesitated.

"Honey, are you sure?" Claire asked. "You're still a bit young for coffee."

Her son ignored her and asked Lucas, "Can't you mix it into a drink with milk or something and some sweet stuff?"

"Hot or cold?" Lucas asked.

"Hot."

"Do you like chocolate?"

"I'm a kid. What do you think?" Grey asked.

Lucas grinned. "You don't have to be a kid to appreciate chocolate," he said. "I've got just the thing."

As he moved away to make the drinks, Claire turned to Grey. "So, no more smoothies and no more soccer. That's the new plan?" she asked.

He shoved his hands into his pockets. "You mean you're cool with no soccer?"

"We're going to have to find something else for you to do. I don't know if Becca is up to having you stay there more than you do already. I hate to even ask her," she said. "She's so strict about their schedule and having it quiet when your uncle Kyle gets home. And you can't be home alone."

"Why can't *you* be at home? You used to work from home all the time," Grey said.

She didn't answer as they moved down the counter. The quiet and isolation of being home were too hard for her. Cranking her music merely held the flashbacks at bay. If she ever stopped to think about the quiet behind the music…

"Maybe you can stay with Gram," she said. "She's always complaining she doesn't see you enough. She wants you to visit some weekend, by the way—spend the night."

"Gram?" Grey shook his head, his voice rising. "I don't want to stay with Gram. I want to stay with *you*. At home. You can work from there, like you used to."

Claire glanced at Lucas, embarrassed the man should witness her argument with her son. "This isn't the time or the place," she said to Grey. "We'll talk about it later."

"I don't want to talk about it later," Grey said. He swiped his sleeve across his face. "I'll go stay with Gram this weekend if I have to, but I'm not staying with her after school. It doesn't make sense."

The sun streamed through the glass front door. Claire focused on the beam of light. If only she could dissolve into the sunshine, she wouldn't have to deal with this. She turned to Grey and touched his shoulder, but he shook her off. Why couldn't he just be happy with things the way they were?

"Grey," she said, keeping her tone steady. "I'll let Gram know you can stay Friday night. We'll talk about the rest later. I have to think about whether I can work from home with you there or see if she's okay with having you three afternoons a week. It's a lot to ask."

Grey stood stiffly beside her. "She won't mind," he said. "*She* likes hanging out with me."

"Americano double shot, two pumps of vanilla, with room. I added a little whipped cream on top." Lucas placed their drinks on the counter. "And a mocha java latte."

With a nod, Grey scooped up his drink. He took

a hesitant sip, then another longer one before saying, "I like it. Thanks."

As Grey headed toward the door, Claire turned to Lucas. "Thank you."

"You're welcome." He paused. "He's just testing his boundaries."

"Yes," she said and glanced at her son, hovering inside the door, sipping his latte.

"I made it decaf. He should be okay."

"I appreciate that," she said. "Caffeine isn't what concerns me, though. It's the quitting soccer."

Lucas glanced at Grey. "Guess that depends on why he wants to quit."

Her gaze settled on her son, still focused on his drink. "I think…he's just tired."

"Tired?" Lucas asked.

What was it about the man that had compelled her to even mention it to him? "We keep pretty busy, like I said, always on the go." She hated admitting it. "I guess it's too much for him."

"I know we've had this conversation, but everyone needs downtime," he said. "Even you."

Heat flooded her. She settled her purse on her shoulder, readying to bolt. "You don't really know me and we *have* had this conversation."

"My apologies. I didn't mean to overstep. It's just that I can see you're a good mother, Claire. And I can't say that I'm an expert, or that I know anything about raising a kid, but I do know it isn't easy. I can't imagine doing it alone."

"I appreciate your concern, Lucas, but I'm not entirely alone. My sister takes him some days after school." She shrugged. "There's my mom, too, and he has a friend he stays with sometimes. I trade off with his mom."

He nodded. "I'm sorry, I don't mean to intrude. It's just that if Grey's anything like I was—and I was raised by a single mom—I can understand your concern about him having too much free time. If his dad isn't around, he could probably use a good male role model. Maybe someone from the Big Brothers Association could help with that." He shrugged. "At least, I wish I'd had something like that when I was his age."

Her gaze met his as she said, "Actually, that could be exactly what he needs. I'll check it out, thanks."

"Of course," he said. "Just a suggestion." He spread his hands and said, "I really don't mean to butt in. I just… I was a little like Grey when I was a kid. My dad split early, thankfully, and it was just my mother and me. I might have avoided some of the…trouble I got into later if I'd had someone looking out for me."

Something about his reference to trouble raised goose bumps of foreboding across her skin. She rubbed her arms. "I've been thinking about finding him someone like that. I'll look into it."

She motioned toward Grey. "I'd better get him to school."

Lucas nodded, a smile curving his lips. “Okay, Claire,” he said. “I’ll see you later.”

The timber of his voice saying her name again made her stomach flutter. She inhaled a steadying breath as she hurried toward Grey. She couldn’t be interested in Lucas. He was too strong, with those shoulders and arms of his. His thin T-shirt did little to hide the definition of his muscles. That much strength was dangerous.

She had to get herself together and figure out how to deal with Grey. She had way too much on her hands to think about a man for now, especially one that pushed her out of her comfort zone.

Everyone needs downtime. Even you.

If she could have downtime that didn’t make her jump out of her skin, she might be inclined to agree. But as things were, that just wasn’t going to happen.

CHAPTER FIVE

"DESTINATION ON YOUR left." The monotone of the GPS was barely audible above the musical notes of Staind as Claire cruised along Edgewood Avenue in Atlanta that afternoon.

She peered at the building to her left. Rows of windows overlooked the street, concrete and glass in the heart of downtown. She found the entrance to the parking garage, her stomach knotting as she finally pulled into a spot.

She smoothed her skirt as she waited for the elevator at one end of the garage. When the doors opened, she saw a man in jeans standing to one side, his width taking half the space.

Her heart sped up as she hesitated, her fingers tingling. He pressed the button to stop the doors from closing. "Are you coming?"

Without speaking, she stepped in beside him, her gaze riveted on the panel of buttons, her pulse kicking up at his proximity. She hated this, how nothing more than sharing an elevator could send her anxiety through the roof. Within moments the door opened and she hurried into the lobby, the wide space and flurry of activity soothing her nerves.

I am safe. I am strong. No one can hurt me.

Five minutes later she stood in front of the receptionist's counter at the Big Brothers and Big Sisters Association of Greater Atlanta. A young man with spiked hair greeted her.

"I'm Claire Murphy," she said. "I'm here to see Doug Straighter."

"I'll let Mr. Straighter know you're here."

"Thank you," she said, and then settled in one of the chairs in the waiting area, shaking the tingling from her hands. The quiet of the place pressed in around her and her heartbeat accelerated again. Pain squeezed up the back of her head, thudding along her skull.

A few moments later a stocky, gray-haired man emerged from a side door. "Ms. Murphy, I'm Doug Straighter. It's a pleasure to meet you."

His deep voice rumbled through her. She shivered and rubbed her arms as she stood. He extended his hand and she took it, even as her instincts urged her to withdraw.

"Thank you for seeing me on such short notice," she said.

"Come on back and we'll see what we can do for you and your son."

He led her down a short hall to an open area with tables and chairs. A younger man with a wiry build moved toward the door as they entered. His gaze swept over Claire and she stiffened, the hairs on her arms prickling.

"George." Straighter shook the man's hand. "Good to see you. How's life treating you these days?"

The new man nodded, though his attention remained on Claire. He said, "No complaints. How about you, Doug? How's the family?"

"Enjoying the cooler weather," Straighter said. He smiled and waved as the younger man continued toward the door. "You have a good one, George."

"You, too," the man said. His gaze swept over Claire once more before he departed.

With that, Claire stood alone with Doug Straighter, the director of the Atlanta BBBS. A big man, he stood over a foot taller than her. He pulled out a chair at one of the tables and gestured for her to sit. Once she was settled, he took the seat to her right.

"George is a great example of what we do here," he said, motioning toward the door. "He came here as a troubled kid fifteen years ago and now he's one of our best 'Bigs.'"

Claire nodded, her head throbbing. Whatever trouble the younger man had been in, it seemed to still emanate from him. A car backfired on the street and she jumped.

She clasped her hands, silently chastising herself as the urge to bolt overwhelmed her. This was an important meeting. She had to find a way to get through it for Grey's sake.

"It seems a little deserted here today. Is it always like this?" she asked.

"Ah, we have events sometimes where we all meet here, but most of the fun happens out in the real world, one-on-one with the kids and their Big Brothers and Sisters."

He shifted and his knee knocked her chair. She jumped, her cheeks warming at her own reaction. She said, "So, what kind of people volunteer to be Big Brothers and Sisters? I saw on your website that you screen candidates."

"We do a thorough background check. We get people of all types, from guys like George—a former street kid turned entrepreneur—to retirees. We even have a former pro basketball player and a former Miss Georgia."

He paused and the buzzing of the overhead light filled the silence. Claire broke into a sweat, her chest tightening with the pounding of her heart. Her seat seemed to shift beneath her. She squeezed her eyes shut and the pressure in her head intensified. Suddenly, she was transported back to that afternoon, a little over a year ago, and the quiet of her house....

The silence blanketed her. The scent of musk drifted in the air as a floorboard creaked behind her. The cold blade of a knife pressed to her throat....

"I'm sorry," she said as the urge to flee drove her to her feet, and she gripped her purse to her chest. The floor seemed to pitch as she tried to remain upright.

"Ms. Murphy, is everything all right? You don't look well," Doug Straighter said as he stood beside her. He reached for her as though to steady her.

She recoiled from his hand. "I'm…fine. I have another appointment I forgot about."

"Well, I'm sorry we didn't get to talk about your son. We can reschedule if you'd like."

She swallowed hard, the need for fresh air overwhelming her. "Yes, I'll reschedule," she said. "I'm sorry."

She fled without looking back.

SOME TIME LATER, Claire turned the corner to Becca's house. She'd made it to her car before the anxiety attack hit her full force and she'd dropped to her knees, right in the parking garage. Shame burned through her. Thankfully, no one had witnessed her breakdown and she'd eventually struggled into the car, where she sat, panicking for who knew how long before she was calm enough to drive.

She pulled to the curb in front of her sister's house. Her mother's car, an old Buick, sat in the driveway. The knot in Claire's stomach tightened. She still hadn't decided what to do with Grey instead of soccer practice. Could she handle working from home with him there?

Besides having to be home for a longer period of time, she'd also have to turn down her music. He'd need the quiet to do homework. Maybe she should talk to her mom about keeping him, but facing her mother while feeling like a complete failure held little appeal.

Janet Bradington, Claire's mother, greeted her moments later as she pushed through the sunroom door. "You're early," she said.

Claire pasted on a smile. She'd had her commute through Atlanta's late-afternoon traffic to recover, but she couldn't quell her disappointment over blowing her appointment with BBBS. Grey still needed a good male role model and she wasn't any closer to finding him one than she'd been that morning.

"My appointment finished earlier than expected. Where's Grey?" she asked.

Her mother nodded toward the open bank of windows. "He's down by the creek with Becca and Amanda," she said. "It's too muddy for me. I just took them some lemonade. Would you like some?"

"No, I'm good, thanks. Did he do his homework?"

"He did it first thing. He said you're okay with him staying Friday night," her mother said.

Claire shrugged. "Sure. You two will have fun."

She inhaled. Maybe she could get some of her running friends to go out with her after their run that evening. At the very least, she'd be able to crank her music all night without worrying about disturbing Grey.

"I'm looking forward to having him to myself," her mother said and nodded to the chair beside her. "Why don't you take a load off? You look like you're about to fall over. Grey, too. Don't the two of you believe in sleep?"

"We sleep," Claire said as she sank into the chair. She should get Grey and leave, but unfortunately her mother was right. Fatigue pulled at her. Maybe she could rest just for a minute.

"Well, not enough by the look of either of you. I get at least seven and a half hours of sleep every night. My doctor says I'm as healthy as a woman ten years younger."

"Good for you, Mother," Claire said and propped her feet on the coffee table before her. She closed her eyes.

"Honestly, hon, I'm worried about both of you."

Claire sighed and opened her eyes. "We're fine." She leaned toward her mother. "I do have a favor to ask, though. If it's too much I understand, but we have a little change in his schedule and I'm not sure what to do about it."

Her mother nodded. "He mentioned he wants to quit soccer. I can't say that I'm surprised. You two can't keep on the go all the time. I can only imagine how exhausting it is. I can't comprehend why you would do that to yourself, let alone to your son."

Claire tightened her jaw in frustration. No matter how old she got, she'd always be an irresponsible kid to her mother, one who never made the right choices—one whose troubles were always her own fault.

"We're okay, and, yes, he wants to quit soccer,"

she said. "But I have to work and he can't be home alone. I feel like we can't ask any more of Becca. You know how Kyle is. Grey's staying longer in the afternoons would be a disruption for them."

"Why can't you work from home?"

Claire waved her hand. Her mother had already proven she would never understand—or accept—the truth. "I might try it, but would you be able to watch him if it turns out I can't work while he's there? It's after school Mondays, Wednesdays and Fridays. If it's too much trouble for you to get him from school, I'd run him over to you, then pick him up afterward. I know it's a lot to ask, but you were saying you don't see enough of him. I just wanted to see if it's an option."

Her mother sat in silence, frowning. At last she nodded. "Of course Grey is always welcome with me. I'm doing a little more consulting these days, though. I can work around his schedule for the most part, but I can't get him until later in the day. He can still go to Becca's and I can pick him up from there. Just let me know what you decide."

"Thank you, Mother, I really appreciate it."

"I'd be happy to see more of him. He's at a good age," she said, smiling. "I can even watch him evenings and weekends. You should be going out more, Claire, dating. It isn't right for you to be single. Both you and Grey could use some male interaction. For obviously different reasons, of course."

Claire pressed her lips together. "No, I'm not interested in dating and, yes, I agree Grey needs a good male role model," she said. "I'm working on it. I'm checking into getting him a Big Brother."

"Really?" Her mother leaned back, arms folded.

"Yes." Claire said. Would she ever be able to set up another meeting? "Really. Why, what's wrong with that? I thought you'd be pleased."

"Nothing, sweetheart—a Big Brother could be a good thing. I just don't know why Grey needs someone who isn't family or a friend. What about Kyle? Can't he spend more time with him? Or how about Ned, my next-door neighbor? His kids are grown and he has more time on his hands than he knows what to do with."

Why did her mother find fault with everything she did? If Becca had suggested the BBBS, would her mother have been open to it? Claire shouldn't be resentful when her mother was trying to help. But still…

"I'm perfectly comfortable with the Big Brother program," she said. "They're people who volunteer their time to be with kids. They're well screened. Which is more than I can say for your choice of friends."

Her mother stiffened at the reference to her former friend, the man she'd admired so much that she'd refused to believe Claire after the attack.

"Phil Adams was an upstanding citizen. He sat on the board of the homeowners association for years and city council wouldn't have been the same without him."

Claire stood. "Well, you and I have very different opinions on what constitutes an upstanding citizen, Mother." She headed toward the screen door. "I'll drop Grey by after school on Friday."

CHAPTER SIX

"KEN, IT looks like we're going to run short on a few supplies before the next shipment," Lucas said to the older gentleman. "I'm going to make a quick run to get what we need to tide us over."

"No problem," Ken said. "I'll hold down the fort while you're gone."

Slipping his jacket on, Lucas pushed through the front door, into the sunlit day. As he patted his pockets for his keys, a familiar brunette rolled into the parking space beside him.

He'd been thinking about Claire since their conversation the other morning. He hadn't been able to stop himself from giving his opinion about Grey's need for a role model. And, of course, he'd pushed again about the downtime. As he thought about it, his whole approach to her was colored by Grey's desire to de-stress their life, but Claire still had no idea Lucas knew about that. She no doubt thought of him as a creep, who stuck his nose in where it didn't belong. He'd been looking for an opportunity to smooth things over with her ever since.

She slipped out of her car and, thankfully, acknowledged him with a little wave. He returned the wave and smiled. "Welcome back."

Now that she was here, he had no idea how to dig himself out of the hole he'd dug with her. She stepped onto the sidewalk in front of The Coffee Stop.

"You're not working this afternoon?" she asked.

At least she was still speaking to him. He again patted his pockets for his elusive keys. "I'm making a quick supply run."

She nodded and adjusted the shoulder strap of her computer bag. "Well, I'm going to get some work done."

"Claire," he said and she paused. "I just want to say I shouldn't have butted in the other day. You know, harping on you about your schedule and suggesting the Big Brother thing for Grey. I was out of line."

Again, she nodded, but then stepped closer to him. "It's okay. You made some valid points." Her cheeks pinked. "I'm going to look into the Big Brother program. It was a good suggestion."

She glanced through his car window as he shoved his hands in his pants pockets, still searching for his keys. "Is that what you're looking for?"

His keys dangled from the ignition.

"Well, that's no good," he said and jiggled the door handle to no avail. He walked around the car, checking all the doors. But all of them were locked.

"Do you have a spare set?" she asked.

"I must have had one at some point, but I have no idea where it would be. I guess I'll call a locksmith."

She pulled out her own keys. "I think I have a coat hanger in my car, if you want to give that a try first."

"I guess it couldn't hurt."

She opened the passenger door beside him and felt around under the seat, but came up empty-handed. "Hold on."

She moved to the back door and tried again from that angle. "I'm pretty sure it's under here."

"It's okay," he said. "I don't mind calling a locksmith."

"No, I'm sure I have one. It was from some dry cleaning and Grey stuck it under there. Let's move the seat up." She climbed into the backseat and leaned over the front, searching for the lever on the left side of the seat.

"Let me get this out of the way," she said as she grabbed a book bag from between the seats and slung it into the passenger seat.

The contents spilled across the blue upholstery, displaying printed pages marked with yellow highlighter. Lucas hurried to gather the documents, but paused as his gaze fell on one of the highlighted phrases.

PTSD Symptoms: Traumatic Flashbacks

"I'll get that," Claire said as she grabbed the papers from his hands.

Before he could comment, she'd shoved everything back into the book bag and resumed fumbling with the lever.

"Let me," he said and she moved aside to let him pull the lever. The seat slid forward and she was finally able to extract the sought-after hanger.

She didn't meet his gaze as she handed it to him. "I knew I had one."

"Claire—" He had so much he wanted to ask her, but the last thing he wanted was to push her again. Was she researching PTSD for herself?

"Why don't you just keep that?" she said as she closed the back door of her car. "I don't need it."

"Okay, thanks." He wanted to reach out to her, tell her he understood too well what she was suffering—if that *was* what she was suffering—but at the same time his stomach tightened at the memory of Toby, gaunt and emotionless.

"I'd better get to work. I have a deadline on a contract," she said, still not making eye contact.

"Sure," he said. "I didn't mean to keep you."

She nodded as she inhaled and straightened. Her gaze met his and as before, it seemed she might say more, but she merely nodded again, and headed into the coffe shop.

THE SMOOTH TONES of jazz floated through the air a short while later as Claire tried to relax into her favorite chair at The Coffee Stop. She glanced around once more to see if Lucas had returned.

What did it matter that he'd seen the articles she'd

printed on PTSD? She had nothing to hide. She was just getting to know the man and if he decided not to pursue their friendship because of them, then she'd count her blessings.

But what if he mentioned the articles around Grey? Even as the question shot through her mind, she chided herself on how foolish she was being.

Lucas probably hadn't given the papers a second thought. If he had, wouldn't he have asked her then? She should have said something at the time, though what that would have been, she couldn't fathom.

She should have just told him she was researching PTSD for herself. There was no shame in that. She'd already picked up a few techniques to help her nip flashbacks in the bud. Not that she'd perfected any of them, but she was trying.

She inhaled and tried to focus on her latest contract. What did it matter to her what Lucas thought? A little voice whispered that it *did* matter, because on some level, she was starting to *like* the man.

It had been too long since she'd had a real friend to confide in. If Lucas knew about her PTSD and accepted her, in spite of that, maybe he'd be someone she could talk to. Heaven knew she couldn't talk to her mother or perfect Becca.

Her gaze wandered around the space, which was sprinkled with other patrons. Sometimes, if she were completely honest, she just felt lonely. Is that why she liked it here?

The music was usually too mellow for her tastes.

The clientele seemed to be more on the quiet side. The afternoon barista was a kid who, like the guy from the BBBS, seemed to radiate a troubled vibe. Yet, people always occupied the upholstered chairs and sofas, as well as the traditional café-style tables and chairs. In its own laidback way the shop provided enough distraction to keep her from jumping out of her skin. There was something of a community feeling here, even if she only felt remotely connected to it.

Besides, somehow she managed to complete her work here, where she struggled to do so in other places.

Why can't you work at home?

Grey's question still haunted her. But just the thought of a quiet afternoon at home sent fear swirling through her, as though that one day had conditioned her to react to those particular circumstances.

Dust motes circled in the beam of sunshine streaming through the window by her seat. They swirled and dropped in a peaceful dance to the strains of a saxophone and horns. The tinkling of the front door drew her attention.

The older couple, who usually sat together on the overstuffed sofa at the back, entered. A younger woman, perhaps their daughter, strode arm in arm with the man.

"Lucas," the older woman said and motioned Lucas out from behind the counter.

Claire straightened at the sight of him. He must

have returned through a back door. The usual adrenaline spiked through her at the sight of his strength. But with Lucas the adrenaline didn't signal something unpleasant, as it did with other strong men. He'd been on her mind since their conversation the other day.

Something about him, the way he blatantly addressed her most pressing issues, the way he apologized for doing so, the way his gaze seemed to see right into her, commanded her respect, even as he pushed her out of her comfort zone.

Lucas glanced her way as he strode to meet the couple and their guest. For the briefest second, his gaze touched hers and her heart raced, sending warmth bursting in her cheeks.

She lowered her eyes, forcing herself to focus on the contract on her laptop monitor. What the hell was wrong with her?

"Lucy here just enlisted. She's headed for boot camp in a couple of weeks," the older gentleman said. He had settled on the sofa between the two women, his arm around the younger one, as if he were afraid to let her go.

Again, Lucas's gaze wandered to Claire. This time she didn't look away, though her heart hammered so hard it surely showed through her blouse. The green of his eyes seemed to darken, as though a shadow passed over him.

His voice was low, but distinguishable, even

across the room. "It takes the right kind of person to make it in the military."

The older gentleman gripped the young woman's hand. "You listen to Lucas, honey. He knows."

The gentleman's wife leaned over him to address the young woman, saying, "Former marine, he served in Afghanistan and Iraq. He was an EMT and medevac pilot."

A chill passed through Claire. She rubbed her arms. She had no business listening. Again, she focused on the contract, but she read the same sentence three times and had no idea what it said.

"He got shot down once," the old guy said and gestured toward Lucas. "Tell her."

Claire held her breath, unable to take her attention off their conversation.

"There isn't much to say," Lucas said, ducking his head, as though he didn't want to tell the story. "We got hit hard. We'd already made two trips out with wounded and had more to go."

He shook his head. "I managed to land us in one piece, but the engine was toast. We had a kid—he couldn't have been more than twenty. He should have been on some college campus, but there he was. He'd taken a frag to the head and several to his back. My copilot, he got out with this first lieutenant who'd lost an arm. They went for help, but the kid—we couldn't move him."

He paused a moment. "I couldn't leave him. You never know what you're capable of until you're in that situation." Again he paused, while the dust motes circled. "I held them off until help reached us. It took them fourteen hours."

He stopped and all remained silent. Claire inhaled. What had happened during those fourteen hours? She closed her eyes.

Fourteen hours. It must have seemed an eternity. Time had a way of stretching during trauma. She'd felt as if she'd been through a time warp that summer day a little over a year ago.

"Like I said, the military isn't for everyone." Lucas's voice kept her in the present. "It turns out I make a better coffee-shop owner than a marine."

The young woman leaned forward on the sofa. "I'm sure you made a great marine."

Claire's gaze swept over the young woman. She tossed her hair and it flowed silkily around her shoulders. Something too much like jealousy swelled in Claire's chest. What did she care if Lucas was interested in the young woman? It wasn't like she wanted to date him.

She had enough on her plate without having to worry with fitting another person into her life. No, dating wasn't on Claire's to-do list and wouldn't be for a long time to come.

CHAPTER SEVEN

"SO, WHY ARE you hanging around with an old lady, when you could be having fun with someone your own age?" Adana Williams, Lucas's mother, waved at her son with her paint roller late Friday afternoon. Baby-blue paint spattered the drop cloth below her.

Lucas grinned and repositioned the ladder before climbing back up with his own paint-soaked roller. "What, and miss out on all this fun?" he asked. "What better way to spend a Friday afternoon than with my beautiful *madre?*"

His mother shook her head as she rolled a streak of blue along the lower portion of the wall of the bedroom section of the efficiency she rented in a friend's basement. "Don't get me wrong," she said. "I love having you around, but I worry about you."

"No need to worry. I like spending time with you. Who else is going to do all your grunt work for you?"

She frowned at him, though merriment shone in her deep brown eyes. She had her mother's dark coloring, her South American heritage showing more than the European blood of her father. "I do my own grunt work," she said. "You just help. Sometimes."

Laughter rumbled through him. "Like when I helped you move into this place last fall?"

"Okay, maybe you did that one on your own. I had that bum knee," she said. "I'm not saying I don't need you at times and appreciate you always, love. I just don't need you *all* the time. Between me and that coffee shop of yours when do you have any fun?"

Lucas focused on coating the roller with fresh paint from the tray attached to the top of the ladder. He worked hard to keep The Coffee Stop afloat and to pass on what he could to his mother. She worked long hours as a receptionist, but she couldn't seem to catch a break financially. Even though it didn't bother her, he hated that she had to live like this.

"I like being busy," he said. "What kind of son would I be if I left you to do this by yourself? And I enjoy the shop and I do meet people there."

"What kind of people?" she asked.

"All kinds. There's the Grandbys, this sweet older couple who like tea and board games. They want to start holding backgammon tournaments in the shop," he said with a grin. "They've talked me into some group deals for them, but they'll bring in a lot of new business, so it's a win-win situation there."

His mother rubbed at a dab of blue paint on her arm, saying, "But what about customers of the female persuasion? Any single young women frequenting that shop of yours?"

An image of Claire Murphy sprang to Lucas's mind, with her auburn hair and those brown eyes carrying the weight of the world. He shook his head and said, "None that I'm dating, if that's what you're after."

"No?" His mother regarded him with arched eyebrows. "That took a little long for you to answer. So, there's at least one woman, but you don't think you can date her. What makes her undateable? She's not married, is she?"

"I'm sure we can find something more interesting than my lack of a love life to talk about," he said. "What about you? How is everything with Richard?"

"He's away on business, which is why he isn't here helping me slap paint on the wall, but everything is wonderful so there's not much to say. And I can't imagine a more important conversation for a mother to have with her best-loved son—"

"Only son," he said. "Only child—"

"—than one about why such a loving, healthy, single man should spend all of his time working or helping out his old-lady *madre*."

"Number one, you aren't an old lady, that would be Grandma and even she puts the other *abuelas* to shame. Number two, I'm happy being single. If I'm meant to be with someone I'll meet her during the normal course of my life."

His mother swept her arm, indicating the room. "Well, if this is the normal course of your life, you're going to be single a long time, my son. I don't have any young available women crowding into my home." She shrugged. "Though maybe I can arrange something if you insist on hanging out here all the time."

Lucas laughed again. "You know I'd put a fast stop to that if I thought you were serious."

"So, tell me about the woman," she said.

"What woman?" he asked.

"The one at your shop. The undateable one."

"Who says there's a woman?" he asked.

She gave him her sternest mom frown.

He blew out a breath. "There's this kid. His mother is beautiful, fit, physically healthy. I wouldn't call her undateable, but I believe she's…distressed in some way."

She stared at him. "Distressed?" she asked. "How so? That's how you describe a scratched coffee table or dented washing machine. Though I suppose we're all a little distressed these days." She again raised the roller toward him. "She's single?"

"One question at a time," he said as he paused to run the edger along the top of the wall. "Yes, she's single—at least she says it's just the two of them. She doesn't wear a ring."

"Ah, so you *are* interested. Go on."

He traded the edger for the roller, glancing at his mother as he rolled it in the tray and asked, "What makes you think I'm interested?"

"You checked for a ring."

He bit the inside of his lip. He could say he did

that with all attractive women, but his mother knew him too well to buy that. "I didn't need to check for a ring. She told me it was just the two of them. And if I did, maybe I was looking for the kid's sake," he said. "He's about ten. He should have a man in his life. I just kind of feel for him, you know?"

"Because she's distressed and that affects him?"

"Well, they both seem a little worn-out, really, but her more so. He's just getting hit with her flack, but it affects him, definitely."

"What's wrong with her? Is she *loco?*"

He blew out a breath. "I suspect she's dealing with a case of PTSD, but I don't really know. She startles, doesn't sleep, seems to be hypervigilant. And I saw she was reading articles on it, which doesn't mean anything, but something's off. I'm just getting to know her."

"PTSD? Like Toby?" she asked, her tone softening.

He nodded. "Yeah, like Toby."

"How long has it been, Lucas? Seems like it just happened yesterday."

"Two years ago last Friday," he said without emotion.

She nodded and rolled more paint on the wall, saying, "Two years already? I know it's still hard for you."

"Yep."

"And I see why you might not want to date this woman."

He paused midstroke and said, "You think she reminds me of how I screwed up with Toby?"

"Did you screw up with Toby?" she asked.

He swiped the roller down the wall. "Maybe. Yes, definitely, when we were younger."

"Helping her won't bring him back."

He turned to her. "I know that."

She met his gaze. "Do you?"

"Yes. I just feel like she could use a friend."

"And you think you'd make a good friend for her?" she asked.

"Yes, especially if she's suffering from PTSD. I could help her. I studied it pretty in-depth after Toby..."

"But why do you feel the need to help her?"

He put the roller back in the tray and spread his arms wide. "Why does it matter? One minute you're asking me why I don't have a woman in my life and then when I tell you I'm getting to know one, you question it."

"Because I know you," she said. "I know how you always feel responsible for other people, even at your own expense."

He stared at her. "What does that mean?"

"When you were young, when your father was still with us, and you know how he liked his liquor—"

"That's all over and done with. Do we need to rehash it?" He picked up his roller and smashed it in the paint. He hated thinking about his father, how he'd hurt his mother and Lucas hadn't been able to stop him.

"The man was an idiot, a cruel idiot, but an idiot—"

"Can we please not talk about him? What does he have to do with this, anyway?" Lucas asked.

"Let me finish. You were seven when he left, so young and so angry."

"Madre—"

"Lucas, listen to me. He'd come home stinking drunk and he'd get mad about a toy you'd left out or a mess you'd made, or something he made up in his head and he'd always yell at you while he struck me and then you took care of me afterward, bringing me the first-aid kit and ice. He made you feel like it was your fault. But it wasn't."

Lucas's throat tightened. He gripped the roller. His father had been a real bastard. It had been a relief when he'd left. "He never deserved you. I don't know why you married him."

"I got you out of the deal, didn't I?"

He nodded, but didn't reply. She thought he felt responsible, but he just felt angry. Even at seven he'd known his father's actions were wrong. How could any of them be Lucas's fault?

"I just want you to think about why you're befriending this woman, Lucas, that's all. It can't just be about her. It has to be about you, as well. You have to get something from the relationship."

He swiped at the wall. "I know that. Like I said,

I'm just getting to know her. And she did help me today. I locked my keys in my car and she gave me a coat hanger."

"Well, good," she said, "but you know what I mean."

"Yes, I know what you mean."

They worked in silence for a while. His mother meant well, but she was wrong. Lucas wasn't trying to save everyone because of some messed-up complex he had over having a sadistic drunk for a father.

He just wanted to do the right thing.

"You're a good man, Lucas," his mother said.

He shook his head. It was impossible to ever be annoyed with her. "I try to be."

"Well, you wouldn't be my *hijo* if you weren't. I'd disown you," she said.

"Yeah?"

"In a heartbeat."

"No, you wouldn't," he said, smiling. "I'm your one and only. Besides, you love me."

"Yes, that is true and you are very lovable, once you get past your whole I-have-to-save-the-world thing."

"I have to save the world?" He regarded her, eyebrows raised.

"Yes, even though it isn't your place, because you aren't responsible."

He groaned.

"Just pointing it out, so you don't forget."

"Yeah, well, I don't think I'll forget that one."

"You might, once you get distracted," she said.

He climbed down and moved the ladder again before responding. "And how am I going to get distracted?"

She took a deep breath then let it out slowly. "I think a young troubled *niño* and his distressed *madre* will prove a very difficult distraction."

"Is that so?" he asked. "And I don't know that the kid is troubled. He's tired for sure, but troubled, I don't know."

"Either way, you won't be able to resist. You're already getting sucked in. I can tell."

Lucas shook his head. He hadn't even mentioned the secret espresso-machine deal. Was his mother right? Would he get sucked deeper into a relationship with Grey and Claire than he meant to? Lucas only wanted to help.

And that did *not* mean he was trying to save anyone.

"So what else is new?" she asked.

"I made Ramsey a night manager. He's been there for almost a year now and he makes a decent barista, especially for someone who didn't know a latte from a cappuccino when he started. But besides that, he's great with the other employees and I trust him completely with the books."

"Won't he be headed to college at some point?"

"I hope so." He didn't offer any further explanation. She'd ask, of course.

"So why give him a promotion if he's leaving?" she asked.

"It will look better on his résumé and it frees me

to do more long-term planning," he said, which was true, but he was thinking about spending some time catching up on the latest treatments for PTSD.

"And…?" she asked.

"And what?"

"And why else did you promote him? Really?"

He lowered the roller and turned to her. "Because he's the right guy for the job, okay? He has a future he's planning for and I think he has potential."

"I see." Satisfaction laced her tone. "Kind of like you when you were younger?"

"Yes, only I wasn't fortunate enough to have someone there to pull me out of it."

"Someone to save you, you mean?" She winked at him when he frowned at her. "Like I said, you're a good man, Lucas."

"I'm a damn softy."

"Yes, but a lovable softy." She lifted the paint can. "We're almost out."

"I'll go. I need to pick up a few things for The Stop at the building supply store."

"Thank you, my love. No hurry, though. Tomorrow is fine. I'm done for the day. It's Friday night. You should be off having fun." His mother set down the can and wiped her hands on a rag. "And, Lucas…"

"Yes, *Madre?*"

"I'm sorry I wasn't there to pull you out of it."

He climbed from the ladder and hugged her. "You

did the best you could for a kid with sadistic-father issues."

She smacked his arm. "You turned out okay. Even though you're still trying to save everyone."

"Well, I'd like to think so."

CLAIRE PULLED INTO her mother's driveway Friday afternoon. She handed Grey his duffel bag from the backseat. "Are you sure you packed everything you need?"

"Yes, Mom, you checked it twice. I have clean underwear and my toothbrush."

"Good. It's just that you don't have extra stuff here, like you do at Aunt Becca's."

"I know." He scrunched his mouth to one side. "Maybe I should leave some extra stuff here."

She frowned. Did Grey want to start hanging out more at her mother's? "Do you mean for more overnights?" she asked.

He shrugged. "Well, yeah, that would be cool. I was just thinking...you know...for after school instead of soccer." He peered at her expectantly.

"Oh." She turned fully to him, scooting around in the driver's seat. "I've been meaning to talk to you about that. I know I kind of left you hanging."

He nodded.

"Well, I did talk to Gram and she said she'd love to have you in the afternoons."

Again, he nodded, but his gaze fell to the floor. He didn't comment.

"You were right, of course. She loves hanging out with you. She can't get enough."

He remained silent, his gaze downcast.

"I was thinking about what you said, though—about me working from home and staying with you after school."

"Really?" His gaze locked on hers. "You actually thought about it?" he asked.

"I did, Grey, and…" She hesitated, almost afraid to say the words, but maybe it was time.

"And?"

"And I think we should give it a try," she said, raising her hands in a wide gesture. "Worst-case scenario, we head to the coffee shop if I go batty. It's actually kind of peaceful there—not sure why I like it—but you should be okay doing homework there."

He frowned. "But we're going to try at home first?"

She squeezed his arm. "Yes, honey, we'll try it at home first, starting Monday. I'll pick you up from school."

"Or I can ride the bus."

"Do you like riding the bus?" she asked.

"It's okay. I don't mind if it's easier for you that way," he said as he opened his door. "Cool, let's tell Gram."

She smiled. At least Grey was happy. Her mom was likely to be disappointed to not be spending more time with him and heaven knew Claire was apprehensive.

But then again, what wouldn't she do for her son?

"Hey, Mom, I know why you like the coffee shop," Grey said, turning to her, grinning, as they headed up the driveway.

"Really? Why?"

"The coffee-shop guy—he's kind of cool."

She stopped, surprised. "Lucas?"

Grey continued up the front steps. "Yes, ma'am, Lucas," he said. "He's a good guy. Don't you think?"

"Sure," she said, frowning. "But why would that make me like the coffee shop?"

His shoulders lifted in an easy shrug. "I think he kind of likes you."

"What? Why would you think that?" Heat filled her cheeks.

"He gave you whipped cream on your Americano."

"So? That doesn't mean anything," she said.

"Really?" Grey shrugged again. "It's extra and you didn't even ask for it, but if you say so."

"I do say so," she said. "It was just whipped cream."

"Okay." Grey smiled. "Well, either way, *I* like him. I think he'd be cool to hang out with."

Claire stared after Grey as he reached the last step. He wanted to hang out with Lucas. She sighed. He still needed a good male role model. She'd have to suck it up and go back to the BBBS.

CHAPTER EIGHT

LUCAS INHALED THE scent of lumber as he headed into the building supply store. He needed Spackle to patch the hole in the wall of the stockroom and new brackets for the shelves he wanted to install once that was done.

A familiar female profile caught his attention as he passed the plumbing aisle. Claire Murphy stood before shelves of supplies, a tube of caulking in her hand.

"Claire," he said. Unexpected warmth filled him at the sight of her. "Fancy running into you here."

She glanced up, her brown eyes wide. "Lucas, hello."

"Are you having plumbing issues?" he asked.

She nodded and hoisted the tube. "My sink and tub are a mess. I thought I'd give recaulking them a try."

He moved beside her. "Ah, and are you a caulking expert?" he asked.

"Do I need to be?" she asked, her eyebrows furrowed. "I mean, how difficult is it? Can't I just finish peeling up what's left of the old stuff and squeeze out fresh caulk?"

"You could," he said, "but there is an art to caulking, if you care about how it looks and, of course, there's the whole functionality aspect."

"Oh. I thought it would be an easy do-it-yourself kind of project."

"It is. You'll do fine. Do you have caulk softener?" He scanned the shelves behind her and handed her another tube. "Here. You'll need to apply this first and let it sit for a couple of hours. It'll make cleaning off the old stuff easier. Do you have bleach, or some other kind of good cleaner?"

"I'm sure I do."

"You'll want to clean the seam really well after you get the old caulk off. It will help the new stuff stick better."

"I see," she said. "I didn't realize there was so much to it."

"Don't worry. It's easy."

"I hope so, though now I'm not so sure," she said, smiling tentatively. "I'm really not much of a do-it-yourselfer."

She straightened. "It's funny running into you. I never see anyone I know here, sometimes at the grocery store, but not here. I guess there aren't as many do-it-yourselfers out there."

"I guess you're right," he said, returning her smile. "So how's everything going?" he asked.

She'd sat at her regular table today, the one by the

window. He'd managed to leave her to her work for most of the afternoon, but he hadn't been able to ignore how the sun lit up her hair, picking out red highlights he hadn't noticed until today.

He *was* going soft, mooning over her hair.

Her smile faded. "Everything's okay."

"Good."

"Lucas." She bit her bottom lip. "I wanted to talk to you about something." She glanced around. "But this probably isn't the best place."

"Oh?" Now he was curious. "Do you want to go somewhere else?"

She shook her head. "It's fine. I shouldn't have brought it up."

"Oh, no, please, it isn't any trouble. I have time if you do. I was going to grab a bite to eat after this. I'd love some company if you don't have to go home to Grey," he said.

"He's at his grandmother's tonight. But you have shopping to do here. I don't want to interrupt that."

"I can come back." He wasn't about to pass this up. "Look, if I have a choice between shopping for building supplies or having dinner with an attractive woman on a Friday night, I vote for dinner." He held up his hands. "Not that dinner means anything. We're just eating, so we can talk about whatever it is you want to talk about."

"We don't have to do dinner. Maybe a drink somewhere."

"All right, if that makes you more comfortable, but I need to eat at some point. Don't you?" he asked.

"I suppose. If you're sure," she said, still frowning. "You can pick the place. I'll follow you in my car."

"I know a good Italian place that isn't too far. Why don't I walk with you while you pay for your caulk and we can go from there?"

She exhaled and then nodded. "Okay."

"I DON'T MIND driving, if you just want to take one car," Lucas said ten minutes later as he motioned Claire toward his car.

She squeezed the strap of her purse. What did she really know about Lucas? Did she feel safe with him? "I can follow you. That way, neither of us has to come back here."

He hesitated, then nodded. "It isn't far, but do you want my cell number, in case we get separated?"

Her fingers felt stiff and clumsy as she entered his information into her contacts. After Grey's comment about hanging out with Lucas, all she'd been able to think about was Lucas mentioning something about the PTSD articles to Grey. Not that that scenario was even slightly likely. But what if Lucas asked her about them and Grey overheard?

"Ready?" he asked. "I'll pull out and wait for you here."

With a quick nod, she headed toward her car.

Claire inhaled slowly, trying to relax. She refused to let her nerves get the better of her.

Five minutes later, she was heading along 400 north, following Lucas. Suddenly, a truck slammed into the car in front of him. The boom of the impact swept over her. She braked hard and her car spun sideways. Claire gasped as the squeal of locked tires tore through the air. Another car plowed into the truck. The sound of crunching steel filled her ears, its echo drawn out as if time had slowed. Then all at once, she was still and silence descended.

She barely had time to pry her hands from her steering wheel when Lucas yanked open her door. Miraculously, no one had hit her and she'd stopped mere inches from his car, which itself was just short of the wreckage.

"Are you okay?" Lucas's hands skimmed over her.

"Yes…I'm fine," she said.

He didn't apologize for touching her—he'd been all business in his quick assessment. Once that was done, he simply reached between her and her steering column to turn on her emergency flashers. Then he was heading for the first vehicle that had been hit.

With her hands shaking, she unbuckled her seat belt, and followed. Lucas had to climb through the passenger door to get to the driver. His shoulders blocked her view, but he turned to her, his cell phone pressed to his ear as he spoke. "We've got a male Caucasian, late twenties to early thirties, unconscious. Laceration to the right temporal brow."

He glanced at her and swiveled the phone away from his mouth. "His air bag didn't inflate. I need something to stem the flow of blood."

"Oh." She glanced around.

"Here." He stripped off his outer shirt. "This will work. I need you to hold it in place."

She took a step closer as Lucas shifted and the driver came into view. A large gash split his forehead. Blood covered his face and ran down his neck, pooling in a deep stain at his collar. Her stomach pitched as Lucas pressed the shirt to the wound. Her fingertips tingled as pain squeezed the base of her skull.

"I need you to take this. Just apply pressure," he said.

When she remained glued to her spot he let go with one hand to motion her forward. "Can you stay with him?" he asked.

She stared at him—at the blood covering his hand—as a ringing started in her ears and her heart thudded. She opened her mouth, but couldn't form a thought, let alone a sentence.

"Claire, I need to check the other drivers," Lucas said, keeping his voice calm.

She nodded, her stomach knotting. She squeezed into the passenger seat and took hold of the blood-soaked shirt as he shifted out. He touched her shoulder as he moved past her. She closed her eyes and pressed hard as the wet warmth seeped around her fingers. She forced herself to take slow, deep breaths.

Lucas's voice floated to her as he reported the other driver's condition to what had to be a 911 operator. The man beside her groaned and she jumped, nearly letting go of the shirt.

With another deep breath, she pressed down again and said, "Sir, you've been in an accident. An ambulance is on the way." She was surprised at how calm she sounded. "We were right behind you and my friend is a former EMT. He was just here checking on you and he called 911. He's checking the other drivers now, but he'll be right back."

At least she hoped he would be.

The man didn't respond. Loud voices reached her as a siren wailed in the distance. She glanced over her shoulder as a big man, nearly as tall as Lucas and twice as wide, weaved toward her, his left arm hanging limply at his side. Rage contorted his features as his gaze locked with Claire's.

"What the hell are you doing?" he asked, his tone angry. Expletives spewed from his mouth, his words slurred as he staggered toward her.

Despite her fear, Claire stayed beside the injured driver, keeping steady pressure on his wound though her fingers had gone nearly numb. The man lurched another step forward, still cursing, his face red. He reached for Claire with his good hand and she couldn't breathe.

Suddenly Lucas appeared, filling the space between her and the man. "I know you're hurt," he said, "but you need to calm down and back away, or you're going to be hurting a whole lot worse."

The man stopped. He stood, scowling at Lucas. "Idiot driver pulled right in my way," he slurred. He gestured toward Claire. "She shouldn't be helping him. This is all his fault."

"He was only in your way because you swerved across two lanes and T-boned him," Lucas said, the anger in his voice barely contained. "From the smell of it, your blood alcohol level will be off the charts."

The man swayed a little as he narrowed his gaze on Lucas.

Lucas grabbed the elbow of his good arm. "I suggest you go back to your truck and wait for the police," he said. "Your shoulder is dislocated, but considering this driver has a serious head wound, I'd say you got off easy."

The man muttered another expletive and stood his ground. Lucas turned him toward his truck. "You're done here. And trust me—you don't want to push me right now."

Claire exhaled as the man moved away. Thank God Lucas had been there. Before she could thank him he slipped to her side.

"How are you holding up?" he asked.

"I'm okay." She nodded toward the injured driver as the sirens wailed ever closer. "I thought he was coming to."

"I can take it from here."

She nodded again and moved aside, being careful

to keep the pressure steady as he slipped his hands under hers. She scooted out, but stayed close, glancing at the truck driver. The tingling sensation in her fingers intensified and she clenched her hands into fists, closing her eyes to the blood staining them.

Please let the ground remain steady beneath my feet. Now was not the time for an anxiety attack.

"Ma'am, are you hurt?" A young female voice startled her. A woman with medic patches on her sleeves and a crash kit in her hand stood beside her.

Claire shook her head and pointed toward Lucas and the driver. "I'm fine. This isn't my blood. He needs you."

The next half hour passed in a blur. As the medics loaded the driver of the first car into the ambulance and the police arrested the driver of the truck, Lucas squeezed her hand. She stared at his bloodstained fingers threaded through her own, as though she were watching someone else. She should be able to feel him touching her.

"Claire?" Lucas asked and folded his other hand over hers.

She met his gaze. In his eyes she found compassion, understanding—a connection. The strength of his presence wrapped around her, comforted her in a way she hadn't experienced once in the past year. Her throat tightened and the night blurred.

"I asked if you're still hungry," he said. "The police said they'd call if they have any more questions. We can go."

"Hungry?" she echoed, the word magnified in her ears.

He grinned and somehow that warmed her even more, brought her back to herself. She gave his hand a return squeeze. "You want to eat after all this?"

He gestured to their attire and said, "I think we can wash most of the blood off. Our clothes are no worse for wear, except for my shirt, which I'm tossing." He tugged on the hem of his long-sleeved T-shirt. "We'll go someplace casual."

"Someplace close?" she asked as her stomach growled.

"Yes," he said, nodding, his hands still holding hers. "Unless you're in a hurry to get home."

"No." At the moment, with the warmth of his fingers surrounding hers, home held even less appeal than usual. "Did you say Italian?"

THE TINKLE OF silverware and clattering of dishes followed Lucas as he passed the kitchen of the small hole-in-the-wall Italian restaurant he and Claire had found not far from the crash site. His pulse quickened. She'd seemed so serious when she'd said she had to talk to him. Was it about the articles in her book bag? He couldn't imagine anything else.

He rounded the corner toward their booth. Their waiter leaned against the table beside Claire, smiling and shaking his head as she spoke. The poor guy probably couldn't help himself. Claire was way too appealing for her own good. Their waiter had been eyeing her since their arrival.

Honestly, Lucas couldn't blame him.

Lucas slowed his pace, letting his gaze drift over her profile. It wasn't that Claire was drop-dead gorgeous, but there had been times tonight when her brown eyes had drawn him in, engaging him on a level he wasn't sure either of them was ready for. And her mouth… He exhaled. He couldn't bring herself to think about her lips, how just when he thought it was impossible to make her lighten up, her mouth would curve into a shy smile.

How would her lips feel if he pressed his fingertips to them?

He dismissed the thought. He shouldn't be thinking about her along those lines. She'd held it together during that collision and then afterward, dealing with all that mess until the EMTs had arrived, but if her shaking hands and distressed eyes were any indication, she'd fought to do so.

Whatever Claire struggled with, he needed to tread carefully.

"There you are," she said, smiling up at him tentatively.

She hid her smile almost immediately, but not before its warmth sank into him. If the fright of their near accident and the trauma of dealing with the aftermath was what it took to make her trust him, then he was grateful for the opportunity.

He retook his seat as the waiter edged away from

the table. Lucas dropped his gaze, forcing himself not to drink in the sight of the candlelight flickering across Claire's face. He warmed with the awareness of her gaze on him.

He inhaled slowly, calming the beat of his heart, surprised at his own reaction. The old excitement rippled through him, the excitement of being in the presence of a desirable woman.

They placed their orders and the waiter left. Claire leaned toward him. "I'm amazed at how cool you were through that whole thing. I was such a basket case."

"I was an EMT and medevac pilot in the marines." He squeezed her hand, the gesture feeling natural now. "I thought you did okay."

She lowered her gaze, but didn't let go of him. "I did okay because you were there."

"Yeah, must have been all that coffee-shop training. You never know when cleaning up lattes will come in handy."

She smiled again, a little longer this time. "Was that something you always wanted to do? Own a coffee shop?"

"I can't say it was. I finished my last tour with the marines and I just… I wanted normal and I thought running a coffee shop would be low-key, but sustaining."

"I understand wanting normal," she said. She straightened and pulled her hand from his, tucking it in her lap. "I wanted to talk to you about those articles in my book bag."

"Claire, you don't have to tell me anything you don't want to."

"The problem is…" She squeezed her hands into fists. "I'd actually rather not say anything…I mean, you hardly know me, but I'm so…neurotic that I can't stop thinking about Grey somehow overhearing something. I've been torturing myself with the thought that now that you've seen them he'll find out."

"Grey won't hear anything from me," he said.

She nodded, her gaze lowered. "Thank you. It's just that he worries enough as it is."

"And if he knew you had PTSD he'd worry more?"

Her gaze met his, her eyes rounded. "He'd want to know everything about it and why I have it."

His stomach tightened as she confirmed his suspicions. He hated that he'd been right. He wanted to take her hand and reassure her, but at the same time memories of Toby swamped him, bringing with them that familiar heaviness.

"I've had some experience with PTSD," he said. "Not firsthand, but I've had buddies with it. My best friend was hit pretty hard." He glanced away. It was probably better not to dwell on what had happened to Toby. "So I know a little about it, if you ever want to talk."

Thankfully, she didn't ask about Toby and merely nodded. "I haven't actually been diagnosed, but from all the reading I've done I'd say I'm a pretty classic case. I'm sorry to even bring it up. I just couldn't stop worrying— Grey can't know."

"I understand."

She shook her head. "He wants normal, poor kid, practically begs for it. And he's stuck with me for a mom." She straightened. "Have you found it? Have you found a sense of normalcy running your coffee shop?"

He studied her for a minute. "That's a tough question. What is normal? I mean, yes, I think I have, but my idea of normal might not be the same as yours. What's normal to you?"

Her gaze locked on his. "Do you mean what's normal for me, as in our day-to-day experience, or what is my definition of what normal should be?"

"Well, both."

She stared off into the distance for a while, until the waiter brought their entrées. Claire thanked him, then waited for him to leave before speaking.

"I think normal for most people is a regular eight-hour workday, and then returning home to their families afterward, laughing, playing, enjoying a quiet meal together, maybe a little TV before bedtime and then finally a restful night of sleep."

"Okay," he said. "Sounds normal enough to me. So what's normal for you? I know you and Grey stay pretty busy."

"I cram as much as I possibly can into every day, just to keep from thinking." Again her gaze drew him in, anchoring him to that spot, that moment. "To keep from thinking about how scared I always am."

Sadness echoed in her laugh as she looked away. "I know that sounds pitiful," she said, "and it is and I have no idea why I'm telling you this, but there it is. You know I have PTSD—which is something I haven't told anyone else—and now you might as well know that. You were just so competent back there and I was so frightened when that big drunk truck driver came after me. I was frozen and you showed up and made him go away and I felt safe." She looked at him again. "For once, I felt safe. And it's been such a long time since I felt that way."

Lucas swallowed past a suspicious lump in his throat. He grabbed her hand from her lap and held it. "Well, it's a good thing that big drunk truck driver didn't pound me into the ground then."

"Yes." She nodded, a small smile playing along her lips. "That's a very good thing."

CHAPTER NINE

A WISP OF cloud drifted past the half-moon as Claire walked with Lucas to her car. So much had happened between the pileup on 400 and then at dinner. It seemed a lifetime ago that they'd left the building supply store.

"I'm sorry tonight took such a bad turn, but thanks for joining me for dinner," Lucas said. "That part was pretty enjoyable, at least for me."

She smiled at his teasing tone. "Dinner was enjoyable for me, too. And not just because of the mousse, which was awesome. As far as the accident, no apology needed. That wasn't your fault and you were quite the hero. The driver who got T-boned was lucky you were there. We all were."

He ducked his head. "I've been trained for situations like that," he said. "It may sound cold, but it's easy when the victims are strangers. It might have been a little different if you'd been hurt."

"It must have been so difficult for you, though… in the marines. When you were a medevac pilot, did you come across victims you knew?"

His chest expanded as he inhaled. "In both Afghanistan and Iraq, yes, I did and it was hard."

Claire waited for him to expound, but he walked quietly, as though lost in thought. "I'm sorry," she said. "I didn't mean to stir up any bad memories."

"It's okay. I don't talk a lot about what happened over there. Most people find it hard to hear."

She glanced at his profile, his head still bowed. His experiences had to be so much harder than what she'd gone through. He functioned as though unaffected, but he had to be. She resisted the urge to touch his arm.

She said quietly, "I'll listen anytime you want."

He lifted his head then and his gaze held hers. "Thanks, I really appreciate that. I'll do the same for you, anytime."

She appreciated the offer and the genuine spirit with which it was made. "Thanks. I don't really talk about it, though. Any trauma I've suffered can't compare to what you've been through."

The warmth of his hand covered hers. "Don't do that," he said. "Don't dismiss your experience. Whatever it was, it's affected you and is no less important than anything that's ever happened to me or anyone else. We all respond in our own way."

He let go of her hand. "I didn't have it so bad," he said. He stood so close that the heat of his body blanketed her.

She breathed in his scent and smiled. "You smell like coffee," she said. "I hadn't noticed before."

His lips curved as he returned her smile. "A bag broke earlier today and I cleaned it up. I don't always smell this way. At least I don't think I do. Between the grime from the accident scene and the painting at my mother's earlier, I'm surprised the coffee's what you notice."

"Well, it's nice. You know I love coffee. I couldn't manage without my espresso in the morning."

"Yes, I know." His gaze hovered over her face.

Adrenaline pumped through her, but whether it was from fear or excitement or both, she couldn't tell. Whatever it was, she was way out of her comfort zone. "I honestly can't thank you enough," she said, "for everything…it was nice having your company tonight, through all of it. I really did enjoy dinner. Thank you for taking the time out for me to… tell you things I'm sure you had no desire to hear. I probably should have kept it all to myself and just put it out of my mind."

The crease between his eyebrows deepened. "I wouldn't have said anything, not around your son."

She nodded. "I overthink things sometimes and then I work myself into a frenzy." She closed her eyes for a moment, then exhaled. "I'm glad I told you. It's a bit of a relief to share it with someone."

He touched her cheek. "You've been dealing with this for a while?"

"A little over a year."

His jaw tightened. He didn't respond, but his gaze held hers.

She couldn't take the short silence. "I'm glad we did dinner and not drinks. I would have scraped together leftovers or something, but this was much better."

"It was definitely my pleasure," he said.

"I feel safe with you." She stood on her tiptoes and slipped her arms around his neck in a hug she hadn't realized she'd intended to give. "I'm not so sure how I feel about that, though."

He lifted his arms to show she was free to walk away from him. "Claire, I don't want to put any pressure on you, but you *are* safe with me. I promise."

His conviction shone in his eyes. Any remaining unease melted from her as his arms gently encircled her and held her against his firm body. Her breasts tingled from the contact. She pulled back, her cheeks heated by her own action. She'd been on her own for too long. She felt like she'd just jumped into the deep end of the pool and forgotten how to swim.

"I'm sorry," she said. "I didn't mean to be so forward."

His hold didn't tighten, but his gaze warmed. "You don't need to apologize," he said. "I'm not complaining."

"No?" she asked as her eyes dipped to his beautiful mouth.

"No." His lips were so close she could almost taste them.

With a small sigh Claire tipped up her face and pressed her mouth to his, his lips soft and so responsive. She welcomed his tongue, stroking it with her own, melting into him. Pleasure rolled over her as he pulled her closer, lifting her from the ground as he deepened the kiss.

Time slowed around them as Claire lost herself in the taste, smell and feel of Lucas. At long last he withdrew, setting her down gently, his arms loosening, so all she had to do was step back to break contact. She did so as the cool night air swept over her.

"I…I didn't realize I was going to do that."

He rubbed a strand of her hair between his fingers. "Again, no complaints here. I just don't want to rush you into anything."

"No, of course not." A small laugh escaped her. Her stomach tightened at the slightly hysterical sound. What was she doing? "I'm sorry, I shouldn't have kissed you. I mean, my life is crazy right now." She spread her hands. "What with all the home repair projects on top of everything else."

He reached for her hand. "Let me know if you need help with anything. You have my number in case you run into any trouble."

"Thanks. I might need you to talk me through how to do the caulking tomorrow."

"Not a problem. Just use the softener first. It'll make a world of difference."

"I don't know," she said. "It sounds so much more complicated than I thought it would be."

"You'll do fine."

"If you say so," she said, frowning.

"Do you want me to come do it for you?" he asked.

"Oh, no, I couldn't ask you to do that."

"I really wouldn't mind."

"Truly?"

"No." He laughed. "We can't have you with a leaky tub."

Claire cocked her head. She did feel safe with Lucas. Maybe it would be okay if he came by the house. "Well, I wouldn't want you to do it for me, but maybe you could be there to give me pointers and make sure I do it right."

"I'd be happy to, Claire."

GREY DROPPED HIS pack of tae-kwon-do gear by the front door and headed for the kitchen the following afternoon. Even though they'd grabbed a quick lunch on the way home, hunger gnawed at his insides. He'd never make it through the park if he didn't at least grab a snack before Mom rushed them out again.

"Hey, kiddo, please don't leave your bag by the door." His mom strode into the kitchen behind him.

"Sorry, Mom, I'll put it away in a minute. I need to eat something before we head back out."

"Head back out? We're not going anywhere." She handed him a banana, then peeled one for herself. "We just ate. You must be going through another growth spurt."

"We're not going to the park?"

"I made other plans. Do you want to go to the park? We can go after."

"After what? What plans? Do you mean we're hanging out here? On a perfectly good Saturday afternoon?" he asked, surprised.

She laughed. "So many questions. Lucas Williams from The Coffee Stop is coming by. He's helping me redo the caulk around your tub."

Curiosity and a little excitement made Grey forget about his banana. "Lucas, the coffee-shop guy, is coming here? How did that happen?"

"I ran into him last night at the building supply store while I was getting the caulk and he offered to help. I hadn't realized it's as complicated as it is."

"Really? So you guys are friends now? Like hang-out friends?" he asked.

She paused a moment. "I guess we are. We went to dinner after we ran into each other. But he's not coming to hang out. He's going to show me the right way to caulk the tub."

Grey's excitement built. His mom really was serious about trying to hang out at home. "That's great," he said. "I like him. He's a good guy." He cocked his head. "So…are you just friends, or do you *like* him like him?"

"Grey! We're just friends." She started rinsing the dirty dishes in the sink. "Maybe I can get him to look at the garbage disposal."

"Is he good at fixing things? Can he fix the shelf in the bookcase in my room?"

She shut off the water and turned to him. "He's probably got better things to do than fix all of our stuff for us."

"But he's helping you caulk and he's a good guy. I'll bet if we asked, he'd help more. We have lots of stuff that needs fixing around here. And maybe we can make him dinner—you know, to thank him. Like a sit-down dinner."

"A sit-down dinner?"

"Yes, Mom." Grey folded his arms.

"Why don't we see how the caulking goes before we load him up on projects?" she said, frowning. "You're probably right about dinner, though."

The doorbell rang and Grey sprinted for the door. "He's here."

Mom hurried after him, but Grey got there first. He opened the door wide. Lucas stood on the stoop, smiling. It was strange seeing him outside the coffee shop. Grey raised his hand in greeting. "Hello."

"Thanks, honey." His mom stepped behind him and gestured for Lucas to enter. "Come on in."

"Want to see my room?" Grey asked. He could show Lucas his shelf and ask him how to fix it. Maybe he could do it himself if he had a few pointers. Mom sure didn't know how to do that kind of thing.

"Grey—" Mom said.

"I'd love to," Lucas said as he closed the door behind him. "How was tae kwon do?"

Grey glanced at his white uniform with his orange

belt; he'd forgotten he still had it on. He shrugged. "It was cool. This way." He led Lucas down the hall to his room.

Mom again followed. "We need to spend a little time in here cleaning up."

"What?" Grey looked around. "It always looks like this," he said.

"Why don't you change and then tidy up in here while I show Lucas where the caulk has peeled away around your tub?" his mom asked.

"Okay, but I should learn how to caulk, too," Grey said. They were actually hanging out at home in the middle of the day on a weekend. It figured, though. They finally had someone cool to hang out with and his mom wanted to hog him.

Mom scrunched up her mouth again, like she always did when she was ready to give in. "You can come help after you change, but then you're going to put your dirty clothes in the hamper and put your action figures away."

"Deal," Grey said. "And then, Lucas, could you maybe tell me what I need to do to fix this shelf? If I could put my books back on it, they wouldn't be all piled on the floor and it would look better in here. Mom tried to fix it, but it just fell apart again."

Lucas bent down to look at the shelf. "I think I could help you with that after we caulk the tub."

"All right!" Grey wanted to high-five Lucas, but Mom was giving him her you'd-better-watch-yourself-mister look.

"This way to the bathroom," Mom announced and Lucas followed her out of the room.

Grey smiled as he pulled a pair of jeans from the pile on his chair. It was Saturday afternoon and they weren't rushing off to the park. They were hanging out at home. All he had to do was keep finding projects for Lucas to help with and they could surely stretch this out until dinner.

CHAPTER TEN

CLAIRE'S SWEET SMELL teased Lucas as he moved beside her. He closed his eyes to enjoy it. Hers wasn't a flowery scent. It was clean and fresh, all that was good and desirable, and he fought the urge to kiss her again. If only he didn't know how soft and responsive her mouth would be.

"I think I got all of the old caulk off," she said as she ran her hand along the seam around the tub.

"It looks good."

"You were right, though. I'm not a pro caulker. I would have just peeled up the old stuff without doing any cleaning. I'm glad you told me about that softener."

"You did a great job on the prep work." He forced himself to focus on loading the tube of caulk into the gun. "Now, we need to cut this tip at a forty-five-degree angle."

He pulled out his pocketknife and flipped it open. Claire inhaled sharply. He felt her tense beside him, but she didn't speak.

Then she stood quickly and said, "I'm going to

check on Grey. He must be having trouble finding the paper towels."

She left and Lucas's stomach clenched as he looked at the blade. Though it was just a pocket-knife, nothing overtly threatening, she definitely wasn't comfortable around it. Had someone threatened her with a knife? Hurt her?

He quickly cut the tip then put away the knife, just as Grey rushed in, paper towels bunched in his fists.

"I didn't know how many you needed, so I brought lots of them," he explained. "I can get more if you want."

"This is plenty, thanks," Lucas said.

He turned to Claire, who stood just inside the door, her expression unreadable, but her posture stiff, her arms wrapped protectively around her middle. He extended the caulk gun toward her and asked, "Would you like the honors?"

She smiled that small smile of hers, though her expression remained guarded as she moved to his side. "Sure. Is there a special technique?"

He took her hands in his to guide her. "You're going to begin here and angle it so you're pulling the gun away from the tip," he said. "We'll start on this short wall. Keep constant pressure on the trigger and don't lift the tip until you reach the corner. Then release the trigger at the end, so the caulk doesn't pool."

She nodded and he let go of her hands, so she could maneuver the caulking gun on her own. She ran a steady bead along the seam. If she'd been disturbed by the knife, she'd recovered quickly or hid it well. Again, he hated the thought of someone harming her.

What trauma had Claire experienced?

"Why is the tub full of water?" Grey asked. "Is someone taking a bath?"

"It kind of settles the tub and ensures we have the tightest seal," Lucas said.

Grey nodded. "You mean the water pushes out the sides of the tub?"

"Exactly," Claire said.

"Cool." Grey moved beside his mom. "Can I help?"

Claire handed him a paper towel and the caulking gun. "Can you be in charge of cleaning the tip?"

"I sure can," he said as he scoured the end of the tube with one of the paper towels. He held it up for inspection. "How's that?"

"Perfect, thanks, little man." Claire smiled at her son as he handed her the caulking gun.

"Grey, can I see your finger?" Lucas asked.

The boy extended his index finger. A giggle burst from him. "Why do you want to see my finger?"

"I need to check the size," Lucas said. "Yes, I think that's just about right." He glanced at Claire, before turning back to her son. "This is an important job. We need you to run your finger along the bead of caulk your mom just laid. That's to smooth it and get up any excess caulk. Can you do that?"

Grey perched on the tub, finger ready. "I can do that."

"You have to wet it first," Lucas said, nodding toward the water in the tub.

Smiling, Grey dipped his finger in the water. "Okay, what do I do?"

"Here, honey, like this," Claire said, then guided Grey's finger along the bead of caulk.

"Perfect." Lucas grinned at the boy and Claire granted Lucas a smile. He basked in that smile for a moment. Including Grey was such a small thing, but well worth it if it made Claire happy.

Lucas was almost sorry when they finished the job a short while later, but Grey turned to him as Claire cleared away the caulking gun and paper towels. "So, can we take care of my bookcase now? I'll bet you can help me fix it right."

"Well, of course, I'll see what I can do," Lucas said and strode after the boy.

GREY'S LAUGHTER FLOATED to Claire over the strains of an old metal band as she slid the chicken into the oven an hour or so later. With Lucas around she'd been hesitant to crank her music as much as she usually did. She peered out the open back window, the weather now unseasonably warm for October. Lucas cocked his head as Grey showed him the gate that was barely hanging together. As Lucas examined the hinge, Grey took off for the backyard shed, apparently to show Lucas where they kept their pitiful supply of tools.

Claire was still so confused over last night with Lucas, but one thing was for sure—Grey really liked him. So did she. Heat flooded her at the memory of his mouth on hers, while he pulled her tight against his hard body. She hadn't known she could still enjoy that.

Grey followed Lucas out of the shed, carrying a screwdriver, while Lucas hefted the rusty old metal toolbox that Claire had had so long she couldn't remember where it had come from. Grey's smile lit his face. He was evidently enjoying every moment. When was the last time he had been this happy?

Claire moved away from the window. As much as she'd enjoyed it, had kissing Lucas been a mistake? What had she been thinking? She wasn't anywhere near ready for a relationship, or whatever else might come as a result of kissing him.

Even though Lucas hadn't meant anything by it, she hadn't been able to control her reaction when he'd pulled out his pocketknife. The sight of that blade had spun her back into that afternoon when her mother's neighbor, Phil Adams, had broken into her house. It had taken all her strength not to drop to her knees in a panic. What would Lucas have thought of her then? Knowing about her PTSD and experiencing it were two different things.

She'd done the only thing she could do.

She'd run. Again.

But how long could she keep up that kind of behavior without him realizing how damaged she was? Would he stick around once he knew how truly abnormal she'd become?

What if Grey became attached to Lucas? She needed to follow up on getting him a Big Brother. Her stomach tightened. Grey lit up around Lucas. Look how he'd manipulated him into staying all afternoon and her into making a sit-down dinner for all of them. They might enjoy today, but what would happen when everything fell apart, as it inevitably would?

She'd have to make sure Grey didn't get too used to having Lucas around. And if she were smart, she'd do the same for herself.

"THIS IS INCREDIBLE," Lucas said as he wiped his mouth with his napkin. "Do you eat like this all the time?"

Grey giggled with his mouth full of broccoli and sun-dried tomatoes. He shook his head, his eyes shining with merriment.

Claire gave a wry smile. "My son finds that question amusing, because we don't eat at home very often." She stabbed a piece of roasted chicken. "We tend to eat on the run."

"Mom hardly ever cooks like this," Grey said, having swallowed the bite, all smiles. "Sometimes she does, but then we pack it to go. Usually it's take-out or something from the drive-through and we eat on our way to practice, and sometimes we take it as a picnic in the park."

Lucas frowned. His gaze swung from mother to son, who both seemed to take their eating habits in stride. "I knew you two were on the go a lot," he said, "but you really don't ever sit down and enjoy a meal?" He gestured to the table covered with dishes, as if for a Thanksgiving feast. "It's just surprising when you can put together such a spread. If I could cook like this, I'd eat this way all the time."

Claire stiffened. "We eat at home every now and then."

Across the table, Grey puckered his lips, but refrained from further comment. He took another big bite of broccoli.

"I just wanted to let you know how much we appreciate all your help today," Claire said. "Grey actually suggested we make you dinner when I told him you were coming. I thought it was the least we could do, especially after you fixed his bookcase and reset the hinge on the back gate after finishing the caulking. You went way above and beyond."

"Yes," Grey chimed in. "I told her we should make you dinner." He glanced at his mom. "A real sit-down dinner, like at Aunt Becca's or Gram's. *They* eat like this all the time."

He leaned toward Lucas and whispered, loud enough for his mother to hear, "Sometimes dinner at my aunt's goes on for hours, especially when Gram comes. We sit around and talk while we eat, then we have dessert, which Aunt Becca usually makes, like apple pie or chocolate cake or her peanut butter cookies, which are awesome, and then we still sit there while the grown-ups have coffee. Nobody has to go anywhere."

"Speaking of dessert..." Claire stood. "We have ice cream with caramel sauce. Who wants some?"

"Me," Grey said, his eyes wide.

Lucas smiled at the boy. "I'm in."

As she scooped the ice cream, she turned to Grey. "When you finish, I'll take you to the park, if you still want, Grey."

Grey's eyebrows furrowed. "Can Lucas come?" he asked.

Claire glanced at Lucas. "You're welcome to join us, but please don't feel obligated. We've taken up enough of your time."

Did she want him to come or was she tired of his company? Lucas glanced again from mother to son. "Actually, I'd love to come, if that's okay with you, Claire."

Her eyebrows arched. "Well, of course, we'd love that."

"Yes!" Grey said as he wielded a spoonful of ice cream. "We'll go to the park and then can Lucas come back tomorrow and help us fix more stuff, like the garbage disposal? And stay for dinner again?"

"Grey," Claire said. "I'm sure Lucas has better things to do than hang out here with us, playing Mr. Fix-It."

"I do need to finish some painting tomorrow, but I'd love to come by after that," Lucas said. "I can look at the garbage disposal and maybe mow the lawn. And your hedges need trimming. Grey can help me, if he'd like."

Grey was all smiles.

"And dinner could be my treat," Lucas said to Claire. "I wouldn't want to put you out again."

She shook her head. "Seriously, I appreciate the offer, but you don't have to do my yard work. I can take care of that. And the garbage disposal hasn't worked for ages. We can manage without it."

"We can at least take care of the outside stuff, though. I have a new trimmer I want to break in. I'd be happy to help. We can all pitch in together and get it done that much faster. And I'll bring dinner, so you won't have to cook, but we can still eat here—another sit-down meal." Lucas winked at Grey.

Claire sat gripping her fork. "Maybe we should wait until next weekend," she said.

"Why?" Grey asked.

Lucas remained silent. She was nervous. Best not to push her. "Next weekend works for me just as well. Why don't you just let me know?"

She nodded. "We have rock climbing tomorrow morning with Becca and Amanda and I'm running in the afternoon. Grey will be at his friend Marty's."

"Mom, we can skip all that," Grey said.

"Grey—"

"It's okay, Grey," Lucas said as he patted the boy's

hand. “We might get to do this again next week-end. And I’ll see you at The Coffee Stop, right?” He glanced at Claire for confirmation.

“Yes, of course,” Claire said.

“And don’t forget, if I do come next week, dinner is on me.”

“Oh, no, if you’re working in the yard, I insist on making dinner again.”

Grey nodded, obviously pacified and pleased at the prospect of another dinner at home. “Mom insists,” he said.

CHAPTER ELEVEN

LUCAS STOOD IN the doorway of Grey's bedroom, while Claire kissed her sleeping son's cheek and pulled the blanket over him. He stepped back as she turned out the light, then closed the door behind her.

"He's so tuckered out," she said.

"When he goes down, he's out for the count, isn't he?" he asked.

Her eyebrows drew together. "Actually, I haven't seen him fall asleep like this in a long time. I hope he wakes up good and rested for a change."

He nodded. Lucas had originally thought the boy was worn out from the nonstop activities, but if he wasn't sleeping on top of that, the poor kid must have been truly exhausted. Was Claire's insomnia disturbing her son's rest?

She touched his arm. "Thanks for coming to the park. I can't remember the last time we had so much fun. That's why he's so tired. I should have gotten him out and run him like that sooner. It's so much better to toss a Frisbee three ways, instead of two, though."

"I'm seeing some Ultimate Frisbee in Grey's future," Lucas said, smiling.

The park had been a blast. Claire had relaxed while she'd laughed at her own misthrows and run after the passes he and Grey never quite got close enough for her to easily catch. Lucas had enjoyed watching her cheeks bloom with her efforts and her easy smile when she triumphed.

She'd been radiant.

But the moment they'd returned to her house, she'd tensed up again, cranking that screeching guitar music, while Grey rolled his eyes, even as he yawned. Lucas nodded toward her right ankle. "Why don't you come sit down and let me look? You were limping a little after that spill."

"It's fine," she said. "Just a twist, not a sprain or anything. I can't believe I was that clumsy."

"Let me look just to be sure," he said and held out his hand to her.

She hesitated only for a moment before letting him lead her to the sofa in the living room, where he had her sit, while he examined the injured ankle.

Her skin was soft and warm to his touch. He pressed in various spots. "Does this hurt?"

She shook her head as she settled against the armrest, a throw pillow at her back. "No, it hurt just a bit when I twisted it, but it's fine now."

"I think you're right. No bruising or swelling. It's not sprained, but it wouldn't hurt to ice it."

"You're probably right," she said and started to rise.

He gripped her ankle to keep her in place. "Stay here. I'll get it."

Her eyes held a glimmer of protest, but she nodded. "Okay, thanks."

He found some ice and a baggie in the kitchen, then returned to the sofa. She'd sat up and had her arms again wrapped around her middle.

What was it about her home that had her so uptight?

"Here, relax," he urged her as he sat at the end of the sofa and pulled her feet into his lap. He settled a dish towel over her ankle before placing the ice bag on top. "Let's see if you can be still for fifteen minutes and let the ice do its job."

"We've kept you so long today," she said. "I'm sure you have better things to do on a Saturday night."

"Not unless you're ready for me to leave."

"You're good company." Her gaze held his. "I appreciate all you've done today, on behalf of my house and my son. I'm sure you could tell Grey really liked having you around." She looked away. "You were right about him needing a Big Brother."

"Have you made any progress there?"

"I went down to their office and met briefly with the director."

"That's great. Did they match him with someone?"

"Not exactly. There's a whole selection process." She took a slow, deep breath. "I had a hard time. I… started panicking, right there in front of the guy. He must have thought I was nuts. I…left."

"You had a panic attack?" Lucas asked.

She nodded, unable to make eye contact.

"Does that happen often?"

"Not usually around other people. I try to fall to pieces in private."

How often did that happen? His stomach tightened as memories of Toby flashed through his mind. He wanted to ask her so much more, but was hesitant to press her. And a part of him wasn't sure he wanted to know.

She bit her lip. "I guess I should try again, call Monday morning, see if I can stop by first thing."

"I think Grey would really like having a Big Brother."

"I'm sure he would," she said. "If I can hold it together long enough to get him one."

"Do you know what caused your panic attack?" He had to ask. "Maybe there's a way to avoid the trigger."

"Oh," she said, "that would be difficult. I…" She shook her head.

"Claire, it's okay. You don't have to tell me anything you don't want to."

"It's just…sometimes I get a little freaked out

when I'm alone with strange men—or with men I know, for that matter."

That statement, along with her reaction to his knife earlier, set off alarm bells in his head. Did he really want to know what had happened to her?

He remembered his mother's words. *I think a young troubled niño and his distressed madre will prove a very difficult distraction.*

Getting involved with Claire would indeed be a difficult distraction. He was just getting to know her and the thought of someone hurting her was already twisting knots in his gut. Could he handle being swept back into the dark place that had already claimed his friend?

"Are you okay being alone with me?" he asked.

Her eyes widened. "Yes, for the most part."

"For the most part?"

She closed her eyes momentarily. "I get flashes sometimes, like little spikes of fear when I first see you, but then it goes away, once I recognize you. I do feel safe with you, especially after the accident."

"Claire, have you talked to anyone about this, a counselor?"

She again wrapped her arms around her middle. "I've been reading up on PTSD—you saw the articles. I can work through it on my own."

"It might help you to talk through it with someone with proper training, though." Someone besides him, a professional, who stood a better chance of helping her.

"Maybe," she said, but she didn't sound convinced. She straightened and smiled. "So, enough of that. Tell me about The Coffee Stop. How's everything going there?"

Part of him welcomed the change in topic. "Business is steady and I have a great crew."

"That's good. Everyone gets along?" she asked.

"Yes, mostly." He pulled the ice from her ankle. "I think that should do it."

"Thank you." She swung her legs around and sat up. "For everything, Lucas."

He nodded. "I've enjoyed it. Thanks for dinner and including me in your day." He *had* enjoyed his time with Claire and Grey. "Let me know about next weekend. I'd love to come back and do it again."

"I will. If Grey has his way, you'll be here." Her gaze dropped. "I'll see what we have planned for Saturday afternoon."

The ripping chords of electric guitar swirled to a stop. "I should probably get going, let you get some rest," he said. "Maybe you'll be able to sleep, too, after all that running around."

"Maybe."

At the door, she undid the bolt and then turned to him. "Thanks again, Lucas, it was really great having you around today."

The openness of her gaze pulled him in. The memory of the kiss they'd shared washed over him. He touched her cheek. "It was my pleasure."

"Grey will be sorry he didn't get to say good-night."

"Well, good luck with getting him a Big Brother."

"Thanks," she said, though concern filled her gaze.

"Claire, would you like me to go with you?" he asked, not wanting to contemplate his motives for asking. "To the BBBS office, for moral support?"

Her eyes rounded. "Oh, I wouldn't want to put you out."

"You wouldn't be putting me out. I'd like to go, if it would help."

She smiled slowly. "That would be nice, but you'd have to let me do something for you in return."

"Whatever makes you happy, but we can worry about that later."

"Thank you, Lucas." She slipped her arms around his neck and hugged him.

"You're welcome." He pressed her close, enjoying her warmth and softness. He exhaled, trying to stem his response to her. The woman had no idea how she affected him.

Her breath fanned his cheek and he turned his face as she shifted and her sweet lips brushed his jaw just before her mouth claimed his. He gave in immediately to her kiss, returning the probing of her tongue with abandon, letting her take as much as she wanted until she slowly pulled away, her arms sliding to his chest.

"I keep doing that," she said.

"You didn't see me stopping you."

He resisted the urge to pull her back into another kiss. He had to be sure of what he was doing with Claire and if he was honest, he wasn't clear on anything where she was concerned.

"So, you'll call me after you talk to the BBBS?" he asked.

She nodded. "If you're sure you're not busy."

"My schedule is flexible. Just let me know and I'll come get you, or you can stop by the shop and we can go from there. Or I can meet you there. Whatever makes you the most comfortable."

Cool air floated over him as she opened the door. "We can go together."

He nodded, placed one last chaste kiss on her mouth, then stepped into the night. He shivered with an unexpected chill as he headed to his car. Helping Claire get Grey a Big Brother was the right thing to do. That she was willing to ride together showed she was growing more comfortable with him.

The memory of the feel of her mouth on his and her body pressed to his stayed with him as he headed home. One step at a time.

SATISFACTION FILLED CLAIRE as she pulled out of the parking lot of the BBBS office and glanced at Lucas. "I did it. At least my interview part. I still need to bring Grey in for his interview. But it sounds like they have some good candidates to match him with."

"He should have someone active," Lucas said. "Someone able to keep pace with him."

"And they have one who's a history buff. He'll score big-time with Grey on that. Thank you so much for going with me. I wouldn't have been able to get through it without you."

"I didn't do anything but sit there like a lump."

"You helped me to keep it together. Remember, I tried on my own and it didn't work so well."

"I was happy to come along for the ride," he said. "So are you coming back to The Stop with me, or do you have a class?"

"I don't have classes on Mondays." She glanced at the clock on her dash. "I'll come in and work for a bit. I have a little time before Grey gets home. This used to be a soccer day."

"You decided to work from home, then, so you could be there with him?"

Her earlier satisfaction drained away as the dread crept in. "We're going to give it a try. This afternoon will be telling."

He cocked his head and said, "Most people would like working from home, but you don't sound all that excited."

She shrugged. "You know how it is with kids around. I'll be lucky to get anything done."

"Really? Grey seems like a great kid. I would think he'd not bother you and do his homework without much fuss."

"He's wonderful and homework is never an issue."

"But being home is an issue."

His quiet statement had her swallowing. "Is it obvious?"

"You were relaxed at the park, but you seemed a little tense once we got back to your house."

She had enjoyed the park. Claire kept her gaze on the road and ignored the throbbing at the base of her skull. "Sometimes being home is difficult, but it'll be fine."

The satellite radio broadcast a cover of an early metal song. She tapped her fingers on the steering wheel and focused on the road, thankful when Lucas let the subject go.

"So, what home fix-it projects are you working on?" she asked. "You mentioned you had to do some painting."

"I'm fixing a hole in my stockroom wall and then putting up some shelves. I was helping my mother with some painting, but that's done."

"That's nice of you. Does she live nearby?"

Lucas nodded. "She's got a little place not too far from mine in Sandy Springs. She's great. It was always just the two of us. Like you and Grey. We're pretty close."

"That's nice," she repeated.

"So, where does *your* mother live?" he asked. "Is she nearby?"

"Ah, yes, unfortunately." She shook her head, her cheeks warming. "No, I don't mean that. That sounded horrible. She's great with Grey and he always has a wonderful time with her. She spoils him shamelessly."

"That's what grandmothers are for, right?"

"Yes, I suppose so."

"I'm guessing you and your mother don't get along as well as you'd like, though," he said.

"No, not at all. She makes me crazy. And I seem to do the same to her."

"I'm sorry to hear that."

She made a swiping motion with her hand. "It's all good. Maybe we'll work it out one of these days."

She merged onto the interstate. This topic wasn't much better than the last. She needed to turn the conversation to something that didn't involve her and her issues.

"So, the marines, what was that like? Why didn't you reenlist?"

He hesitated before answering. "It was great…at first. Definitely what I needed at the time. I learned so much—acquired skills, grew up fast. I got my certification as an EMT, like I told you, and I trained as a medevac pilot." He paused as a horn sounded in the distance.

"The military was good for me…don't get me wrong," he said. "I needed the discipline. My mother was wonderful. She did the best she could, but I made some bad choices when I was younger. I got into trouble. Being in the marines straightened me out in a way nothing else could have."

Lucas gazed out the front window. A chill passed

through Claire. She had so many questions about him. It seemed the more she learned, the more she wanted to know.

"What…what kind of trouble did you get into when you were younger?"

He took so long to respond she was afraid she'd pushed too far. "I'm sorry, I didn't mean to pry."

He touched her shoulder and surprisingly, she didn't flinch. The feel of him was comforting, rather than threatening. "It's okay," he said. "It's just not a part of my life I'm particularly proud of."

"You don't have to tell me, Lucas."

"Things were always tough for us. My mother did the best she could, but it was hard to make ends meet. Some months we didn't have electricity. I got a job bagging groceries when I was fifteen, but then she lost her job. She'd been working in a diner. And…well, we started to get hungry.

"I got mixed up with the wrong crowd, a bunch of gangbangers. They were into a lot of questionable, but…profitable activities." He shook his head. "At first I thought it was worth it. The money sure beat what I made bagging groceries. I was able to put food on the table and help keep the lights on, but I'm not proud of what I did."

He stopped again, his gaze shifting once more to the road as she exited the interstate. He exhaled as if the weight of the world bore down on him. "I ran deliveries," he said. "I didn't always know exactly what I was carrying, but I knew it was drugs or stolen goods—even weapons. I thought, if not me some other kid would do it and I wasn't *doing* drugs or *stealing* anything. How bad could it be?

"I only meant it to be for just a little while. Just long enough for my mother to get back on her feet. But the weeks stretched into months and then a year or more had gone by. We got into it with another gang. Things went bad in a hurry. I was running a delivery in a respectable neighborhood. It was way out in the suburbs, though, on the west side. I didn't have my license or a car, so a friend of mine drove. We got to the place and it was deserted and quiet—too quiet."

The tension in her skull increased as her pulse thudded. Claire gripped the steering wheel as the dreaded tingling started in her fingers. "What happened?"

She felt Lucas glance at her from the other side of the car. "We got jumped," he said. "It was bad. I'd been in fights before—we had regular beat-downs—but nothing like this."

They passed through a yellow light, and then turned down a side street. "I was lucky. I walked away, crawled, really, but no permanent damage. The guy with me, my driver, he wasn't so fortunate."

She swallowed her apprehension. "What happened to him?" she asked.

"He didn't walk for months." He shook his head. "And he never seemed quite the same after that. That's on me."

"But you can't feel responsible for him. He chose to be there. He must have known what he was getting into."

She risked taking her eyes off the road and his gaze met hers. "He was my friend—my best friend. I talked him into running with me because I needed him to drive. He only went because he was trying to keep me out of trouble."

Claire's stomach clenched. She shivered, but remained silent. She hadn't been in Lucas's shoes.

"I'm sorry about your friend," she said.

"Toby was tough as nails. We got out of the gang after that. Before all that trouble I never would have thought anything could get him down. We joined the marines together. He saw things…did things… and he couldn't get over it. I didn't know then how much he really wasn't handling it…."

She turned a corner and The Coffee Stop came into view. Claire bit her lip. She should probably ask, but did she want to know what had happened to Lucas's friend?

"I'm sorry," he said. "I didn't mean to be such a downer."

"It's okay," she said as she pulled into the parking lot. "I know how it is once you start to unload. I've told you plenty. I appreciate that you feel you can confide in me."

She pulled the key from the ignition and flexed her fingers. Thankfully, the tingling had subsided. "Will you let me buy you dinner or something to repay you for going with me today? Or maybe I can help you with your shelving or painting. Not that I'm good at that kind of thing, but I'll be your gofer, if you'd like."

"Claire, you don't owe me anything. You listened just now. I'd say we're even."

"Oh, no, you've already put up with some of my craziness. You said whatever made me happy and I'd be happy to either help you or feed you. Your pick."

He smiled as they exited her car. "I don't want to make you cook and I'd rather take *you* to dinner."

Lucas wanted to take her to dinner. That and the thought of doing chores with him lightened her mood. A breeze swept over her and she inhaled the fresh air. The pounding in her head also seemed to ease.

"So I'm your gofer," she said. "When are we putting up shelves?"

CHAPTER TWELVE

CLAIRE GRITTED HER teeth later that afternoon and straightened as she heard a tap on the kitchen window. She was strung as tight as a bow. Hadn't it been enough that they'd had a proper dinner with Lucas on Saturday? How had she let Grey talk her into that? She moved to the window to make sure it was still the same branch that had made the sound earlier. Maybe she could get Lucas to trim that tree the next time he came by. The branch hit the glass every time the slightest breeze caught it.

Satisfied the culprit was indeed the old maple, she again took her seat at the table across from Grey. A car rolled along the street outside. She remained alert until it passed, then tried to focus again on the contract she was reviewing. The house was too quiet.

She'd turned off her music earlier so Grey could concentrate on his homework. She was afraid to use her earphones, since even that seemed to bother him. He hadn't complained, but she was keenly aware of his every squirm, cough or glance and he hadn't been able to focus. The kid had supersonic hearing.

Surely, she could stand the quiet for the amount of time he needed to do his homework.

Grey glanced up from his spot across the table. He'd been so excited to have her there when the bus dropped him off, she hadn't had the heart to work in her home office. Besides, if she weren't right there with him she'd be obsessively checking to make sure he was okay.

"What's wrong?" he asked. "Why aren't you working?"

"I'm working."

"No, you're not," he said, frowning. "You didn't have to turn off your music. It doesn't bother me."

"You weren't concentrating when I had it on," she said.

He drummed his pencil on the table. "Please, Mom, try again. I promise it won't bother me." He jumped up and headed for the television set in the adjoining living room. "I'll put the TV back on, too."

"Honey, it's okay."

But he'd already turned on the TV. She sighed and put her earphones back in and cranked the heavy metal. She finished reviewing the contract, then opened the proposal for one of her newest clients. The movement of a drumming pencil caught her attention again.

Grey sat with his head in his hand, feet swinging, pencil keeping a constant beat on the table, his homework forgotten in front of him. She pulled out her earphones. "Do you need help, little man? What are you working on?"

"Vocabulary. I just have to write sentences with these," he said and showed her a list of about twenty words. "I can do it."

"How much have you gotten done so far?"

He turned his notebook toward her. She scanned down the page. It held two completed sentences and the start of a third sentence, smudged with eraser marks.

"I think maybe we should try again without the television," she said. When he opened his mouth to protest she held up her hand and moved toward the other room to turn off the TV. "I'll keep my earphones in this time."

He nodded, responding only by putting pencil to paper and scratching out the rest of the sentence. Claire smiled as her phone buzzed, announcing a text. Her pulse quickened as she checked the display. It was from Lucas.

how's working from home?

She glanced at Grey, who'd stopped writing to watch her. She motioned for him to continue, then sent Lucas a return text. idk. working on it.

good luck. if u need to u can come back here.

She frowned. After this past weekend and this morning, she wasn't sure she'd be able to ever work around Lucas again. She'd spent her time after the BBBS meeting alternating between thinking about his gang past and remembering kissing him.

And she couldn't let go of the picture of him with that knife in his hand. Even now the image washed over her, triggering the squeezing again at the base of her skull and the tingling in her fingers. She struggled more and more these days to maintain a state of normalcy around him.

will give it more time. not ready to give up yet, but thanks for the offer.

She set down her phone as Coldplay came on her internet radio. She smiled again. When had Coldplay snuck into her library? Perhaps hanging out at Lucas's coffee shop had mellowed her.

Grey remained hunkered down over his vocabulary, though a quick glance at his paper revealed more eraser marks than sentences. The tree branch tapped again at the window and she stiffened, but ignored it as she pulled out a red pen to mark the drafted contract.

Fifteen minutes later, the drumming again drew her attention to Grey. She placed her hand on his to still his pencil.

"Little man, how are those sentences coming?" she asked.

He frowned and covered his paper with his arm. "They're coming."

She nodded as she turned off her earphones. "Okay."

The quiet of the house settled around them as Grey bent his head over the sheet of paper, his pencil now working across the page. Claire swallowed and turned back to the contract. The branch tapped the windowpane. The overhead light buzzed quietly.

She squeezed her eyes shut. Outside, the wind blew and the house groaned as it settled on its foundation. The buzzing of the light magnified as her breath became shallow and she broke out in a sweat. When the tingling in her fingers started, she pushed back from the table.

Grey paused in his writing, glancing up at her, his eyebrows arched. "Are you okay, Mom?"

She nodded as the floor seemed to tilt beneath her. "I think we should try this at the coffee shop. What do you think? Lucas is still there."

"Sure, if that's what you want. It would be cool," Grey said, though disappointment weighed his words. "Is it because I didn't get more sentences done?" He showed her his paper. "I did more. See?"

She nodded. "Good job, honey." She flexed her fingers to try to stop the tingling. Thankfully, the floor seemed to have leveled below her feet. Still, she wasn't taking any chances. Grey had yet to witness her in a full-blown panic attack and today would not be the first time.

Not if she could help it.

The buzzing of the light continued and it was all she could do not to turn it off. They had to leave.

"I'm going to get my purse. Pack up your stuff and we'll head to Lucas's shop," she said.

Grey nodded without responding and Claire escaped to her bathroom where she splashed water on her face before grabbing her purse. When she stepped back into the kitchen, Grey had not only packed his school bag, but he'd also loaded up her computer bag with the papers she'd been working on.

"Thanks," she said as she slipped the bag over her shoulder.

Heavy metal blared from the car radio during the ride to Lucas's shop. Grey stared out the window without speaking, his arms crossed. Claire inhaled slowly, again flexing her fingers to make sure the tingling had stopped.

Why had she thought she could do it? She shouldn't have gotten Grey's hopes up.

But the day hadn't been a complete loss. She'd had some success in her mission to find him a Big, as they called them at the BBBS. "I have some good news."

"What?" Grey asked, slumped in the passenger seat.

"I went to the Big Brothers and Big Sisters organization today. If you think you'd like it, I've started the process of finding you a Big Brother."

"What is that?"

"It's someone who can hang out with you."

"You mean, like a stranger?"

"Well, he'll been screened by them and I'd meet him with you and we'd make sure we were both comfortable with him before we planned anything." She glanced at her son as he sat frowning beside her. Maybe she should have discussed this with him first, prepared him better.

"Lots of kids have Big Brothers, Grey. I think you should give it a try."

"Are you just trying to find someone else to palm me off on?" he asked, staring at her.

"No, why would I do that?"

He turned away, shaking his head.

"Grey, it would be good for you," she said, frustrated now. Somehow, she'd managed to mess up again.

She'd no sooner parked in front of the shop than Grey bolted from the car and raced inside—away from his failure of a mom.

GREY STARED AT the teenager behind the counter. Stubble covered his cheeks and jaw. A cast encased his left forearm.

"Where's Lucas?" Grey asked.

"He's in back. Did you need him for something?"

"No, it's cool." Grey glanced toward the entrance as his mom came in and headed in their direction. Why did she think he needed a stupid Big Brother? And why did they call it that? It wasn't as though the guy would really be his brother. Who would want to be a part of their family?

He shoved his hand into his pocket and his fingers closed around the ten-dollar bill Aunt Becca had given him for chores. It was a payment on the espresso machine. He blew out a breath. He'd have to find a way of getting it to Lucas without Mom seeing.

Mom stepped up beside him, her fake smile in place. Grey hated that smile. Why did she have to pretend she was happy?

"What are you having, little man?" she asked.

Heat rose in Grey's cheeks at the use of the nickname. He glanced at the kid behind the counter. A smoothie might be nice, but the kid already thought he was a baby. "Espresso."

"Make that a decaf mocha latte and I'll have the same," Mom said.

"Yes, ma'am, coming right up. Do you want whipped cream on those?"

"No," Grey said. Only babies had whipped cream.

Without looking at his mom, he moved to a nearby table and dropped his book bag by a chair. Maybe Lucas would come out and he'd find a way to slip him the money. But he still had to figure out how to get the espresso machine to the house.

Would his plan even work? If Mom couldn't sit still at home for an hour in the afternoon, would she be able to manage breakfast? She had managed on Saturday, though, and they could still blast her music.

She stood at the counter, her back stiff as the new kid chatted while he made their drinks. She obviously asked about his cast, because he waved it, no doubt telling her the story. His sleeve slipped upward on his good arm as he reached for a mug, revealing part of a tattoo on his arm.

Who was this tattooed kid? How long had he been working in Lucas's shop?

With a shake of his head, Grey pulled out his notebook. What did he care? He should at least finish his homework. Then maybe they could head home again and he could shut himself in his room. Why bother trying to hang out with his mom? She'd just blast her music and it wasn't like they could talk over it. And obviously she didn't want to hang out with him, if she was trying to push him on this Big Brother guy.

A short while later his mother joined him. "Here you go," she said as she placed his coffee drink beside him.

"Thanks," he said and then sipped the drink.

"Honey, I'm sorry. I should have talked to you about getting you a Big Brother beforehand, but it doesn't mean I'm palming you off on him. I love hanging out with you. We hang out a lot. I just think it's important that you have a good male role model."

"If you love hanging out with me, then why can't we hang out at home?" he asked.

Her shoulders rose, then sank. “It’s difficult for me.”

“Why?” He stared at her. Why would hanging out at home be a problem? It never used to be.

“We hung out with Lucas this past weekend.” She gestured with her hand. “I made dinner.”

“Fine, then let’s do it again.”

“Fine, I’ll ask Lucas if he can come hang out this Saturday, but then I want you to give this Big Brother thing a try.”

He shrugged and sipped his drink. “Fine.”

At least they’d get to hang out with Lucas again. Besides, if Mom didn’t want to tell him what was really going on, he might as well try out the Big Brother. Maybe he’d tell him stuff.

“Don’t fill up too much. We can stop for dinner when we’re done here.”

Grey nodded. Of course they’d stop somewhere. Why would they do anything so crazy as to have dinner at home, like normal people? “I’ll bet Aunt Becca is making a nice dinner.”

Mom stopped and stared at him a minute. “I’m sure she is. My sister is great about doing things like that.”

Grey felt bad about hurting her feelings, but he couldn’t seem to stop himself. Had she even tried to work at home? What was wrong with her that she couldn’t manage something as simple as that?

He shrugged and focused on his paper. He had a billion more sentences to write and then he still had math to do. He focused on the page. The bell on the front door jingled as a group of laughing teenagers entered.

At least they were having fun. An upbeat song came on and Grey tapped his pencil to the beat. Why did his mom think this place was mellow? Just because Lucas didn't play acid rock didn't mean there wasn't a lot going on.

"Here are my favorite espresso drinkers." Lucas appeared beside their table. "How's it going, Grey?"

Grey nodded and said, "Okay."

"Got a lot of homework?" Lucas asked as he peered over Grey's shoulder at his sentences.

"A little. I have to finish these sentences, then I have a math worksheet."

"Well, my man Ramsey has been hitting the math pretty hard these days. If you run into trouble, maybe he can help you." Lucas nodded toward the scruffy teenager behind the counter.

"Your man Ramsey has a tattoo," Grey said. "I saw it when his sleeve rode up."

"What kind of tattoo?" Mom asked, frowning.

Grey shrugged. "Couldn't see all of it, but it looked like some kind of letters or something."

"He's a good kid," Lucas said.

"Is he old enough to have a tattoo?" Mom asked. "Don't you have to be eighteen?"

Lucas's eyebrows arched. "I don't think he got it legally," he said, "but he's still a good kid. He may have gone astray at one point, but I'd say we've gotten him back on track."

"Astray in what way?" Mom asked. "Did he really fall down some stairs?"

"Mom," Grey said, "he just works here. If Lucas says he's cool, then he's cool."

Grey glanced at his mom. She still seemed intent on this Ramsey kid. Hurrying, he pulled his notebook into his lap and jotted a quick note.

Need to give u $ and ask u something.

He tore the note from the page and slipped it to Lucas under the table. Lucas read the note, then glanced at him and nodded.

"Hey, Grey, can I borrow you for a minute? I need to get some cups from the back. I thought you could help me," Lucas asked and glanced at Mom.

She frowned. "Well, only for a minute, okay? He's got to finish his homework."

"I'll have him right back," Lucas said as he pulled out Grey's chair. "Follow me."

Grey smiled at his mom as he hurried after Lucas. She didn't suspect a thing. Boy, was she going to be surprised on her birthday. They slipped behind the counter and then down a short hallway, before reaching a door marked Staff Only.

Grey smiled as Lucas led them into the supply room. Shelves of coffee, bottles of varying shapes and sizes and all kinds of boxes surrounded them. Grey dug in his pocket and pulled out the ten-dollar bill.

"Here," he said and handed the bill to Lucas.

"That makes just another thirty dollars I owe you, right?"

Lucas took the bill as he bent low to look Grey in the eye. "That's right, but it's not too late to change your mind," he said. "I mean, are you sure this is something your mom wants?"

"Yes, she's going to love it," Grey said.

She *had* to love it. He didn't have a Plan B and he'd go nuts if something didn't change soon.

"I still have a couple of weeks until her birthday," he said. "Her birthday is the weekend before Halloween. I need your help getting the espresso machine home, though. Maybe you can bring it over for me—you know, like we could get you to come to fix stuff and then you can stay and we'll surprise Mom and celebrate or something. Maybe I can ask Aunt Becca to help me bake her a cake." He frowned. "I'm not sure how to sneak that over if it's part of the surprise, but I could try to figure it out."

Lucas straightened. "Maybe, but don't worry. We'll figure something out if that doesn't work."

"Why wouldn't it work? Aren't you going to come back to our house to help us again? Mom says she's going to ask you about this Saturday, but we've got lots of stuff that still needs fixing, so one day won't be enough. We'll have to stretch it out, until I can pay you the rest of the money. I'll help you with fixing stuff and doing yard work."

"It's not entirely up to me, buddy. I'd like to say we're going to fix lots of more stuff together, but I can't say what's going to happen tomorrow, let alone in a couple of weeks. But I'll do what I can to help."

Grey was more frustrated than he ever remembered being. Why was Lucas saying this? Didn't he like them?

"Hey, you'd better take these out front, or your mom will be on to us." Lucas handed him a stack of disposable coffee cups. "Give these to Ramsey. He'll know where to put them."

Grey took the cups and glanced at Lucas expectantly, hoping he'd come back out front and hang out with them, but he'd already turned toward an office tucked away at the back of the stockroom.

"Okay, thanks," Grey said.

Lucas turned to him and smiled. "You've got it, Grey. I'll be back out front in a little bit."

Well, that hadn't gone quite the way he'd thought it would. Grey found Ramsey at the far end of the counter, cleaning out some kind of metal filter. He'd have to ask Lucas to show him how to make espresso, so he could make some for his mom when they had their own machine at home.

"Here," he said, handing the cups to the tattoo guy. "Lucas said you'd know where to put these."

"Sure." Ramsey took the cups. He removed them from the plastic bag and carried them to a spot mid-counter.

Grey trailed along behind him and asked, "So, how long have you worked here?"

"Like, almost a year."

"How come I haven't seen you? We're here every morning."

"I'm only here after school."

"You're in high school?"

"I'm a senior."

"And where did you get your tattoo?" Grey asked. "My mom thinks you're too young to have one."

Ramsey frowned and rubbed his arm. "It's just something stupid I did. My mom got really pissed."

"Mine would kill me if I did that." Grey glanced at his mom. She was watching him and she didn't look happy. She motioned for him to come back to the table, pointing at his notebook.

"You shouldn't get one, then," Ramsey said. "Not at least until you're old enough."

Grey turned so he couldn't see his mom. "Why did you get yours?" he asked.

Ramsey busied himself fidgeting with the big espresso machine. "I was stupid. I was into things I shouldn't have been into," he explained. "But Lucas gave me a job here and helped me to get out of a bad situation."

"Were you in a gang? Is that why you have the tattoo? I saw a special on the History Channel about gangs and they showed tattoos kind of like yours."

"Look, it's not something you talk about." He shook his head. "Lucas is cool. I couldn't have turned things around if he hadn't been there."

"Yeah, he's cool." Grey glanced at his mom again. She was giving him her mom frown. "I've got to go."

"Okay, see you."

He trudged back to the table, back to his homework and his mom, who continued to frown at him as he slipped into his seat.

"Sweetie, please try to concentrate now," she said. "I think it's best if you go to Gram's after school a few days a week from now on."

Grey picked up his pencil and didn't answer. Why argue? She'd made up her mind. Great, now he'd be spending more time at Gram's. At least *she* seemed to like having him around. Maybe he could spend the weekend with her or Aunt Becca. These days any place was better than at home.

CHAPTER THIRTEEN

LATER THAT WEEK Lucas paid his bills online as Ramsey settled in the chair beside his desk. Lucas's decision to promote the kid had proven right. Ramsey had turned out to be a good manager.

"What's up, Ramsey?" Lucas asked.

"I was thinking we should schedule an extra person Saturday mornings. We've had a lot of new groups showing up and it can get hectic with just two of us up front. Not for the entire shift, but starting midmorning would be good."

"Why don't you see if you can work it out without us having to hire any additional staff? I gave you access to the schedule last week. Let me know the next time you log in and I'll walk you through it."

Ramsey nodded. "Thanks. That'd be great. I really appreciate you giving me this opportunity."

"Well, I appreciate the work you do around here."

"Cool. Good." He gestured toward Lucas's cell phone on the corner of his desk. "I can get you a deal on a new cover, if you'd like."

Lucas picked up his phone, with its simple black cover. "You don't like my cover?"

The kid's shoulders rolled in an easy shrug, as a rare smile curved his lips. "A guy needs to stay current," he said. "You know, to gain the interest of the ladies."

"Ah, you think I'm an old fogy."

"No, not at all." Ramsey shifted in his seat. "I think we all just need whatever help it takes."

Lucas shook his head. There was no way Claire had even noticed his cover. "I think this one's fine, but I'll give it some thought."

"It's not a bad cover. It suits you. And really, I still feel like I owe you. If you change your mind let me know and I'll get you one."

"Thanks, Ramsey. I'll let you know."

"I'm going to do my best around here."

Lucas grinned, resisting the urge to ask the kid to explain just how the plain black cover suited him. "I gave you the opportunity," he said, "but you wouldn't still be here if you hadn't shown you were up for a challenge. Now, how's school going? You've been putting in a lot of hours here. I don't want your grades to suffer."

"Oh, no, it's all cool. I'm doing okay. I was having a little trouble with physics, but I have a friend tutoring me now." He smiled. "I made an eighty-four on my last quiz."

"Good job." Lucas patted him on the back. "We can adjust your schedule if we need to. Just let me know."

Ramsey shrugged. "My plans for Saturday fell

through. I can work that morning until closing, since Ken is taking off."

Lucas cocked his head. He'd planned to spend the morning working in the back office, but be on hand in case it got busy. Hopefully, he'd be at Claire's that afternoon, though he wasn't going to push her. "I can't remember the last time I slept in and took an entire Saturday off."

"You should totally do it," Ramsey said. "I'll come in and you can do whatever you want that day. I mean, you're the boss. You should be able to take time off when you want, right?"

"Thanks, kid. That's actually not a bad idea."

"Cool. I'll add myself to the schedule then." He nodded. "I'd better get back out front."

As Ramsey left, Lucas leaned back in his chair. His mother's boyfriend had returned from his trip and was available to help her with projects, or to do whatever the two of them liked to do. With The Coffee Stop covered, Lucas had plenty of options.

A vision of Claire drifted through his mind. She'd mentioned that afternoon that Grey would be at his aunt's all day Saturday and Saturday night, so they'd postponed his visit until Grey would be there.

What would it be like to spend the day with her, without doing handyman projects? They could do something outside and active. She'd been so relaxed at the park last weekend. It was bound to do her good.

It can't just be about her. It has to be about you, as well.

His mother's warning echoed through his mind. Why was it a bad thing that he wanted to help Claire? And getting outside with her would be good for him, too.

Would she be up for it, though? He picked up his phone in its plain black case. There was only one way to find out.

"I DON'T WANT to go to Aunt Becca's," Grey said early Saturday as they made their way to Claire's sister's. "We were supposed to hang with Lucas today. All of us. It isn't fair."

"I'm sorry I forgot about your plans with your cousin, Grey."

"You should have remembered," he said.

"I don't always remember everything." She focused on the road. Her memory issues were getting to be a problem. "We'll reschedule with Lucas. Amanda is excited about you coming. Aunt Becca is taking you guys to the zoo and the Cyclorama. You love the Cyclorama and I thought you had fun at Aunt Becca's house." She pursed her lips. "They have dinner at the table the way you like."

"But you get to hang with Lucas and we eat at the table when he comes. I like being at our house then. Why can't I stay and hang out with you guys?"

Claire's head pounded so hard her scalp felt tight. Why had she agreed to go with Lucas this afternoon? She didn't know the trail he'd picked to hike, she'd gotten even less sleep than normal fretting about it and now Grey was getting upset.

"We only had dinner together once. And we won't even be at the house today. I'm meeting Lucas at the trailhead. You know I'd love to have you come hiking with us, but we already made these plans with Amanda and Becca. It would be rude to back out now."

He crossed his arms and pouted. "So, can you ask Lucas if he wants to go hiking again next weekend, with both of us?"

She wasn't sure she'd make it through today with Lucas, let alone next weekend. "Grey, I know you like Lucas—"

"Of course I like Lucas. He's a cool guy. He's *normal*."

"—but I don't want you to get too attached to him."

Grey stared at her. "Why not?" he asked. "Because you think he'll leave?"

She felt a rush of empathy for her son. He'd been through so much and the effects were starting to come out. "Not everyone is like your dad, honey. In fact, Lucas is very different from your dad, but, even so, he might not stick around forever. That's normal. People come and go."

"Sometimes they stay. Why wouldn't he? He likes us. He'd come over more if you'd let him."

She blew out a breath. "You can't say that after just one afternoon. And even if he likes us, he could change his mind. You just never know. I don't want you to get your hopes up. Besides, I'm…used to being on my own. It's an adjustment for me to be around another person so much."

"You're always around other people," he insisted.

"Yes, that's true, but they're mostly just other people who happen to be sharing the same space. I mean being around someone I'm…interacting with."

Claire could see his frown even from the corner of her eye. "I get it, Mom. You can't have relationships."

His perceptiveness surprised her. "Grey—"

"It's true. You don't get along with other people. You and Gram don't get along. That's why we never see her. Aunt Becca gets along with you, but she gets along with everyone. I guess Dad didn't like being with you, or he would still be with us."

She glanced at him, stunned. "That's how you see me?" she asked.

He shrugged, his eyes downcast, but he didn't deny it. They drove in silence the rest of the way. When they got to her sister's, Grey jumped out of the car with his bag and raced up the front steps before Claire could unbuckle her seat belt. As he disappeared into the house, her phone buzzed with a text from Lucas.

Stopped by the shop. Bringing ur espresso. C u soon.

She shook her head as she backed out of Becca's driveway. After this episode with Grey, she couldn't say for sure she was looking forward to seeing Lucas, but one thing was certain. She needed that espresso.

THE SUN CAST a dappled light around the trees as Lucas hauled himself up a boulder the size of a small car. Claire turned to him from her spot on the rock. She pointed to the Chattahoochee River as it rolled by along the other side of the trail they'd just left.

"The geese are still here. I guess they stay year-round," she said.

He settled beside her, forcing himself to look at the geese instead of her. "They don't want to leave a good thing. I don't think the winter will be too hard for them. It feels nice out here today."

"Yes, it does, though I'm sure we'll have another cold spell soon," she said. "I'm glad I left my jacket in the car."

"Me, too." He shook his head. "You move at a pretty good pace, though. If I'd known we were going to take this at a near jog, I'd have worn running shorts."

Her gaze drifted over his cargo pants and T-shirt. "You're dressed fine. And you were the one setting the pace. I was just trying to keep up."

He chuckled and said, "If you say so, though I think you could outrun me any day."

"But I was the one who wanted to take a break. Remember?"

A goose honked from somewhere farther upstream. A fly fisherman swung his line, casting it with a precise arc. A slight breeze ruffled the little flyaway hairs framing Claire's face.

"I wish I had the patience for that," she said, nodding at the man standing thigh-high in the river.

"You mean to fish? You don't like the sport?"

She crinkled her nose. "Too much downtime."

"That's right. You like to stay on the go, but look at him." He leaned closer to her, gesturing toward the man. "Doesn't he look peaceful?"

Her shoulder bumped him as she shrugged. He didn't withdraw. "Maybe it works for him, but I couldn't just stand there with nothing going on."

"Nothing going on?" Lucas cocked his head. "Listen."

She was silent for a while. After a moment, she leaned toward him, her shoulder brushing his again, deliberately this time. "Right, nothing going on."

"What about the splash of the river, the call of that bird—is that a hawk?—and the whispering of the wind? Peaceful."

She chuckled softly. "The whispering of the wind? Is that what you hear?"

His laughter came easily with her. "Yes, and I don't care how goofy that sounds. We all need to hear the wind when it's soft like this. Come on, try it."

"You're killing me," she said, but she smiled.

He drew back slightly to look at her. He said, "After all the hustle and bustle of life, you can honestly tell me you can't appreciate a little quiet, a little peace?" His gaze floated back to the fisherman. "I know I've had moments that were so insanely chaotic that all the peace in the world wouldn't soothe the memory of them." He turned to look at her again. "But it helps."

Her eyes filled with empathy. "I'm glad you can find peaceful moments. It must have been really hard for you."

She waited, but when he didn't elaborate, she shook her head. "I'm not saying peace and quiet are bad things. I appreciate the benefit they offer… for other people. For me…it's difficult."

He touched her arm. "Why, Claire? What is it about quiet that bothers you?"

She shook her head again, but didn't respond for so long, he thought she wouldn't. Still he remained silent, giving her the opportunity to work through her thoughts. Why *did* quiet bother her? For Toby it had been the noise. Crowds, music, any situation with a lot going on set him off. He couldn't handle anything but the quiet.

"It's deceptive," she said. "The quiet. It closes in around you and it seems peaceful…safe."

He took her hand, lacing his fingers with hers. "But it isn't always?"

She looked away, but kept her fingers entwined with his.

"So, you don't feel safe when it's quiet."

She stiffened next to him and whatever opening he'd had seemed to have evaporated. "Are you ready to get moving again?" she asked. "We're eight miles out and need to make it all the way back. Are you up to it?"

"Sure." He jumped from the boulder, then reached up to help her down.

As they headed back along the trail, he took her hand again, satisfied when she made no move to pull away. "How's Grey doing?"

"Grey? He's great. He hates me, but he's great."

"Your son doesn't hate you."

"Really?" She turned to him. "He couldn't get out of the car fast enough when I dropped him at my sister's. He didn't even say goodbye."

"Did the two of you have a fight?"

"We had a discussion. We seem to have them more and more. I'm not sure I'd call it a fight. He's just not happy these days." She was silent again for a moment. "I seem to just rub him the wrong way most of the time. Actually, he was upset that he couldn't come hiking with us."

"I thought he was going to the zoo and Cyclorama with his cousin."

"He was. I guess you're his new favorite person, though. He likes hanging out with you."

Lucas nodded. "I like hanging out with him, too—with both of you. We could come back another time and bring him along, if that would help."

She smiled, though there was still something sad in her eyes. "He'd like that."

They walked along and he didn't comment. What

made her sad about that? Was she worried about Grey spending time with him? Did she trust him with her son?

He held a branch aside for her to pass. "You say he'd like to come hiking with us, but I get the feeling *you* might not like that so much."

"It would be nice."

"But?"

She shook her head, continued a few more steps, before turning to him. "I'm just afraid he'll get attached. You know, we talked about how he needs a man in his life and he evidently does, because he's taken to you like a duck to water, but..."

"You're afraid he'll get attached and then I won't be around anymore."

"Yes," she said as she started hiking again. "Not that you'd ever deliberately do anything to hurt him. I know you're a decent guy. I appreciate that you care about him." She shrugged. "That's part of the problem. Your decency is like a beacon to him. That doesn't mean you need to take him on, though. I know you already have a full life. You didn't sign on to befriend my son."

What could he say to reassure her? He'd actually started talking to her because he wanted to help her son. She was right. As much as he'd like things to work out between him and Claire, there were no guarantees. In fact, as skittish as she seemed to be, any romance between them was likely to be short-lived.

What then? Where would that leave Grey?

"Listen, I didn't tell you that to make you feel guilty," she said. "He's my kid. He means everything to me. I would just hate to see him disappointed."

"I get it. Honestly, I have the same concern. I wouldn't want to disappoint him, either. Or you, for that matter."

"Me?" Her eyebrows arched. "You couldn't disappoint me. If there's any screwing up to be done here, I'll be the one doing it."

"That's generous of you to say, but I've disappointed plenty of people in my life."

Her gaze met his briefly, before flitting back to the trail. "That makes two of us. Mostly I've disappointed Grey, though. I'd really like to break that trend. I just don't know how."

"He's ten?"

She nodded.

"Do you think any parents manage not to disappoint their kids at that age?" he asked.

"I'm sure there are plenty."

"I'll bet they're rare. And I'm sure it will get worse as he gets a little older."

"Great. Can't wait for that." She stepped around a puddle in the trail.

"I'm no expert, but it seems to me for the most part the two of you get along. You talk, right?"

"We do."

"And communication is key. I think if you have

that down you have a head start on working through the bumps along the way," he said.

"I really hope so." She sounded forlorn.

Was she only concerned about working things out with Grey, or was something else worrying her? He gave her hand a reassuring squeeze. "You two have a solid relationship. He wanted to be with you today, right? Wasn't that part of the problem?"

"He wanted to be with *you* today. I'm in the mix by default."

"I think he likes the idea of all three of us together." He kept his gaze on the trail, but didn't let go of her hand. "And if I'm going to be honest, I'd have to admit I do, too."

This time she was the one to squeeze his hand. "It has its appeal."

A burst of pleasure rolled through him, though he tamped it down quickly. He'd have to approach any advances in his relationship with both Claire and Grey with caution. If he really were a decent guy, wouldn't he be satisfied with being friends with her? That would certainly be the safest way to ensure he'd be around a little longer. The sunlight glinted off her hair, again picking out the red highlights. He watched the gentle sway of her walk as she strode quickly along the path. The memory of their last kiss washed over him.

What if they moved beyond the friend zone? The truth was, they'd already done so with those kisses. Could he even be just friends with her, when the sound of her voice sent pleasure rippling over him? What if they became more than friends and the relationship actually worked? Didn't he owe it to himself to explore that possibility?

CHAPTER FOURTEEN

THE HALF-MOON hung low in the sky as Claire reached her car and turned to Lucas, key in hand. A pole light illuminated their corner of the parking lot. As before, she hated to see her time with him end, though her logical side warned her that Grey wasn't the only one in danger of getting attached.

"You shouldn't have let me take us out so far," she said. "I'd forgotten how early sunset comes this time of year. We should have headed back a mile or so sooner. It was a good thing you had that miniflashlight on your key ring."

He held up the light. "I have a thing for little gadgets. You never know what will come in handy. Besides, we made it back in one piece. No worries."

She nodded. "Well, thanks. I had a good time."

A cool breeze whipped around them and Lucas stepped closer to her, shielding her from the chill. "I did, too."

The heat of his body radiated out to her. She racked her brain for something to say. She should tell him good-night, then jump in her car and go. But it felt so good just to stand close to him, not touching, as anticipation rose in her.

He traced the curve of her jaw with his finger. “Claire…”

She couldn’t bring herself to look at him. She wasn’t ready for this. He was so…present…in the way his energy wrapped around her, in the way his body seemed solid and real, in the way he focused on her and her alone, as if no one else existed.

She shook her head, but couldn’t form a sentence. Her lips tingled with the memory of his lips caressing them. She should just turn away, but instead, her hand found its way to his chest. His heart beat under her fingertips.

“I would never hurt you, Claire.” His voice was unsteady, heavy with emotion.

He blew out a breath, then he moved to turn away. Her fingers closed around the fabric of his shirt, holding him in place. He looked down at the T-shirt bunched in her fist as she stared in surprise, willing her wayward hand to let go.

Then he smiled, the light in his eyes filling her with peace, with the clear realization he hadn’t wanted to leave any more than she’d wanted him to. His hand covered hers, as his other arm scooped her close, bringing her up to meet his kiss.

Her heart raced and she again found herself lost in the beauty of kissing Lucas. In his arms she felt at ease…safe.

How could this not be right?

Eventually he pulled back to look at her. "I'm not ready to go home yet."

"I'm not ready for you to go home, either." She wrapped her arms around his neck to draw him closer.

CLAIRE INHALED SLOWLY as she parked in her garage and peered in her rearview mirror at Lucas's headlights stopping behind her in the driveway. She needed to calm down, but a sense of anticipation raced through her.

She'd invited him to her house for a thrown-together dinner of whatever she had in the fridge and he'd said yes. And now they'd arrived. Yet, the speeding of her heart wasn't from fear the way she might have expected. No, this was excitement.

She wasn't afraid of Lucas. When she was with him, she felt safe, enveloped in that special something that made him who he was. The little spikes of fear she'd once felt had ceased as she'd gotten to know him. He'd shown her and Grey nothing but kindness and consideration.

As she got out of her car the memory of that first night with him when he'd gone into action at the scene of the accident flowed over her. He'd been every bit the hero that night, sharing his strength and calm with her. The knowledge he'd keep her safe had comforted her through that evening and the feeling hadn't left.

He walked from his car to tower over her. Her

heart continued its rapid dance as he took her hand and turned her toward the door. He said, "I believe you mentioned food."

"If you don't like what we have, we can order in." Relief overwhelmed her. At least for a while longer, she wouldn't have to bear being alone in her house.

He rubbed his stomach with his free hand. "I don't know, you put me through the paces out there. I've worked up quite an appetite. I may clean out your fridge and still need to order something."

Her stomach rumbled in response, making them both laugh. She pushed open the side door. "I think it's safe to say we'll use whatever's on hand for starters, then."

"It all sounds good to me," he said as he followed her into the living room.

She flipped on the TV, then detoured into her home office to boot up the computer. Again, she was careful to keep the volume lower than normal, but once the house was filled with sound she led him to the kitchen. "How about a drink first?" she asked.

"Water would be great."

She passed him a glass from the cupboard, then pointed to the water dispenser at one end of the counter. "The water's over there."

"Yes, I remember this from my last visit. You take the hydrating thing seriously."

She shrugged as she pulled an assortment of bowls and covered dishes from the refrigerator, depositing them on the heavy oak table. "It's important, given how active we are. Besides, coffee is dehydrating, so I have to drink my water if I want my espresso."

He set her glass of water on the table as she pulled two dishes from another cabinet and said, "So tonight we have a smorgasbord of spinach, pecan, avocado and feta cheese salad, roasted chicken—I'll make whatever we don't eat tonight into soup tomorrow to take to my sister's—mac and cheese, made with quinoa pasta, and tuna salad. Oh, and grilled veggies."

He spread his hands wide. "Seriously? We won't need anything more than this. This is a feast. For someone who doesn't like sit-down meals you really know how to throw together dinner."

"Just because I don't like formal meals doesn't mean I don't cook. We still have to eat." Her stomach again growled as though making her point.

Lucas smiled and shook his head. "Eat, then. Have dinner with me. I really appreciate your doing so."

"And I appreciate your coming by to have dinner with me." She glanced around, past the open archway to the rooms beyond. "I'm not crazy about being home alone."

She didn't know why she could tell him these things, but somehow sharing her concerns with Lucas made them less daunting. She forced a smile. "It's too empty without Grey. Not that he takes up so much space, or would be much help in an emergency."

Lucas nodded, his fork idle in his hand. "I'd bet he'd be more help than you think, but I get what you mean." He paused. His gaze dropped to his plate as he stabbed at the salad he'd heaped on it. "I spent a little time in therapy. Actually I went in and out for a while between and sometimes during my deployments."

"You did?" Somehow the change in topic didn't seem jarring.

"It helped. I didn't think I had so many issues, but I'm glad I went. I think it's important not to keep things bottled up. My friend Toby, the one I told you about, he wouldn't talk about what happened over there."

He lifted his hands. "Not even to me and I was with him. I know what happened. I helped him get in to see someone, made the appointment and drove him there. He seemed better after. I thought he was continuing with his treatment, but..."

She covered his hand with hers, hoping he'd continue. It seemed Lucas, at least, needed to talk.

He took a deep breath. "I thought he was better and I stopped checking on him for a little while. He wasn't better, though he hid it well. Our other friends didn't suspect how wounded he was and I certainly didn't realize it." He pressed his free hand over his chest. "Wounded here."

She kept her hand on his and nodded, still without speaking. She, too, was wounded in her heart. Some days it hurt so much, almost like a physical pain. She gave his hand a squeeze to encourage him to continue.

"He killed himself one night." He cleared his throat, then continued quietly, "He left a note about how hard it was and how he couldn't keep it bottled up anymore." He turned to her, gripped her hand and looked her straight in the eye. "I don't understand why he kept it bottled up."

His face before her blurred. She blinked. "Maybe he tried talking about it, but it didn't work."

He leaned closer to her. "Is that what happened with you, Claire? You tried to talk to someone and it didn't help you?"

Help her? Her mother had nearly yelled at her for daring to mention anything so inappropriate. Worse, her mother, the one person she should have been able to count on, hadn't believed her. She smiled through the pressure building up the back of her skull. "Maybe talking makes things worse. Maybe sometimes it's easier to push it all down and move on."

"But can you honestly say that's working?" His eyebrows furrowed and true concern shone in his eyes, until she had to look away.

When she tried to pull her hand from his, he held it tighter. "Please, Claire, don't push it down. I don't think that's the better alternative. It'll make it worse, make you sick. I'm not a counselor, but my guess is if you saw one he'd tell you that PTSD is a very treatable condition. Whatever happened to you, it's still with you and ignoring it won't make it go away. I still say you should talk to a professional, but I swear you can also talk to me and I won't judge. I'll listen, really listen. Maybe that's all you need to get you started on beating this thing."

She closed her eyes, torn between wanting him to let her go and comforted by the support flowing through his hands to her. He meant well and he meant what he said. Of that she was certain.

"It's hard," she said, flexing her fingers around his. "The headaches get bad when I just think about it and talking…talking…it's so hard, Lucas, you don't understand. It literally brings me to my knees reliving stuff, just in my head. How can I talk about it?"

"You have to, sweetheart. I promise, I'll do everything in my power to keep you safe, to help you find the right person to talk to. Please, trust me."

Sweetheart. When was the last time anyone had called her that? When was the last time anyone had offered her this kind of support, clear and honest from the bottom of his heart? For whatever reason she felt safe with Lucas, but trust wasn't an automatic byproduct of that security. Trusting was even more difficult than talking.

But how she wanted to trust him.

Claire finally disengaged her hand and rose. "I want to, really. I know I'm screwed up. There, I've admitted it. I totally get that I'm not normal. Grey reminds me of it every day, because all he wants is normal. Imagine that, the kid wants normal and he's got me. I make him crazy." She shook her head. "I make us both nuts, but I can't figure out how to live any other way."

Lucas stood, then moved toward her. "You can have normal, if you really want it. Not that normal is all that it's cracked up to be, but you can have the life you want for yourself and for Grey." He cupped her cheek. "Don't you want that?"

She stood before him, her heart swelling with the thought of everything he offered, emotion clogging her throat. "Yes, I want that. I don't want to be scared anymore."

His smile spread slowly, as warm as sunshine. She wanted him. She hadn't been with anyone since the rape, but maybe that was her first step back toward normal. Heaven help her, she hadn't been sure she'd ever want a man again the way she wanted Lucas in that moment.

She opened her eyes. "Will you do something for me?"

"Anything." His thumb stroked the curve of her jaw.

The woman in her reveled at the desire in his eyes, even though he held himself apart, no doubt denying himself because she was such a mess. Why would he want to get more involved with her?

"Promise?" She smiled slowly as his body eased, seeming to sway toward her.

He cocked his head and answered with a cautious tone. "I think so…."

She looped her arms around him, joining her hands behind his neck, pulling his mouth closer to hers, until her lips brushed his, then she leaned back to look at him. Again, she felt as if she were diving into the deep end, but as huge a step as this was, she needed it.

"Stay with me tonight," she said.

His eyes widened slightly. "Claire, you know I want to, but… You have to know how much I want to—how much I want you. I don't know that I have the willpower to stay and not…and to remain a gentleman."

Laughter bubbled up inside her. For once, she was headache free. That had to be a good sign. "You didn't seem so worried about being a gentleman when you were kissing me."

"Well, we weren't alone in your home at the time."

"Ah, so you're worried about spending the night all by ourselves here."

"I'm worried about pushing you into something you might not be ready for."

She held his gaze, filled with the confidence that regardless of whatever might come tomorrow, tonight she needed to be with this man. "I'm ready, Lucas. I want you, and not just because of your sexy body, but because of that noble heart of yours. I find it irresistible. Unless of course, *you're* not ready."

He shook his head, though at last he pulled her

close. “Sweetheart, the way you make me feel, if you’re really sure this is what you want, I’m ready. Absolutely ready.”

With that he dipped his head and again claimed her mouth.

CHAPTER FIFTEEN

BRIGHTNESS SURROUNDED LUCAS as he slowly awoke. Everywhere he looked, white filled his vision. White curtains covered a row of windows framed in a wall of white, a white comforter rolled along the pleasant curves of the woman tucked in beside him, her body spooned against his, warming him to his core.

He smiled and propped himself up on his elbow to better see her. The internet radio and TV she'd turned on last night still warred with each other in the other part of the house, but in here peace reigned. In sleep, Claire appeared younger, relaxed in a way he'd never seen her. If she'd been suffering from insomnia, she wasn't any longer. He touched her arm, but she didn't stir.

He moved with care, extricating himself from the tangle of her legs and arms, missing the warmth of her body as soon as he emerged from the puffy comforter. The television and radio beside her bed switched on simutaneously, startling him, both evidently set on timers. He glanced at Claire, but she remained asleep, so he turned them off. Better to let her rest while she could.

He glanced around the room again. Funny how when he'd been here last he hadn't seen her bedroom. He wouldn't have guessed her private domain to be quite so…heavenlike.

With a shake of his head, he found his clothes in a trail along the white carpet. Mixed with hers, the garments were splashes of colors detailing their route to her bed the previous night. He should probably berate himself for taking that step, but last night had been too full of wonder for him to harbor regrets now.

He smiled, letting himself indulge in watching Claire's face as she slept. He sat on the edge of the bed to put on his socks, relishing the intimacy of the room.

When he was dressed, he padded into the kitchen, where he searched for a coffeemaker while he phoned the shop, then scolded himself. Of course she didn't have a coffeemaker. That's why Grey wanted the espresso machine.

Ramsey answered the shop phone on the third ring. "The Coffee Stop."

"Ramsey, I thought you were off today and Ken was back from his break."

"Oh, hey, Lucas. Ken called yesterday to see if we could swap days. He has a hot date today. I emailed you about the change. Should I have called or texted instead? I didn't think I should disturb you."

"Email was fine." Lucas glanced in the direction of Claire's bedroom. "I did get a couple of alerts, but haven't had a chance to check them. Thanks for covering again, though."

"No problem. I like it here." Ramsey laughed. "Keeps me out of trouble. Besides, there's been a girls' high school track team or something in here this morning."

Lucas smiled. "I'm sure you haven't minded taking care of them."

"No, sir, I didn't mind at all. Did you enjoy your day off?"

"I did. I was just checking in to make sure you don't need me for anything today." After last night, he wanted to be prepared for whatever happened when Claire awoke.

Would she want him to leave right away, or would she need him to stick around? He seemed to have made some headway in at least her feeling comfortable around him and he'd like to press on in that direction if she let him.

"Everything's great," Ramsey said. "Hank will be in at eleven and I'm here for the rest of the day, so we should have plenty of coverage. Besides, Rachel is here and she says she's here until we close."

"Well, let me know if you need me for anything," Lucas said.

"Will do. Have a fun day off."

"Actually, I have a big favor to ask you. Is it busy, or do you think Rachel can spare you for a little bit?"

"She can handle it. Rach is like a drill sergeant.

She can handle anything. I'm at your service. What can I do for you?"

Lucas gave him a small breakfast order, including Claire's regular espresso, and asked him to deliver it to Claire's address. As he hung up he glanced toward the bedroom. How long would she sleep? Should he head out to work in the yard?

Better to stick close until she woke. The last thing he wanted was for her to wake up and think he'd fled. He yawned. She'd given him all he could handle well into the night. It seemed once Claire shed her fear of him, she couldn't get enough.

But how would she feel in the bright light of day?

And Grey… If he were to find out, how would he feel about Lucas having spent the night?

He was a bright kid. Would he sense the change in Lucas's relationship with Claire? At ten, was he old enough to feel he had to be her protector?

When was he due home?

The musical notes of a cell phone sounded from the direction of the living room. Lucas retraced his steps to the room, but between the TV and radio he had trouble telling where the sound was coming from. He paused and listened again. With a shake of his head, he turned them both off to better hear.

This time when the phone rang he tracked it to Claire's purse, which she'd dropped near the garage door. He retrieved the purse, but the ringing had stopped by the time he reentered her room.

Claire still slept, undisturbed by the phone or

other noises from the living room. He placed her purse on the nightstand by her bed, then paused. From the look of it, she'd be out for some time. He could leave her a note to let her know he'd be in the yard and that he'd have his phone on him in case she needed anything.

Satisfied with his plan, he left the note on her purse, then headed to the shed in the backyard. If he recalled correctly she had a set of hedge clippers in there. He could get a little work done before breakfast arrived.

CLAIRE AWOKE WITH a start. Something was wrong. Adrenaline pumped through her as she sat upright, feet on the floor. Silence pressed in all around her. Her heart raced.

Why was it so damn quiet? She hit the button on her radio then got up to turn on the television. As the sounds of a traffic report and an ad for laser hair removal filled the air, she calmed down enough to feel disappointed.

Lucas had left.

The doorbell rang and she jumped. Who could that be? She glanced at the clock as she felt around on the bench at the foot of her bed for her robe. She slipped into the garment and went to answer the door. She couldn't believe it was after nine in the morning and she'd slept through the night.

The back door opened as she hit the entry hall. She caught the shape of a man and the old fear spiked through her, but she quickly recognized Lucas. A smile lit his face. "Good morning, beautiful."

Relief mixed in with her fright and the unease over waking to the quiet of her house. "You didn't leave."

"I left you a note," he said. "I didn't want to wake you. I was out back trimming your hedges."

"Oh," she said. "I didn't see your note. You were trimming my hedges? That's so nice." She was babbling, and took a breath to calm her racing thoughts. "It was quiet when I woke up."

His eyes widened. "I'm sorry. I wasn't thinking. I turned everything off."

The bell rang again and Lucas moved toward the door. "That's breakfast."

"Breakfast?" She trailed after him as he opened the door and greeted the troubled-looking kid from his shop.

"Good morning," the kid said and raised a bag and a drink carrier with two coffees to go.

"Ramsey, this is Claire Murphy." Lucas took the food and drink. "Claire, Ramsey Carter. He's my manager at The Stop. I don't know if you two have officially met."

Claire tightened the belt on her robe, her unease mounting. Ramsey had a hardness about him that made her uncomfortable. Lucas trusted him, though, and she needed to get over being skittish around every strange male she encountered.

She extended her hand to the young man. "We've spoken, but no, we haven't officially met."

"It's a pleasure, ma'am." Ramsey took her hand and smiled.

"Thanks for dropping this by," Lucas said to Ramsey. "I'll add a little something to this week's paycheck."

"Oh, no, that's not necessary, boss. It was nice to get out a bit."

"It was very good of you," Claire said, her gaze swinging between the two men. "Nice of both of you."

Ramsey gestured toward the food. "I'm going to head back now and let the two of you get on with your breakfast. See you back at The Stop."

They thanked him again and Claire closed the door behind him. She followed Lucas into the kitchen, where he deposited the goodies on the table then swept her into his arms. "Now for a proper good morning."

Before she had a chance to catch her breath, his lips descended on hers, capturing her mouth in a kiss that left her weak in the knees. He kissed her long and deep, before letting her up for air.

"Oh, my," she said. "I think I'm a little speechless."

He brushed his lips over hers again. "Maybe that's not a bad thing."

He kissed her thoroughly and all the fear and doubt left Claire's mind. She stood instead in a place full of the delicious sensation of being in Lucas's arms, his tongue hungrily stroking hers.

At long last, he raised his head. "That was my way of saying I'm sorry I left you in the quiet this morning."

She nodded. "Oh, that… I *was* a little freaked out when I woke up. You know, I tend to leave everything on and my TV and radio work kind of like an alarm duo to wake me in the mornings. I guess the…*quiet* must have woken me. That's so not the norm around here."

"I'm sorry, Claire. I was awake when they came on and you were still sleeping. You looked so peaceful. I wasn't thinking. I know you told me the quiet bothers you, but I wanted you to sleep. Then your phone started ringing and I couldn't find it with all the racket out here, so I turned off the TV and radio in your living room and I found your purse. I left it on your nightstand, but your cell had stopped ringing by then. I left the note on your purse."

"I didn't see the purse or the note, but it's all okay." She turned toward her bedroom. "I'd better see if that was Grey calling me to come get him. I never sleep in like this." She laughed. "Actually, I never sleep."

"Here." Lucas pulled out a chair for her. "You sit and get started on breakfast and I'll get your purse."

Shc hesitated. "Why don't we take breakfast to go? I can show you a new spot at the park."

"Oh." He looked at the bag of food. "Right, meals

on the go. Except we did have a couple of nice dinners here."

"Yes, but again, not the norm and breakfast is all packed up. I'll just see if Grey called and then I'll get dressed. Give me five minutes, ten tops?"

"Sure." He saluted her with one of the coffees. "I'm going to have my coffee while I wait, though."

"I'll be right back." Her cheeks warmed as she hurried to her room. What had Ramsey thought about bringing them breakfast?

On her way through the living room, she turned on the television and stereo. Sure, they were only going to be here a few minutes, but she wanted to erase the unease of the earlier quiet. She found her purse on her nightstand, where Lucas had told her he'd left it.

She read his note with a smile, and then dug inside, until she found her phone. The missed call display indicated her sister's home number. Surely it had been Grey. She dialed the number.

"Hello?" Becca answered after a couple of rings.

"Hi, it's me. How's my little man?"

"Hey, Claire, he's doing fine. He and Amanda are helping Kyle in the garden. He's got them pulling weeds. Grey is trying to cram in as many chores as he can. He's being sweet to put up with Amanda helping. He's good with her, most of the time."

"That's great. I had a missed call from your number. I assume it was him. Did he want me to come get him?" Claire asked.

"I don't think so. He said he wanted to stay and do more chores. He asked me to make him a list. Honestly, I can use him if you let him stay. He's cheap labor. And then I thought I might take them to a movie as a thank-you treat. You know, he seems to like it here and we love having him."

Disappointment filtered through Claire. Of course Grey liked it there. Becca's house was normal. She herself would like to take Grey to a movie. They could do more of that, if that was what he wanted.

"Of course he can stay," she said. "Can I talk to him? I just want to make sure he doesn't need anything."

"Sure. Hold on a sec and I'll get him."

Claire moved to her dresser and pulled out clothes to wear to the park. She dressed quickly while she waited. A glance in the mirror had her frowning. A ponytail was going to have to do this morning.

"I can't get him out of the garden," Becca said when she came back on. "He says he'll call you later. You should enjoy your day, Claire. Take some time for yourself. Unwind a little. No offense, but you're looking kind of ragged these days. We've got Grey. If you want a longer break, he can stay again tonight."

Claire frowned. "Thanks, Becca, but I wouldn't want to impose and it's a school night. Besides, I miss him. I'll check in this afternoon."

She hung up, finished getting dressed and cleaned up, then made her way to the kitchen. "He still hates me," she said to Lucas. "He wouldn't even come to the phone."

"Sweetheart, I promise he doesn't hate you. He's just busy, like kids get. Playing with his cousin or something."

"He's doing chores."

"There you go, even better." He moved closer to her. "And it gives us more time to spend together."

"Okay, but no more quiet if you're going to be… hanging out here. I didn't like that." She bit her lip.

Why would Lucas even want to hang out here? Her own son couldn't wait to get away and didn't seem interested in returning anytime soon.

He nuzzled her neck. "No more quiet. I promise."

"Thank you, Lucas."

He straightened to meet her gaze. "For what?"

"For understanding how abnormal I am, and for accepting me anyway. I know I'm no picnic. Evidently, I send most people running in the opposite direction."

I get it, Mom. You can't have relationships.

"I'm not running anywhere." He shrugged. "We all have our baggage, me included."

"Yes, well, I think mine's more along the lines of a steamer trunk." She slid her hand over his. "And you should have tons of issues with all you've been through, but you seem to have it all perfectly together."

"I'm not so sure about that, but thanks."

She nodded and picked up her coffee. “Are you ready for the park?”

“Breakfast to go, yes, ma’am. Let’s do it.”

CHAPTER SIXTEEN

"I THINK THIS is the last of it, right?" Grey's question the following weekend drew Lucas's attention from the towel bar that he was installing in Claire's bathroom.

Lucas shifted his gaze from the boy to the rolled bills in his hand. The uneasy feeling he'd had when they'd struck the secret espresso-machine deal hit him. He set down his hammer, but made no move to take the money.

"Are you sure you want to do this, Grey? It's not too late to get her something else."

Grey's eyes widened. "Why would I want to get her something else?"

"I don't know. Your mom seems a little touchy about changes in routine and an espresso machine is definitely a change."

"But that's the point. This will be a good change."

"Yes, but you should try to understand this won't be easy for her. Don't get me wrong. I get what you're trying to do…."

"So, it'll be fine."

"She couldn't work at home. How will this be any different?"

Grey crunched the bills in his fist. "It'll be different. We had dinner at the table with you. That was a change. We used to have more dinners like that before…before she got so…against that kind of thing."

"But how many have we had since then?"

"We'll have more and then we'll start having breakfasts at home again, too," Grey said. "You'll see. We used to eat at home all the time. She'll get used to it again."

"I hope you're right, Grey," Lucas said, laying his hand on the boy's shoulder. "Just be prepared, in case she needs to warm to the idea."

"She's going to like it," Grey said and shoved the money toward him. "Please take it. We had a deal."

"Yes, we did." Lucas held out his hand and Grey deposited the cash in his palm.

Lucas's stomach tightened as he shoved the roll in his pocket. How would Claire react to Grey's gift? How would she feel when she realized Lucas had helped Grey with his plan?

"What are you two up to?" Claire appeared in the bathroom door frame. She had that wide-eyed look he'd learned meant she was getting antsy. "Who's up for a walk in the park? We've got a little time before we have to pick up Amanda and Becca for rock climbing."

"Give me five minutes to finish this and I'm in," Lucas said.

Grey sighed. "I'll get my jacket."

CLAIRE PULLED HER coat close around her as they headed into the park fifteen minutes later. She'd awoken in a sweat, the smothering nightmare fresh, her heart pounding. She hadn't been able to shake it and the sense of unease she normally felt at home had followed her into the overcast day.

"It's chillier out here than I realized," she said.

"Here, I think I have a hat with me somewhere." Lucas felt around in his jacket pockets. He withdrew a beanie from one. "Do you want to put this on?"

"I'm okay," Claire said, shivering. "I'll warm up as we keep moving."

"Are you sure?" Lucas asked. "I have gloves, too. Would you rather wear those?"

"I appreciate the offer, really, but I'm fine." Her head pounded. Why did he feel the need to take care of her when she was perfectly capable of taking care of herself? "Thanks, though."

Chastising herself, she forced a smile. She shouldn't be so defensive. Lucas meant well. "You've got some big pockets."

He patted his jacket. "A guy likes to be prepared."

A gust of wind blew by them and Claire glanced at Grey, who'd run ahead along the trail bordering the Chattahoochee River. "Grey, honey, are you warm enough?"

He gave her a backward wave. "I'm fine, Mom." He stopped and pointed to a spot along the river where a number of people clustered around a small dock, fishing poles in hand.

"Look, Mom, Marty's here. Can I go say hi?"

"Sure, just be careful and don't get too close to the edge of the dock."

He took off at a full run and Claire exhaled. "He *looks* like a happy kid. So maybe he has small periods of time when he's actually not miserable."

"We all get frustrated now and then," Lucas said. "But he seems okay overall to me. He's a smart and complicated kid. You're going to have to expect things to not always run smoothly. I think he looks happy most of the time."

"You don't see him all of the time," she said. "It's not easy. I try to do the right thing. I'm not always successful." She was silent a moment, the old frustration building. "I haven't made any more progress in getting him his Big."

"Why don't we schedule his interview this week? I'll go with you. I think that it will do wonders for him."

Her cheeks warmed. "I'm sure it would. I just…I hate that I have to get you to go with us. I hate that I can't get through a meeting on my own without feeling the need to flee." She shrugged. "Seems simple enough. Get through Grey's interview, meet with the enrollment team, approve a match."

He took her hand. "I can be with you through all

of it. If it would help, I'm more than happy to do that."

Her aggravation only increased at his offer. "You're missing the point. I don't want to have to count on you. This is important for my son and I can't manage it on my own. It seems so...overwhelming. I panic just thinking about it. I know I should do it, but I let the days slip by and here we are."

Thankfully, Grey's questions about his father had stopped since meeting Lucas, but that only increased her concern about Grey getting too attached. "I just want what's right for Grey. It isn't his fault his father couldn't cut it."

"Does his father truly not have any contact with him?" Lucas asked.

Claire shook her head. "Not for years and before that it was sporadic at best. I don't even know how to reach him anymore."

"If the guy was stupid enough to walk from the boy's life, that's proof enough he didn't deserve him."

She said, "I'll call BBBS in the morning and set up an appointment."

Lucas nodded. "Let me know if you want me to come. No pressure either way." He paused. "If it's any consolation I love spending time with him."

Her heart warmed, despite her frustration. "He loves spending time with you. He talks about you nonstop when you're not around. It's just...you know, hard not to worry about him getting attached."

"I know. I worry about that, too." He tugged her a little closer. "I guess that's more motivation for us to really give this relationship a shot."

Her stomach tightened. She was thrilled to be with Lucas. He was so caring and considerate, and she did feel safe with him. At least, most of the time.

"Mom." Grey ran back to them, his cheeks flushed. "There's a dog—it's hurt. Come on. I'll show you." Grey grabbed her hand and pulled her toward a thicket of trees off to one side of the dock.

Claire felt Lucas follow as her son led them to where a small group of people had gathered. She stopped and pulled Grey close to her when they got there. A dog lay on its side in a nest of leaves. Blood splattered its coat, open wounds appeared across its flank and shoulder and its ribs showed through matted hair.

"Stay back." Claire held on to Grey as Lucas knelt beside the animal. Her stomach tightened. "Poor beast."

"Was he in a fight?" Grey asked. "Is he going to be okay?"

"He's a she," Lucas said. He ran his hands over the animal, checking the extent of its injuries. "And I don't think it was a fight. These are cuts, maybe from a whip."

He ran his hand along her neck, pulling back the matted hair to reveal scarring where a too-tight collar had cut into her. He turned to Claire. Anger creased his brow and glittered in his eyes. "This is abuse."

Claire stared at the man who'd held her hand and offered her support only moments ago. That man was hardly recognizable in the deadly countenance before her. Though his anger was clearly directed toward whomever had abused the animal, she shivered in fear and stepped back.

Grey's friend Marty and his mother walked over beside them. The towheaded boy peered at the dog, eyes wide. "Is it going to be okay?"

Lucas exhaled. "I don't know." He glanced around the group of people gathered. "Does anyone know this dog?"

Heads shook and murmured conversations broke out. One man said, "We could call someone, maybe the SPCA, or the animal shelter."

"She needs a lot of attention," Lucas said. "Even if she receives the appropriate medical care and heals physically, she's going to need a ton of TLC."

He bowed his head for a moment, the anger visibly draining from him, until he was the old Lucas again. Claire exhaled. He was such a caring man. What was wrong with her that she'd ever be afraid around him?

She knelt beside him and gently laid her hand on the dog. It looked to be possibly a German shepherd mix. What kind of person could do this?

Was the owner looking for the dog?

"I'm going to take her," Lucas said. He met Claire's gaze. "I can treat her superficial wounds, but she'll need a vet to check for internal damage. The vet will report this to the proper authorities, as well. Can you stay with her while I get my car?"

Claire's pulse quickened and her fingers tingled. What if the owner showed up while Lucas was gone? She closed her eyes as Lucas waited for a response. Why was this so difficult for her? She'd worked hard to be able to defend herself. She shouldn't be such a coward.

Finally, she managed to nod, acutely aware of the attention from the other people around her. She swallowed, unable to look at Grey. Did he see the shaking of her hands?

Lucas left and Claire focused on drawing deep breaths. She could do this. Now was not the time to lose control. Even if the dog's owner showed up, she wasn't alone. A number of the group drifted back to the dock, but Marty and his mother remained near Grey, chatting quietly.

"Mom, are you okay?" Grey placed his hand on her shoulder.

She flinched, startled by his touch.

"What's wrong?" he asked. "Lucas will be back and he'll take care of her."

She had to get a grip. She couldn't break down in front of Grey and his friend. She nodded and tried to paste on a smile, though her gaze remained on the dog.

"I know, honey. He's a good man."

Ten endless minutes later, Lucas returned with a big towel that he wrapped around the poor dog. Claire and Grey followed him as he carried her to his car. Once Lucas had the animal safely loaded in the backseat, he turned to Grey.

"Hey," he said, stooping to Grey's height. "I'm going to take her to a friend of mine who's a vet." He smiled. "He's a veteran, as well as a veterinarian and a great guy. We're going to do everything we can to help her, okay?"

"Okay," Grey said. "Will you call my mom and let her know how she is later?"

"You bet I will." Lucas then turned to Claire, rubbing her arms as he spoke. "I'm sorry to run off like this."

"It's fine, Lucas. Please go do what you have to do." She put her arm around Grey. "We've got a full afternoon. We'll see you later."

"Thanks for understanding, sweetheart," Lucas said.

He glanced at Grey, who had his nose pressed to the window as he waved at the dog. Lucas gave Claire a quick kiss while her son wasn't looking. The tenderness in that sweet contact made Claire wish she could wrap herself in his arms and feel safe again.

"Have fun rock climbing, Grey," he said to the boy.

Grey frowned. "Okay, but what are you going to call her? She needs a name."

Lucas's gaze met Claire's briefly. The concern filling his eyes told her he wasn't sure the dog was going to make it. "Why don't you think of some names and I'll think of some, too, and we'll talk later and maybe pick one for her then."

"Sure." Grey nodded, his expression grim. "I can do that."

"That would be great, buddy," Lucas said. "I'll talk to you later, then. Okay?"

"Okay," Grey said. "Bye, Lucas. Bye, dog."

Claire turned to Grey as Lucas's car pulled out of the parking lot. "Come on, honey, let's head back and get ready for rock climbing."

He fell into step beside her. "Don't worry, Mom. Lucas will fix the dog. She'll be okay."

"Grey, don't get your hopes up. He's going to do his best, but that poor animal has been badly hurt. You know there's a chance she won't make it."

"But Lucas fixes everything," he said.

"Nobody can fix everything."

"I don't know. Lucas is pretty good at it. He fixed the tub, the gate, my bookshelf, Ramsey."

"Ramsey?" she asked.

"Yes, the guy at The Coffee Stop, the one with the tattoo on his arm."

"I know who he is. What do you mean Lucas fixed him?"

Grey shrugged. "He used to be in some kind of trouble. Maybe a gang or something, but now he works for Lucas and he isn't doing stupid stuff anymore. I'd say that's fixed."

"Why do you think he was in a gang?" Claire asked.

"I just wondered and he didn't deny it when I asked him. He said you don't talk about those things. That's the same as admitting it."

If Grey was right, that explained the feeling she got around the teen. She held Grey back from the street until it was clear, then hurried across with him. "Even if Lucas helped Ramsey, that doesn't mean he can fix this dog. I want you to be prepared for that, all right?"

Grey pressed his lips together. "Fine, but I say he fixes her. You'll see."

Claire shook her head as the cold breeze wrapped around them. Was that why Lucas was with her? Because she needed fixing just as badly as everything else? If so, what would happen when he decided she was unfixable?

CHAPTER SEVENTEEN

THE FIRE IN the hearth at The Coffee Stop popped and crackled the following morning as Lucas settled his new charge on a big pillow before it. “Here you go, girl. You’ll stay warm by the fire and you can see everything that’s going on.”

The bell on the door tinkled and Grey barreled in with Claire close behind, a gust of cool air entering with them. The dog whimpered and readjusted her position on her makeshift bed. Lucas petted her as Grey made a beeline for them.

“How is she?” the boy asked. “Mom said the vet said she’s hurt inside.”

Lucas nodded. “She had some internal bleeding, but it seems to have stopped, so we’re going to let her rest and see if she gets better.”

“Can I pet her?” Grey looked from Lucas to his mother as she knelt beside them.

“Sure,” Lucas said.

“Be gentle,” Claire reminded him.

Grey nodded as he sank his hand into the dog’s fur. “She looks better all cleaned up.”

"She probably feels better, too, but she still has a lot of mending to do." Claire touched Lucas's hand.

While Grey focused on the dog, Lucas threaded his fingers through Claire's. They'd decided to keep their relationship discreet in front of Grey, until they knew where they were headed. Claire didn't want to get his hopes up.

"What are we going to call her?" Grey asked as he stroked the animal behind her ear.

"I don't know," Lucas said. "I've kind of just been calling her 'girl,' but that's not really a name. Do you have any ideas?"

Grey shrugged. "What if we call her Lady, because that's how she should be treated? Like a lady."

"That's great," Lucas said. "Simple, but respectful. I like it."

"Hello, Lady." Grey leaned forward to gingerly hug the dog. "We're going to take good care of you."

Claire smiled cautiously and gestured toward the counter. "I'd better order our drinks. Do you want an espresso or smoothie this morning, Grey?"

"A smoothie is fine," the boy said, without taking his attention off Lady. As Claire left them, Grey turned to Lucas. "You'll make her better."

"I'm going to give it my best shot, Grey, but there aren't any guarantees. You should know the vet wasn't overly optimistic."

"Doesn't he know you're the guy who fixes things?" Grey asked.

Lucas chuckled. "I can fix your bookshelf, but

that doesn't mean I can fix a dog. I appreciate the vote of confidence, though."

"Sure you can. You fixed Ramsey."

Lucas tilted his head in surprise. "What do you mean, I fixed Ramsey?"

Grey shrugged. "Well, he was doing stupid stuff until you gave him a job and helped him to stop. And Mom told me how you fixed people while you were in the military and how you fixed that guy at the car accident. If you can fix people, a dog should be a piece of cake."

"Did Ramsey tell you I fixed him?" Lucas asked.

"He told me you helped him out. Was he in a gang? Did you get him to quit? That's why he has the tattoo, isn't it?"

"What do you know about gangs?" Lucas asked.

"I saw a show on them on the History Channel."

Lucas inhaled. "I didn't fix Ramsey. I gave him an opportunity and he was smart enough to make the best of it. I'd say that Ramsey fixed himself."

Grey turned away from Lady to face him. "But you *do* fix things. And you can fix people. I know it."

Lucas's stomach tightened. "Grey…"

"You fixed Ramsey and now I need you to fix my mom."

Lucas squeezed his eyes shut. What had the boy gotten into his head? He opened his eyes and met Grey's hopeful gaze. "Grey…look…"

"What is wrong with her? She's…not normal."

The boy glanced at his mother at the pickup counter. "She didn't used to be like this."

Lucas touched the boy's arm. "Listen—"

"You can help her be like she used to be."

"I promise you I will help her in any way I can."

A smile lit the boy's face. "Yes, I knew you could do it."

Lucas glanced at the counter as Claire collected their drinks. "I haven't done anything yet and anything that happens will be completely up to your mom."

As Claire approached, Grey stood. He threw his arms around Lucas's neck. "Thanks, Lucas."

Lucas wished he deserved the boy's gratitude. The concern he felt over the espresso machine was nothing compared to the dread filling him now. Grey expected him to fix Claire. Lucas would laugh if his stomach weren't tying itself into knots.

"One banana-strawberry smoothie," Claire said as she reached them and handed the drink to Grey.

She gave Lucas a questioning look as Grey bid Lady goodbye. Lucas raised his hands and shrugged, but couldn't meet her eyes. She'd likely ask him about Grey's enthusiastic hug later. That was a conversation he wasn't looking forward to.

"Thanks, Mom." Grey took the drink, and then smiled back at Lucas as they headed toward the door.

After they'd gone, Lucas turned to the dog by the fire. "Lady, what are we going to do?"

THE LATE-AFTERNOON sun hung low in the sky by the time Lucas maneuvered out of traffic and found his way back to The Coffee Stop. He and Claire had just dropped Grey at her sister's after the interview at the BBBS. Though the interview had gone well, Claire had remained unusually quiet on the return ride.

She finally broke the silence. "Thanks again for going with us."

The sadness in her tone pulled at him. She'd made it clear yesterday that she'd wanted to be able to do this alone. Obviously, it still bothered her that she couldn't.

He drew a deep breath before replying. "You're welcome. I think it went well."

They exited the car without saying anything more. When she was depressed like this he couldn't help but think of Toby. The heaviness pressed down on him as he remembered his mother's words.

You always feel responsible for other people, even at your own expense.

Did he feel responsible for Claire? If he were honest with himself, he definitely felt responsible for Toby. He didn't want to make the same mistakes with Claire and he was determined to be there for her, but what was he supposed to do when his being there got her this down?

They entered the shop, where Lady still lay before the fire. Ramsey nodded to him from behind the counter. Lucas returned the nod. "How did she do?

"She drank a little water, but she hasn't eaten anything."

Lucas turned back to the dog to find Claire on her knees, petting the animal. He knelt beside her, stroking the golden fur with her.

"I'm sorry I made you leave her," she said, her voice choked with emotion.

"Ramsey kept an eye on her." He slipped his arm around her and she leaned into him.

"She isn't going to make it, is she?"

"I don't know," he said. "I don't think so, but you can never tell."

He'd learned never to second-guess death. He'd seen injured soldiers pull through when he didn't think they stood a chance. Then there were instances like Toby's, where he'd thought the danger was long past.

Claire straightened. "I don't feel like working and I have time before I have to pick up Grey. Do you want to put up your shelves? I totally owe you and I want to repay my debt. Can Ramsey keep an eye on her?"

"Sure." He stood, then held out his hand to her.

He nodded toward Lady as they passed Ramsey. "Can you watch her while I'm in back?"

"Sure," Ramsey said.

When they were alone he turned to Claire. "You don't owe me, sweetheart, but if it will make you feel better to do something, then we can certainly work on the shelves."

"I watched a video last night. I get the gist of it. If you work the power tools, I can work the level. That much I can do." She pressed her lips together. "I just need to feel like I can be useful."

The distress in her eyes increased the heavy feeling in his gut. Between her and the dog, his mood was definitely plummeting. Maybe putting up the shelves would be good for both of them.

He gave her a quick kiss. "Let me get you the level."

"HERE, TAPE THIS." Grey angled the large box toward Lucas, kneeling beside him on his bedroom floor the day before his mom's birthday. Excitement rippled through him. Tomorrow they'd have breakfast at home, a nice, quiet breakfast.

Lucas smoothed a piece of tape over the seam. "Nice wrap job, Grey," he said. "Where did you get the paper?"

Grey scanned his handiwork as Lucas took the box from him and added more tape. "I swiped some out of the stash in her bedroom. I didn't see any with flowers, so I thought stripes would be okay. There's a pink stripe." He pointed. "That's girly enough, don't you think?"

"Sure. Do you have a bow?" Lucas searched around the scraps of wrapping paper scattered around them.

"A bow? Yeah, hold on." Grey ran to his closet and dug around for the bag of toy cars he'd gotten from his cousin last Christmas. He still kept them in the gift bag. "Here it is," he said as he yanked the bow from the bag. "It's a little squished, but will this work?"

"It's perfect," Lucas said. "We just need a little tape to make it stick."

"I can put it on." Grey held out his hand for the bow as Lucas stuck tape on the back. With a flourish, Grey stuck the bow on the top of the box.

"She's going to be so surprised." Grey stared at the gift, smiling. "Then we can have breakfast at home in the mornings. Maybe you can show me how to use it and I can get up early and make espresso for her."

"Sure, I'll even show you how to steam the milk for lattes. You can do all kinds of things with this little baby."

Grey sat back on his heels, feeling remarkably satisfied as he surveyed the present. She was going to love it. Yes, this was going to be a birthday his mom would never forget.

"I HAVE NO idea what I'm doing." Lucas walked into his *madre*'s kitchen later that afternoon and headed for the refrigerator.

His mother glanced up from the desk tucked into a nook on one side of the space. "So what else is new?"

"I'm not kidding," he said as he slipped into the seat across from her.

"Have you eaten? Richard is making me dinner

at his place at seven, but I'll have a snack with you, if you're hungry," she said.

He rubbed his stomach. "I don't know—I'm really not that hungry."

"Really?" She moved to the refrigerator and pulled out a half-full pie tin, which she set on the table. "Not even for my homemade key lime pie? Oh, wait..." She turned back to the fridge. "If we're going to be bad and have dessert for our snack, we may as well break out the whipped cream."

Lucas sighed. She wouldn't be happy until she'd fed him. He gave in and grabbed plates and silverware. The knots Grey had put in his stomach intensified.

Where was Toby when he needed him?

"Out with it," his *madre* said. "What is it you're doing that you don't know about?"

"I'm...dating...her."

Her eyes widened. "Who? The undateable one?"

"Yes." He bowed his head, his fork still. Why had he let himself get sucked in by Claire's soft eyes and amazing touch, by her ability to make him feel complete? "And now her son thinks I can fix her."

"I see."

"You see? That's all you have to say? You're the wise one who said I have to save everyone. I didn't ask for this."

She took a bite of pie and chewed it thoughtfully before she answered. "You want to help her, right? So help her."

"Did you hear the part where her son wants me to fix her? Her *son* asked me that."

"Of course I heard. There's nothing wrong with my ears. We all need fixing. The real question here isn't whether or not you can fix her, which, of course, you can't—"

"Well, I can't fix her by myself, but I can help her—"

"—it's whether or not you *want* to date her."

"Well, I *am* dating her, so the answer to that is yes. I want to date her. She may have issues, but like you said, we all do, and she's an amazing woman. The question is how do I avoid disappointing Grey. He has no idea what's wrong with her. All he wants is to have the life they used to have."

"There's no going back. They've moved beyond that point. Even if she were to get help, they can never go back to before." She shrugged. "Life is different if for no other reason than that you're a part of it now."

"But for how long? What happens when Grey realizes I can't fix her? And what if she decides she doesn't want to be fixed?"

His mother leaned toward him, holding his gaze. "If you want to stick around at that point, then you need to find another purpose for being there."

"What do you mean? I'm there because I want to be there."

"And do you want to be there because you want to fix her?"

"I want her to get better for both her and her son," he said.

"And you think you're the man to make that happen?"

"I don't know. No one else was helping and I couldn't just let them keep going as they were." Why did this have to be so complicated?

"So you're there because you want to help her get better."

"Is that a bad thing?" he asked.

"You tell me. You're dating her because you want to fix her. Is that a bad thing?"

Lucas frowned. "I'm not dating her because I want to fix her. I have feelings for her, for both of them. I want to be a part of their lives. I'm there to be a support to them," he said. "Though I don't know how to get her to help herself."

"Is she aware she has these issues, or is she in denial?"

"She's aware. We've talked about PTSD. I've encouraged her to get help, but I can't force her. She has to be ready to do that herself. I wish…I wish I could help Grey to understand that."

"He may not be able to right now, because you're telling him something he doesn't want to hear. This is a boy without a father, right?"

Lucas nodded.

"So you're probably the first man in a while to give him the attention he needs. He idolizes you. He sees you as being able to fix his problems."

"Right, but I'm not that guy. No one is."

Light sparkled in her dark eyes. "You're more that guy than you realize. But you were right when you said that all you can do is be a support to them."

"But how? What do I do when I can't fix her and she isn't ready to get the help she needs?"

She patted his hand. "It's easy, dear one. You wait."

He straightened. "I wait?"

"For her to realize she needs to help herself and for him to realize no one else can fix her."

How was Lucas supposed to just stand by and wait? The train wreck was coming and he needed to do something.

"Wait," his mother repeated. "You'll see. It'll either work itself out or it won't. Either way, there isn't anything more you can do at this point. *You,* my dear one, can't fix this."

The unease in his stomach intensified. No, he couldn't fix this, even he realized that. "Okay, I'll wait."

CHAPTER EIGHTEEN

THE ROCKING OF the Goo Goo Dolls and the blaring of the TV news broadcaster provided the soundtrack to Claire's morning round of checking the doors and windows. She shivered as she touched the latch on the last window in the living room before heading into the kitchen. The cold air seeped through the pane. October wasn't normally this cold in Georgia. Did the chilly temperatures have to accompany her birthday?

She padded into the kitchen and stopped. A large box sat on the floor by the kitchen table, wrapped in her favorite striped paper and topped with a crushed bow. She smiled. From the looks of it, Grey must have used an entire roll of tape wrapping the gift.

"Happy birthday."

His voice behind her made her jump. She turned to him, her hand pressed to her heart. "Honey, please don't sneak up on me like that."

He shrugged. "I didn't sneak. You just couldn't hear me, because the television and computer are making too much noise."

She pulled him to her and hugged him. "You got me a present. That's so sweet. Thanks."

He hugged her back, then moved to the box, turning it toward her. "It was too big for me to put it on the table. I slid it out from my room last night. Do you want to open it?"

She frowned. "Now? Shouldn't I wait until after dinner tonight? That's what we normally do."

"Who says we have to do things like we normally do? I think you should go ahead and open it now."

She glanced at the clock on the wall. "We need to head out soon."

"But it's your birthday. We should take our time, enjoy the morning."

"Take our time?" A nervous laugh bubbled up in her. "Since when have you known me to enjoy taking my time, especially when it comes to getting out of here in the mornings?" She smiled, hoping he would return it, but he frowned, his gaze on the floor.

She lifted his chin. "I'm sorry, honey. You must have worked hard on this. I'd love to open it. We can stay long enough for that."

A wide smile broke across his face. "All right. Just tear into it."

She turned the package around, trying to find an easy spot to rip. "Do you think you used enough tape?"

"Lucas helped. Hurry, tear it," he said as he bounced on his toes.

She tore off a long strip of paper. "Lucas helped you wrap this?"

Grey nodded. "When you were with your running group yesterday and he stayed here with me."

She exhaled. Whether she liked it or not, Grey was getting as attached to Lucas as she was. And she was definitely getting attached.

"Here, let me help," Grey said, peeling back more of the paper.

"I've got it," she said as one side of the box emerged from the wrap. Her heart seemed to skip. Surely, her present was just in a box with a picture of an espresso machine on it. Grey wouldn't have actually bought her an espresso machine. Would he?

"Honey, what is this?" she asked.

"It's an espresso machine." He pointed to the picture. "Like at The Coffee Stop, only for home."

"But I don't drink coffee at home. We roll out every morning and grab coffee at Lucas's shop. Why would I need one here?"

"So that maybe sometimes we won't have to roll out so fast in the mornings. Maybe sometimes we could have a quiet breakfast at home."

A sick feeling formed in the pit of her stomach. "You mean sit-down breakfasts."

"Yes." He smiled wide. "Sit-down breakfasts for just you and me. Here, at home."

"Honey..." She stared at him, trying to find the right words. "You know I *like* to roll out in the mornings. We don't have time for breakfast at home."

His smile faltered. "We could *make* time. Like we used to. Remember? You used to like that."

Claire closed her eyes. Why did she have to be the bad guy here? How could she ever make her son understand that, for her, staying home any more than they absolutely needed to was torture?

"Grey, I'm so sorry, this is a lovely thought and I appreciate the gift, but I don't want to have espresso at home. Don't you like going to The Coffee Stop? That's how we met Lucas."

Grey heaved out a breath, his expression downcast. "He told me you wouldn't like it. I said you would, but I guess he knows you better than I do."

His bitter tone surprised her. "What does that mean?"

Grey narrowed his eyes. "It means I'm not a baby. I know you two *like* like each other."

"What are you talking about, Grey?"

"I saw him kiss you the other day, at the park when he left with Lady. Why do you keep stuff like that from me? You know when you don't tell someone the truth it's the same as lying to them. You've been lying to me about Lucas, just like you've been lying to me about you."

"I'm lying to you about me? What does that even mean?" she asked.

"It means there's something wrong with you. You don't act right, but you pretend like everything's fine when it isn't. That's lying. Why won't you tell me what's wrong? I can handle it. What I can't handle is you rushing me out every morning, and then rushing me around for the rest of the day. I want normal, Mom. We used to be normal." He gestured to the box. "That's what this was for. It's supposed to help you want normal again."

Claire pressed her lips together. Her fingers tingled and the floor seemed to dip ever so slightly. She inhaled slowly, trying to calm the rapid beat of her heart. She couldn't deal with this now.

"Back up a minute," she said. "*Lucas* said I wouldn't like the espresso machine. So he knew you were getting it for me?"

"Yes, he cut me a deal and let me pay a little at a time. That's why I've been helping out with chores so much here and at Aunt Becca's—to earn money to pay for this thing. And now you don't even want it." His voice cracked.

Claire tried to put her arm around him, but he slipped away, saying, "I'm going to go get ready. I know you want to leave as soon as possible and I wouldn't want to make you late for The Coffee Stop."

"Grey, wait," she said, but he stormed down the hall and slammed the bathroom door.

She stared at the espresso machine, her throat burning and tears filling her eyes. How could Lucas have done this? He had to have known she wouldn't be able to accept it, yet he'd helped Grey buy the thing. The way Grey had stormed away he might never forgive her. How could Lucas have let this happen?

"HEY, BOSS?" KEN called to Lucas from the door to the stockroom a short while later.

Lucas slid a box of coffee onto the shelf, then turned to look at his employee. "Yes, Ken?"

Ken ducked his head, his eyebrows drawn together. "That nice lady and her kid are out front. The little brunette. She wants to see you."

"Okay, thanks. I'll be right out."

"She doesn't look very happy," Ken said.

Damn. It had to be the espresso machine.

Claire stood at the end of the counter when he got to the front, the espresso machine still in its box before her. Grey stood a short distance away, his arms crossed, his expression sullen. Lucas stepped around the counter to Claire.

"Good morning, sweetheart. Happy birthday," he said.

"How could you have gone behind my back and helped Grey do this? Surely you knew it was an… inappropriate gift." She kept her voice low, though her anger came through loud and clear.

"Claire—"

"He wants to have breakfasts at home." She glanced away for a moment, toward the light streaming through the window. "He wants normal. I thought you of all people understood my…shortcomings, understood how difficult this would be for me. I feel like you deliberately set me up for failure."

"Honey, I'm sorry."

"I don't know how to make this right with my son, Lucas. I can't believe you put me in this situation."

"It's just an espresso machine."

She flinched as if he'd struck her. "He wants us to have *normal,* Lucas. You know I can't do that."

"You could, though. You could have whatever life you wanted. All you have to do is get help. Look, I'm sorry you're angry, but he meant well and I couldn't crush the kid's hopes. I really care about you, about both of you. Please, Claire, let me help you. We'll find someone for you to talk to and I'll go with you if you want. We can fix this, together."

Moisture gathered in her eyes. "There is no we, Lucas. I'm not angry so much as I'm hurt," she said. "I thought you understood me better. I thought you accepted me the way I am. I'm sorry—I get that I'm no prize, but I come as is. I thought you were okay with that. I thought you got me."

His throat tightened. "I do, sweetheart, but I can take it better than Grey can. He needs his old mom back."

Tears spilled down her cheeks as she touched the box. "Well, she doesn't exist anymore. I can't do this, Lucas—this thing with you and me. I can't be with someone who wants to change me."

"I don't want to change you. I want to help you. If not for your sake, then for Grey's."

"I think you've done enough already. I'm sorry, Lucas, but I'm one project you can't fix." She turned and headed toward the door.

Grey stared at him for a minute before asking, "Where's Lady?"

Oh, God, not that, too. He crouched to Grey's level. "I'm sorry, Grey, she wasn't doing well. I had to take her back to the vet's. Apparently she started bleeding again inside. He's keeping her for a while to see if he can make her better."

Grey nodded. "I hope she'll be all right."

"Me, too." As the boy turned to catch up with his mother, Lucas stopped him. "Grey, wait."

Lucas opened the register and counted out the money Grey had given him for the espresso machine. He handed it to the boy. "I'm so sorry the espresso machine didn't work out."

"It's okay. You told me she wouldn't like it. I should have listened to you." His gaze met Lucas's. "Am I going to see you and Lady anymore?"

Lucas swallowed past his burning throat. "I don't know, buddy. I hope so."

"Me, too." Grey paused. "I'd better go. Guess we're headed for another coffee place. She has to have her espresso."

"Okay, you take care."

Grey nodded, and then threw his arms around Lucas's neck. "I'm sorry I messed up. I should have listened to you."

Lucas pulled back to look at the boy, his chest

tight. “It isn’t your fault, Grey. You didn’t do anything wrong, okay?”

The boy nodded, tears spilling down his cheeks. “Who’s going to fix my mom now?”

“She’s going to have to fix herself.”

“Grey, we need to go,” Claire called from the door.

Lucas pressed Grey close one last time. “If you ever need me, I’m always here for you.”

Nodding, Grey slipped away and hurried to his mom. Without a glance in Lucas’s direction, Claire turned and left with her son.

How had he screwed everything up so completely? He’d lost Claire and upset Grey. Even the dog probably wouldn’t make it. Some Mr. Fix-It he’d turned out to be.

CHAPTER NINETEEN

LUCAS HAD TO see Lady, to make sure she was okay, to reassure himself not everything he'd touched had been destroyed.

He pushed through the animal clinic door, where his friend, Dr. Danny Brenner, had operated on Lady that morning. Lucas stopped at the front counter, where Danny's young receptionist greeted him.

"Good morning, Mr. Williams, I think Dr. Brenner is done with the surgery. If you'll have a seat, I'll see if you can go back."

Lucas thanked her and sat in the quiet waiting room. A woman spoke softly to a fur ball of a cat across from him. Classical music drifted from a hidden speaker. The roll of tires sounded along the street outside.

Lucas shook his head. Claire wouldn't have been able to sit still here. The door beside the reception counter opened and Danny Brenner waved him in.

Danny offered his hand, his expression grim. Lucas gripped his friend's hand. "How did it go, Danny?"

"Not as well as I would have liked. Her vitals are

low. I've done all I can for her, but she may not be strong enough to pull through."

Lucas's throat tightened. He hardly knew this dog, but her survival seemed crucial to him. A memory of Grey hugging Lady flashed through his mind. Since he couldn't fix Claire, he would will Lady back to health if need be. She just had to be okay.

"Can I see her?" he asked.

"Of course." Danny walked him back to the sterile room, where a nurse tended to the dog. A dressing covered Lady's abdomen.

Lucas stroked the animal's matted fur, his anger rising again over the abuse she'd suffered. Lady whimpered softly and licked Lucas's hand. "You're going to be all right, girl."

He turned to his friend. "Can I take her home?"

"Sure." Danny lifted a sheet of paper from a nearby counter. "Here are her home care instructions. There's really nothing you can do other than to make her comfortable and wait. I'm sorry, Lucas, but I wouldn't get my hopes up if I were you."

Lucas nodded. "I understand. Thanks for all you've done for her, Danny. I really appreciate it."

"Not a problem. I wish I could have done more." His friend walked him to the front as Lucas followed, carrying Lady.

He thanked Danny again as he helped him load the dog in the backseat. Before he turned to leave, Danny said, "Call me if you need anything."

Lucas nodded, then buckled himself into the driver's seat. "Ready to go home, girl?" he asked as he pulled out of the parking lot.

The drive home was quiet, with the exception of the soft tones of Dave Matthews on the satellite radio. Lucas stopped at a light, saying, "We're almost there. It's too warm for a fire, but we'll just hang out, okay?"

Lady lay still, unmoving. Lucas's heart thudded. He reached back and pressed his hand to her side, feeling for the slow movement of her breath. Only after a couple of moments of frantically searching did he find what he sought.

When he arrived home, he settled her on the big pillow in the living room and sat beside her to wait.

GREY STARED OUT of his grandmother's window at the damp, overcast day. At least he didn't have to play soccer in this mess. The other kids would be covered in mud for sure.

"It's dreary out there," his grandmother said as she lowered herself into the seat beside him, mug in hand. "Are you sure you don't want some tea?"

Grey straightened. "No, thanks. I drink espresso now, like my mom."

"I see." Gram eyed him with her eyebrows raised. "I take it you drink decaf espresso?"

"Of course." His mom might be a little nuts, but she still took good care of him and she'd never let him drink the real stuff.

"I can brew you some decaf coffee, if you'd like."

"No, thanks. I'm fine." He settled back into the soft cushions of Gram's sofa as she clicked through the TV stations. She stopped on a boring news show.

"Can I call someone?" he asked during a commercial.

"Sure, hon, who do you want to call?"

"Lucas Williams."

"Who's that? Is he a friend of yours?"

"Yes, he's a friend of mine and my mom's at The Coffee Stop. He's taking care of a dog we found that was hurt and I want to see how she is. Can I use the computer to look up the number?" he asked.

"It'll be faster to use my phone to find it," she said as she reached for her phone. She paused and handed it to him. "Would you like to look it up yourself? You can call him directly, too, that way."

"Cool," Grey said and took the phone. Mom never let him play with her phone. He clicked on Gram's browser and searched for The Coffee Stop. He turned the screen toward his grandmother.

"This one?" he asked as he pointed to one of the links.

"That's it. Touch it and let's see what you get."

Another page popped up and this one had Lucas's name. "I found it. It's right here."

He touched the phone number in the entry and the phone indicated it was calling Lucas's shop. Grey smiled at his grandmother. "It's ringing."

"Good afternoon, The Coffee Stop," a man answered, but it wasn't Lucas. It sounded like that older guy, but Grey didn't know his name.

"Is Lucas there?" he asked.

"I'm sorry, Lucas isn't in this afternoon. Would you like to leave a message for him?"

Grey frowned. How was he supposed to find out how Lady was? "When will he be back?"

"I'm not sure, but he's usually here in the mornings. Can I tell him who called?" the man asked.

"Sure. Can you please tell him Grey called and ask him to call me? Tell him on the house phone tomorrow night. We won't be home until late, but he can leave a message. Just tell him I'm checking on Lady."

After thanking the man, Grey hung up and handed the phone to his grandmother. "Thanks. Mom doesn't let me do stuff like that on my own. She still treats me like a baby."

"Anytime, Grey," she said. "I promise you, I won't treat you like a baby. Maybe I could even teach you to cook. Would you like that?"

"Sure, that would be cool." He grinned. Maybe it wasn't so bad at Gram's, after all.

"Your mother should be here soon," she said, checking her watch.

The earlier argument rolled back over Grey, weighing him down. He nodded, his gaze on the carpet. Another miserable night at home, only this would be worse, because of the espresso-machine fiasco.

Why hadn't he listened to Lucas? And now Mom

was mad at Lucas, which was totally stupid. What had Lucas done to make her so upset? And why would she get so bent out of shape over Grey wanting to eat breakfast at home? He felt a bit bad about telling her she wasn't normal, but how could she not know that?

"What's wrong, hon?" Gram asked. "You don't look happy."

"I'm fine."

"Grey." Gram put down her mug. "Tell me what's going on at home. Is everything okay?"

"Everything's…fine. Why?"

"You don't seem happy. You're always tired. I don't know how you stand it with your mom's insane schedule."

"I'm okay, Gram."

She frowned. "I wish your mother would slow down."

"Why is she like that, Gram? She wasn't always. Did something happen?"

Gram blinked. "I think she's just tired, too." She stood. "I have to get dinner started."

"Do you want me to help?" he asked.

"No, dear, I've got it covered."

So much for teaching him how to cook. As she headed into the kitchen Grey stared out the window at the night. The wind rustled the trees outside. Gram was right, Mom would be there soon. And whatever was wrong with her, no one was talking about it.

CLAIRE'S STOMACH TIGHTENED as she turned the corner onto their street the evening after her birthday. Wasn't coming home supposed to make a person happy? At least she was exhausted enough that she might actually sleep tonight. She hadn't had a decent rest since that night with Lucas.

"Mom, hurry up," Grey said, impatience punctuating his words.

"I'm not going to speed, honey, it's a residential zone. What's the hurry?"

"Lucas is going to call to tell me how Lady is. He had to take her back for the vet to fix her. She was bleeding inside again."

"Oh, Grey, that doesn't sound good," Claire said, casting a glance at her son. Tension radiated from him. How had he gotten so invested in the dog?

"You're really worried about her, aren't you?" she asked.

"Of course I am. She might die."

"What did Lucas say?"

"Just that he had to take her back to the vet."

"And he's calling you tonight with more information?" she asked.

"He should be. I left him a message at The Coffee Stop."

Claire didn't respond. Grey had called Lucas at his shop. Not seeing Lucas was going to be hard on him. She pulled into the garage. Not seeing Lucas was hard on her.

Grey raced from the car into the house. She followed him more slowly. Her son wouldn't take the dog's death well if it happened. And if Lady recovered, Grey would want to see the dog regularly. Maybe she could work something out with Lucas as far as visitations with the dog.

She sighed. She was too tired to think about dealing with Lucas right now. The quiet of the house pressed in around her. As she moved through the living room she turned on the TV and computer.

She found Grey in the kitchen, staring at the answering machine.

"He didn't call," he said.

"He'll call."

"What if he didn't get my message, or what if she didn't make it and he just doesn't want to tell me?" he asked.

She pressed her hand to his shoulder. "He'll call. Why don't you get ready for bed? It's late."

He shrugged her hand from his shoulder. "I know it's late. It's always late."

He'd taken just a few steps from the phone when it rang, making Claire jump and her pulse quicken. She fisted her hands to keep from picking up the receiver as Grey hurried to answer it.

"Hello?" he said.

Please let the news be good. Grey didn't need anything more to upset him.

Grey nodded. "I know, you told me. So, how is she? Did you bring her home?"

He glanced at Claire, but she couldn't read his

expression. Again, he nodded. "And you hung out and talked to her?"

She pressed her lips together to suppress the urge to ask what Lucas was saying. She'd find out soon enough.

"Okay, I see," Grey said. "Thanks for calling."

He hung up, then headed again toward his room. Claire followed, pausing in his doorway. "Grey, what did Lucas say? How's Lady?"

Grey lifted his presidential pajama bottoms from the end of his bed and shook them out. He didn't look at her. "She didn't make it. She died last night."

Concerned, she stepped into his room. "Honey, I'm so sorry."

He caught her eye and the sheer exhaustion she saw there stopped her in her tracks. "I don't want to talk about it, okay? I'm fine, Mom. Now, if you don't mind I'm going to bed. I'm tired and I want to sleep."

Claire's throat tightened and her vision blurred. He was exhausted because of her. She nodded and closed the door behind her as she left.

CHAPTER TWENTY

THE YOUNG WOMAN behind the counter at the new coffee place smiled expectantly at Grey. Grey kept his gaze on the floor, stubbornly refusing to answer her request for his order. Claire frowned. How could her child be deliberately rude?

"He'll have a banana-strawberry smoothie," she answered for him.

"I don't want a smoothie," he said.

Relaxing her jaw, Claire attempted a smile. "You have to have something, Grey. I'm not dropping you at school with an empty stomach."

"Um, we don't have smoothies," the girl said. "Only coffee and tea. How about a coffee cooler? It's a blended drink."

"That's fine," Claire said. "Thank you."

"I don't want it. Coffee isn't breakfast," Grey said.

"And a bagel with cream cheese," Claire said.

The girl nodded as she busied herself getting their order. Grey frowned. "I'm not hungry. I hope you got all that for yourself."

Claire pulled him away from the line of other waiting customers. "Listen, I'm trying to be patient here. I know you're sad about Lady and about Lucas and you can be mad at me all you want. But you can't be rude to other people just because you're having a bad day. It isn't okay, Grey. Do you hear me?"

"Isn't that what you did, though? You were in a bad mood because I gave you the stupid espresso machine for your birthday and because you don't want to have breakfast with me at home, so you were mean to Lucas. Isn't *that* what happened?"

Heat flooded Claire's cheeks. She glanced at a woman in the nearby line. The woman looked away as though she hadn't been listening. Grey made her sound like a monster.

She kept her voice low. "I don't expect you to understand why Lucas and I aren't friends anymore, but it isn't because of the espresso machine, though admittedly I wasn't thrilled about that."

"Then why? Why were you mean to him? I finally have someone cool who wants to hang out with me and you ruined it."

"We're going to talk about this when we get to the car," Claire said, glancing at the barista to see how close she was to completing their order.

"Fine. I'll wait in the car."

"Grey, hold on." Claire tried to stop him, but he slipped from her grasp and headed toward the door.

"Here you go," the barista said, setting a small bag and drink tray in front of her.

"Thank you," Claire said as she hurriedly paid.

Grey was already in the car with the doors locked

when she got there. She unlocked the driver's door, and then maneuvered into her seat with the drinks. She set the bag with the bagel in the console beside Grey, along with his coffee cooler.

"Sometimes things don't work out between people—" she began.

"I know. We've already been over this," Grey said. "You suck at relationships."

Claire tightened her grip on the steering wheel. "That's really unfair, not to mention disrespectful. I don't see how I deserve that."

"I want to have a funeral for Lady."

"Is Lucas having a funeral?"

"He will if I ask him." He turned to her. "Mom, please will you ask him, or take me by there and I'll ask him?"

"Honey, it might be too late," she said. "It's been a couple of days. I'm sure Lucas has…taken care of that by now."

"We can ask."

"Okay, we don't have time now, but I'll stop by there after I drop you off and I'll talk to him."

Hope filled his eyes. "Promise, Mom? Because she should be treated like a lady, remember? And a lady would have a proper funeral."

Claire blinked moisture from her eyes. Her son could be rude, but he was also a very thoughtful young man. "Yes, Grey, you're right. I promise. I'll talk to Lucas."

Guns N' Roses rocked quietly from the overhead speakers as Lucas emerged from the back. The scent of coffee welcomed and soothed him as it always did. He glanced at Ken and nodded toward the speakers. "What's that?"

"Guns—"

"I know who it is. I'm just wondering who changed the station."

"Oh, that was Ramsey. We jammed to that yesterday. I meant to switch it back," Ken said.

Lucas arched his eyebrows. "*You* jammed to that?"

"I like a little hard rock now and then," Ken said as he headed to the stereo to change the track.

"It's fine, Ken. You can leave it. I don't mind," Lucas said.

Ken nodded and turned around as the bell on the front door sounded. "I think you have a visitor, boss."

Lucas's pulse quickened as Claire headed toward him. He hated still having this reaction to her. He'd called numerous times to try to work things out, but she'd never answered or returned his calls. He should be angry, but instead he was just sad that she was shutting him out.

He'd known all along the risk of getting involved with her. What a fool he'd been. Bracing himself, he nodded his greeting as she stopped in front of him.

"Good morning," he said.

She paused, the lines of her face drawn taut. Evidently, she wasn't any happier about being here than he was to have her here. "Good morning, Lucas."

"Is Grey okay?" he asked, racking his brain to figure out why she'd come.

"Actually, no, he's upset about—" she waved her hand "—everything, but more specifically he's really sad about Lady and I realize it may be too late, but I promised I'd come ask." She looked away, and then met his gaze. "He wants to have a funeral." Her voice faltered. "He says that's what a lady deserves."

Lucas's throat tightened. "I buried her in my backyard, near the garden. I thought about inviting the two of you, but I figured it would be too hard. I'm sorry."

She nodded. "Of course. I told him it was probably already too late." She nodded again. "Thank you, anyway."

As she turned to leave, Lucas called her name. She stopped and turned back to him. He said, "We could still have a funeral, say a few words, lay flowers on her grave, that kind of thing. Whatever you think might help Grey feel better."

Once more she nodded. "Thank you, Lucas. That would be really good. Could we do it today after Grey gets out of school? We'll have the ceremony and let him say goodbye before I take him to my mother's house."

"Sure, Claire, whatever works for you."

"Four o'clock?"

"Sure, four o'clock. I'll see you both then. I'll get

some flowers. Is there anything else I should do?" he asked.

"No, that's okay. I'll take care of everything." She seemed about to leave, but stopped once more. "Thanks again, Lucas. Under the circumstances I would have understood if you didn't want to do this."

"It isn't a problem. I'm happy to do anything for Grey—for both of you."

She parted her lips, as though she might say more, and then walked out the door.

GREY SCANNED THE long line of cars in the carpool pickup lane, searching for his mom's car. He'd gotten a message that she was picking him up today, not Aunt Becca. Mom was always late, and today wasn't any different. He resettled his backpack and stood alongside the other waiting kids, avoiding eye contact, so he wouldn't have to talk to anyone.

"Are you all right, Grey?" Miss Ambers, one of the teachers who supervised the pickups, stepped beside him.

"I'm fine," he said.

She looked at him curiously. Why did everyone look at him that way? "Are you sure?"

"My dog died," he said, just to make her stop.

She frowned in sympathy. "I'm so sorry."

"It's okay," he said.

She patted his arm, and then moved on to help a parent and child safely across the driveway. He shrugged off the hint of guilt at his lie. He'd found

Lady. He'd gotten his mom and Lucas to help. If things had worked out differently, they'd be sharing Lady with Lucas. They'd all be one happy family. Was it really wrong he'd called her his dog?

Nearly fifteen minutes later his mother finally showed up, way at the end of the line. It figured she'd be last to get him. They'd spend an uncomfortable trip to Aunt Becca's with her awful metal music blasting, then she'd dump him at her sister's, because she couldn't freaking be at home with him. Yet no one—not Gram, not Aunt Becca, not Lucas—wanted to talk to him about what was wrong with her.

Fine. They could all act like everything was normal, but he was done with that. He wasn't going to pretend anymore.

He walked along the line of cars. The blaring sounds of Mindless Self Indulgence reached him ten cars before he reached his mom's old beat-up Honda. He hated that he knew enough about metal bands to recognize the song. His stomach knotted as he slipped into the passenger seat. Surprisingly, she turned down her music a notch.

"Hi, little man, how was school?" Mom asked as she pulled from the curb.

He stared at her. "I hate it when you call me that."

Her smile faded. "I'm sorry, Grey. I won't call you that anymore."

He focused on the road ahead. "Thank you. Did you talk to Lucas about the funeral for Lady?"

"I did. I stopped in to see him after I dropped you off this morning." She paused as she checked traffic and changed lanes.

"And?"

"And he buried her in his backyard already, but we're going to still have a funeral."

"When?"

"Now, if that's okay. I told him we'd meet him at his place as soon as I picked you up."

He nodded. "Thanks."

"I'm sorry I'm late. I stopped to get some flowers. I mean, Lucas is getting flowers, too, but you can never have too many at a funeral." She gestured toward the back. "I got some dog toys, too—a chew bone, grooming brush and other little stuff. I thought it might be nice to get her some things she should have had. If there's something in particular you'd like to add, we can make another stop. Whatever you want, Grey. This is for you."

"It's for Lady," he said.

"Of course. Look, I'm sorry you didn't get a chance to get to know her."

He didn't respond. It was cool they were going to Lucas's house. They turned into a neighborhood lined with neat yards and matching mailboxes. Grey tried to imagine Lucas living in one of the brick houses, but he couldn't quite picture it.

Mom checked her phone's GPS, then turned down a side street. They passed a lawn that needed mowing, and another that had sprouted wildflowers instead of grass. One house had a mailbox that looked like it belonged in an old-time railroad station. Grey nodded to himself. This looked more like Lucas's neighborhood, at least what Grey imagined it to be.

"Here we are," Mom said as she pulled into one of the driveways. It wound back a ways and a small kind of arbor with overhanging branches framed the end of it. She parked beside an old pickup truck.

Grey slipped out of the car. A soft breeze wrestled some of the lingering leaves from the overhead branches. They floated down, taking their time to hit the ground. Mom stood beside him, her gaze scanning the expanse of yard around them. "Lady would have loved it here."

Nodding, Grey let his gaze follow hers. Lady would have loved it, all right. And he would have, too.

CHAPTER TWENTY-ONE

CLAIRE'S BREATH CAUGHT as Lucas rounded the side of the building and headed toward them. Grey saw him about the same time. Without warning, her son launched himself at Lucas. Lucas caught him in a big hug, lifting him off the ground and holding him tight.

Claire swallowed past a lump in her throat. Part of her wanted to launch herself at Lucas, too, but he'd betrayed her trust when he helped Grey buy that espresso machine. Her fragile relationship with her son had gone downhill since then.

"Hello, Claire," Lucas said as he set Grey on the ground. "Thank you for coming by and arranging this."

"Hello, Lucas," she said. He looked tired and his hair needed cutting, but the woman in her still jumped at the sight of him. "And it was all Grey's idea. He was pretty insistent."

"Don't we have some stuff in the car?" Grey asked.

"Yes," she said. "Lucas, I know you said you'd get flowers, but I saw these and thought it wouldn't hurt to have more."

She lifted the bouquet of roses, lilies and other assorted flowers. She shrugged. "I liked this—the colors are bright and happy and I thought maybe we could all use something to lift us up."

"They're pretty, Mom. I'm sure Lady would have liked them," Grey said as she passed him the bouquet.

She grabbed the rest of the items and Lucas led them toward the back of the house. He picked up another bouquet from a bench as they passed. Grey clung to his side.

"See this, Grey?" Lucas asked, pointing to a gazebo as they rounded the corner to the backyard, a yard that seemed to stretch on without boundaries.

Greenery of various shapes and sizes surrounded the structure, while flower baskets adorned hanging planters and pots, which were strategically placed throughout the area. The flowers had lost their blossoms to the cooler temperatures, but this must have been breathtaking a month or so ago.

"This was a kit I bought. I thought it would be a weekend project," Lucas said. He glanced at Claire. "It took me six months to finish the thing."

Grey raced up into the gazebo. "It's awesome. If we'd known you then and Mom had let me I would have totally helped you build it."

"I wish I'd had your help," Lucas said. "It was so much more complicated than I thought it would be. I do enjoy it now, though."

"It's lovely," Claire said, stopping beside him as Grey leaned over the railing and waved at them.

She rubbed her arms. Normally, Lucas would have pulled her to his side. Her throat tightened and she moved away as moisture blurred her vision. It would have been so much easier if she'd been able to just drop off Grey and not have to actually see Lucas. She couldn't have done that, though, and not further damaged her eroding relationship with her son.

Lucas gestured to an area beyond the gazebo. "This way to the garden."

They headed down a short path that opened onto the garden. Claire stopped short as Grey raced to a circular clearing at the path's center, lined with Adirondack chairs and old wooden end tables. The foliage and flowers here still had a hint of their former glory. Claire turned to Lucas. "It's beautiful, Lucas. Did you do all this? I can't imagine what it was like when everything was in bloom."

"I hired a crew, but I helped with the planning and some of the work. I have help keeping it up, as well, though I do what I can." He shrugged. "I really created this for my mother. She enjoys it when she visits and I'm hoping she'll eventually come here to live. She loves a good garden."

"You did this for your mom?" Grey asked.

"That's right."

"That's cool. She's one lucky mom." He scooted

down the steps of the gazebo. “Where did you bury Lady?”

Lucas’s smile faded. “Over here.”

He showed them down a side path to a lawn surrounded by more foliage and flowers. A small mound of dirt and a wooden cross marked the grave tucked into an alcove with what appeared to be rosebushes.

“Are these roses?” Claire asked.

Lucas nodded. “They bloomed early this year. We had that cold weather earlier and they didn’t make it. It’ll be pretty when they bloom again, though.” He gestured to the cross. “I threw that together with scrap wood, but we can make something else if you’d like, Grey.”

Grey tilted his head. “I don’t mind the cross, but a headstone would be nice, if they don’t cost too much.”

Lucas glanced at Claire. “I think we could find something that would work. If your mom doesn’t mind, maybe we can go together to pick it out, the three of us. That’ll give us a chance to figure out what it should say.”

Grey nodded, his forehead creased in thought. “Yeah, we’ll have to come up with something good. I’ll think about it.” He glanced at Claire. “Mom, you’re good with that stuff. Will you help? Oh, and is it okay for us to go with Lucas to find a headstone?”

A bit of happiness rippled through Claire, even though the circumstances were sad. Grey so seldom sought her company lately, she was glad to have this opportunity to spend time with him…and with Lucas. She glanced at Lucas, gratitude filling her. "Of course it's okay and I'll think about an epitaph."

"Epitaph?" Grey asked.

"That's whatever we write on the headstone," Lucas said. He gestured toward the grave site with his bouquet of flowers. "Do we know how we want to do this?"

Grey looked to Claire and again she felt touched. It was good to have him looking at her for direction for a change. She didn't know how much more disdain and anger she could take from him.

"Why don't we each take a turn saying something about Lady and then laying either flowers or her other gifts on her grave?"

"Okay," Grey said. "Can I do the toys and chew bone and the brush, too?"

"Of course, honey." She traded the items for the bouquet he'd carried from the car. "Do you want to go first?"

Grey straightened. "Is that okay, Lucas, or do you want to go?"

"Be my guest," Lucas said.

Grey stood before the grave. "Lady, we just met you and all we know about you is that somebody was really mean to you." His voice caught and he paused. "They didn't treat you like a lady at all, but that's what you deserved. And that's what we would have done if you hadn't died." Again, he faltered and stopped to compose himself.

He knelt and laid out the rawhide bone, squeaky toy, brush and rubber ball. "These are for you and I'm sorry you can't play with them." He glanced again at Claire and then said, "But it's our way of showing you we love you and we would have spoiled you if you were still here to make up for all the meanness you had to live through before. I hope you're happy now."

He stood, then stepped back beside Claire. She squeezed his shoulder. "That was really nice, Grey."

"It was," Lucas agreed. "Do you want to say anything?" he asked Claire.

"Oh," she said, glancing at Grey. "Okay, I can do that."

Bouquet in hand, she stepped forward. "Poor Lady, like Grey said, we're so very sorry for all the abuse you suffered." The chill of fear she'd experienced that day, when she thought of the type of person it would take to hurt an animal so badly, came over her again.

Her fingers tingled. She knelt and placed the flowers beside the gifts Grey had set on the grave. "These are for you to show you how much we cared for you, even for just the short while you were with us."

As she rose, the ground seemed to shift beneath

her and she willed the panic to subside. They were safe in Lucas's backyard. No one would harm them here.

Grey slipped his hand in hers and she bit her lip as tears rolled down her cheeks. She wouldn't have guessed she'd get this emotional over the dog's funeral or over her son's quiet acceptance of her. It seemed she'd been craving the latter for so long.

"Thanks, Mom," Grey said.

Lucas moved to the graveside. His voice was low and soothing as he said, "I had hoped you'd stick around with us awhile, girl. I did everything in my power to give you a fighting chance, but I think the fight had gone out of you long before we found you. I could tell, though, that you were a gentle soul and you deserved a better life. I hope you have that now, wherever you are. I hope we were able to provide you some comfort in your last days."

He knelt and laid the flowers with the other offerings, then he stood beside Grey and Claire. The wind ruffled the treetops around them, where birds sang in the late afternoon. After a period of quiet, Grey turned to Claire. "I know you have to take me to Aunt Becca's now, but can I please have some time alone with Lady before we leave?"

"Sure, if that's all right with Lucas."

"Of course," Lucas said. More quietly, he said to Claire, "And maybe we can have a moment."

She couldn't find words to respond, but she nodded.

He took her elbow and steered her away to give Grey privacy.

"I called," he said, without a trace of accusation.

"I know, Lucas, I'm sorry I didn't call you back. I was upset and I didn't know what to say."

"Maybe you could have listened instead," he said.

"I'll listen now."

He glanced away, then back. "You were right. I had a bad feeling about that damn gift from the start, but I kept telling myself, it's just an espresso machine. What harm is there in that? I should have listened to that feeling and convinced Grey to get you something else. I should have known it would make you feel pressured to do something you're not ready to do. If it helps, he planned to buy it before you and I even met.

"I just want you to know I'm sorry, Claire. I would never willingly do anything to hurt you and I'm so very sorry my shortsightedness did that. I know you may feel you're not ready for a relationship and I don't know if you'd ever give me another shot, but I've missed you and Grey and I'd do anything to be back in your lives again."

The tears tracked unheeded down her cheeks. She was an emotional wreck, but somehow Lucas helped stabilize her in a way nothing else did. The tingling had left her fingers and the earth remained steady beneath her feet.

Lucas swiped his thumb over her cheek. He pulled a glove from his pocket and dabbed at her tears.

"So, do these tears mean you're sad about Lady or are they happy tears that we get to hang out again? Does it mean you forgive me?"

She inhaled. "I know how hard it is to talk Grey out of something. Of course I forgive you, if there's really anything to forgive." She frowned. "And if you forgive me. I'm sorry I overreacted."

"There's nothing to forgive. You can't help the way you felt."

"But I'm such a basket case. Are you sure you want this? Even if I'm a neurotic mess?"

"Yes, I want this." He cupped her face. "Right or wrong, I want to be with you, Claire. I want to be with you both."

Her heart leaped and she wanted to tell him she wanted that, too, but the words stuck in her throat and then he was kissing her and she lost herself in the warmth and security and fire that was Lucas.

CHAPTER TWENTY-TWO

LUCAS ROLLED OVER and covered his head with the pillow. He'd hardly slept last night with metal music cranking from the stereo in the living room and old movies playing on the television all night. Now, some traffic reporter was going on about an accident on Interstate 285, while rap music from the radio next to the bed had joined the cacophony.

How was a guy to get any rest?

He finally groaned and sat up, blinking at the brightness of Claire's white room. Her side of the bed was empty and she was nowhere to be seen.

He switched off the rap alarm and dressed quickly, trying to shake off the grogginess. It had been two weeks since Lady's funeral. He'd spent nearly every night here with Claire and Grey, but he was having trouble gaining his footing in the chaos that was Claire's world.

Grey's voice mixed in with the jumble of the music and television. Lucas followed the sound to the kitchen. Claire stood at the counter, packing the insulated bag she used for their on-the-road food. She glanced at him as she turned Grey toward the hallway, her eyes wide with that look he was coming to understand signaled her need to flee.

"Please, Grey, go get dressed. See, Lucas is awake and we need to hit the road," she said.

"But, Mom, Lucas is here and it's the weekend. Why can't we hang out again? He still hasn't looked at the garbage disposal. Please? I don't want to get dressed. I want to stay here."

"I'm not arguing about this. Get moving, now, please."

Grey frowned and headed toward his room. "I hate this. I should have stayed with Gram or Aunt Becca again."

Claire closed her eyes and squeezed her fists. Lucas kissed her cheek. "Good morning, sunshine."

She didn't open her eyes. "Good morning."

"What's wrong?" He wrapped his arms around her. "How long will Grey take to get dressed? Do I have time to drag you back to bed?"

"I have to move the laundry along," she said as she pulled away from him.

He grabbed her arm. "Claire?"

She stopped and finally looked at him. "Yes?"

"What's wrong?"

"I just haven't had a chance to get to the laundry and if I don't move it now it won't be ready later," she said.

"Okay," he said, letting her go. "I'll help you."

She squeezed her hands into fists again. "No, it's all right. I can manage the laundry on my own."

"Sweetheart, did I do something wrong?"

"No."

"Are your hands okay?"

She frowned. "Why do you ask?"

"You keep making those fists. Do you want to take a swing at me?"

She pulled her hands, still fisted, to her chest. "No, why would I want to hit you?"

"Because I seem to be annoying the hell out of you right now," he said.

She closed her eyes again and her entire body seemed to nearly tremble with tension. "No, it isn't you…exactly."

He clasped her fists, still pressed to her chest. "It's okay, Claire. You can talk to me. We're in this together, remember?"

"That's the problem. I'm…not used to all of this…togetherness. It's hard…for me."

"Breathe, sweetheart. Take your time. Just talk to me. Believe me, I've heard it all. Nothing you say can drive me away."

She slowly exhaled through her mouth. "I'm having…a…rough morning and I'm not used to…being around someone…so much." She flexed her hands. "I had another…nightmare last night. My fingers are…tingling and the floor is slanting and my…head is pounding…." She paused and breathed again. "I don't want…you to see me…lose it."

"You're having an anxiety attack, right? And you're worried about doing it in front of me."

Tears spilled down her cheeks. "It is…so much harder…with you here. I have to keep it…together all the time…and I can't…do that."

"You don't have to. You can lose it with me. I promise I can handle it," he said as concern rippled through him.

Her gaze locked with his. "But I…can't. I need to leave…now." She pushed away from him again and headed for the basement, running down the steps to get away from him.

He followed her to the basement doorway, afraid she might fall in her state. He stopped at the top step. She made it to the bottom and sank to her knees, almost in the fetal position.

He scrubbed his hands through his hair, torn between going to her to comfort her and the knowledge that she didn't want him there. His stomach knotted as he stepped away to give her privacy. What horror had she suffered to put her in that state?

How was he supposed to help her, if his very presence made it harder for her? He was in over his head with Claire. He needed to find a way to convince her to get professional help.

"OKAY, BOYS, Grey's mom is here," Marty's mom said as she stood in the doorway to the den where Grey and Marty were playing a video game.

"Hold on, Mom. We'll be done in just a sec," Marty said as he worked his controller.

Grey jumped to his feet, his controller in hand. “Zombie to your left, Marty. I can’t get him.”

“It won’t fire!” Marty jammed his thumbs into the buttons. “I’m out of ammo. Crap, he’s got me.”

“Ugh, you’re toast, dude,” Grey said. “There’s too many of them. I’m trapped.”

“Grey, what are you playing?” Mom asked from beside Marty’s mom.

“Mom?” Grey glanced in her direction. His video character stalled. He tossed the controller onto the sofa. “They got me.”

“You’re killing zombies, now?” Mom asked.

“It’s just a game, Miss Claire,” Marty said. “We’ll be ready for the zombie apocalypse. Right, Grey?”

“Sure,” Grey said. His mom wore her running clothes, with her hair in a sweaty ponytail. She looked wild and unkempt next to Marty’s mother in her jeans and sweater. Why did his mom have to always push it so hard?

“Are you guys ready to go?” she asked.

Guys?

“Let me get my bag,” Marty said as he darted from the room.

Grey stared after him. “Why is he getting a bag?”

“I thought I told you, honey. Marty’s spending the night, while Cynthia goes out,” Mom said.

Marty was going to spend the night? The high of the zombie apocalypse crashed and burned. They’d dragged Marty around with them before, but he’d never been to their house and now he was coming for the entire night?

Hopefully he wasn't expecting to get any sleep.

"My mom has a hot date," Marty said, grinning as he returned with a bulging backpack.

Miss Cynthia ruffled his hair. "You like Reed, don't you, Marty?"

"He's cool." He turned to Grey's mother. "I'm all set."

Moments later, Grey slipped into the backseat of the car. Marty took the front passenger seat. He jammed with Mom all the way home, head banging, like that was something he did all the time.

Grey felt nauseous by the time they reached the house. The driveway was empty. "Where's Lucas's truck?" he asked.

Mom pulled into the garage and killed the engine. Grey sucked in the brief respite from the noise before they walked into the house. She'd leave the TV and stereo on all the time, if Grey didn't turn them off whenever they went out.

She glanced at him, but her gaze didn't quite connect with his. "He's helping his mother with something. He said it would be late when he finished."

Grey stared at the back of her head as she pushed through the side door. She'd done something to run Lucas off again, hadn't she? She'd finally found someone who, for whatever reason, put up with all her crazy and she kept driving him away.

Cranking on the music and television on her way

in as always, she showed Marty to Grey's room, where, obviously she expected Marty to stay. He dropped his bag on Grey's bed.

"Mom, how are we both going to sleep in here?" Grey asked.

His normal routine of shutting himself away in his room with his earplugs wouldn't work with his friend here. Grey glanced at his bed. If only they'd go away and he could climb into his bed and cover himself with the comforter and a pillow or two. He was tired enough tonight to sleep through the chaos.

"This is a good song," Marty said, playing air guitar. He didn't look like he was going to be ready to sleep anytime soon.

"It's a double bed, Grey. Can't you share?" Mom asked.

He was supposed to sleep in the same bed with Marty?

Mom sighed. "Okay, we can pull out the sleeper sofa in the living room and you guys can hang out there and watch movies. Marty can sleep there. And, Grey, if you would rather sleep in your own bed, you can do that."

"Okay," Grey said, turning to his friend. "Let's go set up the sofa and see what's on."

Marty nodded as he strutted his way into the living room after Grey, brandishing his air guitar. Half an hour later the metal music had moved to Mom's bedroom and a disaster movie played on the television in the living room. Pajama-clad, he and Marty shared a bowl of popcorn as they watched a giant asteroid plummet toward the earth.

While a top team of astronauts attempted to save the planet, Mom made her third circuit of the windows and doors. Grey's stomach tightened. Maybe Marty hadn't noticed.

Marty leaned in close. "Why does your mom keep doing that? Does she have OCD? Is she a checker?"

Grey was too embarrassed to look at his friend. "I don't even know what that is. She just does it. I guess it makes her feel better to know we're locked in safely for the night."

"But she keeps doing it. It's obsessive compulsive something. I saw it on the Learning Channel. It's when someone can't stop doing the same thing over and over. Like some people keep washing their hands until they bleed and some people check stuff, like if the oven is off, that kind of thing, but they do it over and over again."

"I don't know," Grey said. Was that what was wrong with her? And here was Marty, just another ten-year-old kid, coming up with a theory when no one else would even admit there was anything wrong.

But having Marty notice how odd she was sent waves of humiliation washing over Grey. Why couldn't his mom just be normal?

Mom passed back through the living room, earphones jamming. She stopped and pulled out one side and the sound of a reeling electric guitar spilled into the room.

"Are you boys okay?" she asked.

Marty jumped up, again strumming his air guitar. "This is another good song."

Mom laughed and jammed on her own air guitar. Grey stared at them. This was going to be such a long night. If he was smart, he'd ask Gram if he could stay with her next weekend. He was just so done with trying to get any rest at his own house.

The front door opened and relief filled Grey as Lucas entered. So Mom hadn't actually run him off. Hopefully, Lucas would keep her occupied and she wouldn't do anything more abnormal tonight.

Lucas greeted everyone, then he and Mom moved on to her room and Marty climbed back on the pull-out. He leaned toward Grey. "Your mom is cool and everything, but does she rock like that all the time?"

Grey nodded, his gaze glued to the television where a giant tsunami threatened the entire East Coast. "Twenty-four seven. It never stops. And the only time we're home for long, except to sleep, is when she's locked in her room and doesn't answer."

"Dude," Marty said. "That just isn't normal."

And there it was, out in the open.

Grey turned to his friend, suppressing the strangest urge to hug him. "Dude, you are so right."

"What are you going to do?" Marty asked.

Grey inhaled slowly as the tsunami broke over Manhattan. "I don't know. Either get her to fix herself, or hope Lucas can do it, or get the heck out of here, I guess."

Settling back into the movie, Marty scooped up a handful of popcorn and nodded. "Good plan."

LUCAS SAT ON the bed as Claire paced around the room, her earphones in, but the volume loud enough for him to hear, even over the old radio on her nightstand blasting heavy metal. Exhaustion tugged at him. It was as though she'd withdrawn from him since her breakdown in the laundry room. Though she responded to his calls and texts and was responsive to him at The Stop when she and Grey had dropped in, she hadn't initiated contact with him since then.

It is...so much harder...with you here.

He moved behind her, his fingers brushing her hip. She turned to him, her lips curving into that shy smile that melted him every time. She slipped her hands over his shoulders, saying, "Hi."

"Hi," he said, though she couldn't possibly have heard him. She brushed her lips over his and he covered her mouth with his. He held her loosely, not wanting the moment to escalate into anything she wasn't ready for. Still, her tongue probed his and she leaned into him.

He drew back and gestured toward the earphones. "Can we?"

She pulled one bud from her ear and booming bass spilled into the room. "I'm sorry?" she asked.

"Do you think maybe you could do without those for now?" he asked. "I just want to hold you and see how your day went. Maybe kiss you some more."

"Oh, of course." She fiddled with her phone until only the sound of the radio filled the air.

"Thank you." He brushed his mouth over hers.

This time her kiss was more tentative, though. Again, he got the feeling she was participating only because he'd initiated. He drew back and caught her gaze. "Sweetheart, are you okay?"

"I'm fine," she said, though her words were clipped.

"Claire," he said. "Can we talk about the other day, when you said it was hard for you with me here?"

She closed her eyes and her fingers curled into his shirt, gripping the fabric. "I'm so sorry, Lucas. I want to make this work."

"Then please get help. You scared me that day. I want to make this work, too, but it's hard for me to watch you suffer."

She nodded. "I know. I'm sorry."

But if she really knew, why wouldn't she do anything about it? "Then let me take you to see someone." He gestured to her radio and the swelling strains of screeching guitar that still filled the air. "You don't have to live like this."

"I know," she said, "but it's…difficult."

"You know you can't go on like this?"

"Yes," she said, the word inaudible amid the the racket in the room.

"So, you'll start counseling?"

She pressed her lips together. "Lucas…"

He couldn't do this. He couldn't make her get help and he couldn't stay if she refused to do so on her own. He'd already watched one person he loved self-destruct. He wouldn't stand by and watch another.

He leaned his forehead against hers, his throat tight and burning. "Please, Claire."

She pulled back and tears rolled down her cheeks. "I…can't."

He blinked against the gathering moisture in his eyes. He held her at arm's length. "Then I'm sorry, Claire. I can't do this."

The heaviness threatened to crush him as he grabbed his jacket and left.

CHAPTER TWENTY-THREE

CLAIRE GRIPPED THE steering wheel and forced herself to focus on the road. Dark pavement flashed by, illuminated by the occasional streetlight. Holcomb Bridge Road was busy for a Saturday night in Roswell. As she weaved around other cars, she cranked up Guns N' Roses on the radio, but the pounding beat did little to stop the swell of sadness overrunning her.

Grey had been adamant about staying at Becca's tonight. Claire rarely resorted to "because I said so," but when he'd asked her why he couldn't spend the night at his aunt's, she couldn't very well tell him that after nearly a week of Lucas avoiding her while she worked from the coffee shop, hoping to keep some connection, the thought of being alone in that house had her drowning in despair.

The light turned to yellow, then red and she hit the brakes, stopping just before the intersection. Her heart thudded and the ache in her grew to all-consuming proportions. She didn't even try to stop the tears as they rolled down her cheeks so the night became a blur of dark with splashes of light. She gave in to the grief as it racked her body in spasms of release.

A horn honked behind her. The light had turned green. She wiped her hands across her eyes, and accelerated. A quick glance in the mirror as she passed a streetlight revealed her puffy eyes and red nose. She inhaled deeply, trying to calm herself. She couldn't show up at her sister's looking like this.

Ten minutes later she pulled into Becca's street. She drove slowly to give herself time to recover. She rarely let herself lose control like that, but even apart from her situation with Lucas the week had been trying. A shipment had been destroyed in a storm and the parties were in a legal battle over the contract terms. She'd lost her analysis of her proposal for a new client and had to redo it at the last minute. One vendor had dropped her all together.

She pulled into Becca's driveway. And Grey… Things with Grey since the sleepover with Marty had gone from bad to worse. Whatever had happened that night hadn't been good. It was as though Grey's attitude had changed. He had zero tolerance for anything he labeled as abnormal behavior and she had a boatload of issues for him to jump on. As far as her son was concerned, she couldn't do anything right and he had no problem letting her know that she had to fix it.

And, of course, she couldn't.

She missed Lucas so much she ached with it. She'd continued to work at The Coffee Stop, hoping to catch a word with him, a friendly smile. What kind of crazy person did that after a man walked away from her the way he had?

And now Grey had evidently arranged for them to buy the headstone for Lady with him tomorrow. How was she going to face him?

I'm sorry, Claire. I can't do this.

His words had brought her to her knees. Thankfully, Grey and Marty had been occupied for the night, because she'd spent it in the fetal position on her floor. All Lucas wanted was for her to get help, for her to get better. She totally got that.

But he didn't understand that just the thought of talking about what had happened to her consumed her with terror. It was like asking her to go back to that day and relive it.

If only she could make him understand. She scrubbed her hands over her face and grabbed her purse from the passenger seat. As if to taunt her, her cell phone slid out onto the upholstery. Before she could change her mind, she'd picked it up and dialed Lucas's number.

Her heart pounded as it rang and she waited. Would he answer? Heaven help her, what was she doing?

"Claire?" His soft baritone flowed to her over the connection.

"Lucas..." Her eyes again filled and her throat clogged.

"Are you okay?" His tone was concerned, not

angry, not hurt, not frustrated—just honestly concerned.

"No."

He was silent on his end.

"I miss you," she said.

"I miss you, too." His voice was tight, as though he were in pain.

That made her cry all the harder. "I'm so sorry. I shouldn't have called. I'll see you in the morning."

She hung up. Lucas had been right to leave her. She was a mess. How she was going to make it through tomorrow was beyond her.

Again, she scrubbed her hands over her eyes, checking her reflection to make sure she was presentable. She wasn't, but she'd been sitting in the driveway long enough to have everyone wondering.

She pocketed her keys as she walked up the steep drive. "Honey, I want to fix myself," she said to Grey although he wasn't there, "but please let me do it in my own way."

Becca answered the door with a worried frown. "He's in the den, but he's not happy about having to leave. It really isn't a problem for him to be here, Claire."

Claire tamped down her frustration. Becca was only trying to help. "I know, Becca," she said. "But I want him home. We have an early start tomorrow."

Claire was ridiculously nervous at the prospect of spending time with Lucas again, even though it was only to appease her son. Grey had been uncharacteristically subdued when he'd told her he'd called Lucas to arrange the outing, though. She'd been too stunned to reprimand him for not asking her first. Would she have denied him?

She found her son busily writing in a notebook while an action movie played on the TV. Kyle nodded to her from his place on the sofa.

"Hello, Claire," he said. He gestured toward the screen. "It's a good one. Would you like to join us?"

"Hello, Kyle. No…thanks, though. It's late and Grey and I have an early morning."

Grey glanced at her, and then bent his head again over his notebook. "You and Lucas can pick me up from here on the way out in the morning."

"Remember, we're having breakfast out first, a sit-down breakfast, and it will be early. We don't want to disturb Becca and Kyle that early on a Sunday."

"They won't mind. They're up early. Amanda never sleeps in," Grey said, without looking at her. "And a sit-down breakfast only counts if it's at home."

Becca stepped into the room, stopping beside Claire. "Here's your jacket, Grey. You can take that notebook with you, so you can keep working on your story."

Grey finally admitted defeat. He accepted his jacket from his aunt and said, "Thanks for letting me hang out with you guys today. I had a lot of fun."

Becca scooped him into an easy hug. Grey hugged

her back with an intensity that made Claire's throat burn. "Come on, honey," she said. "We should get going."

"Maybe he could stay next weekend," Becca suggested as she walked them to the door. "For the entire weekend. Amanda would love it. We all would. We'll go to some of the historic houses in Roswell. You'd like that, wouldn't you, Grey?"

"That would be great," Grey said.

Claire opened the door as the night blurred again. She blinked and took another slow breath to keep from losing it again. "Thanks for having him, Becca. We'll see you at Atlanta Rocks tomorrow afternoon."

"We wouldn't miss it." Becca gave her a quick hug, then closed and bolted the door behind them. Grey didn't speak to her for most of the way home and she was too exhausted to try to mend things with him, so she cranked the radio and focused on the road.

They'd turned onto their street when Grey broke his silence. "What did you do this time?"

"What do you mean?"

"To drive Lucas away. The last time you were mean to him because he helped me get the espresso machine. What happened this time?"

There was no way she could tell her son about the panic attack she hadn't been able to hold at bay. "We just needed a little break. He's coming by in the morning, right? We're going shopping for Lady's headstone."

"He's coming because *I* asked him to come. He was practically living with us and then he wasn't. Why did you need a break? Who asked for it?"

She pulled into the garage and got out of the car. Grey followed her into the house. "We both needed it. It isn't easy being with someone all the time. We should have taken things more slowly at the start. We just jumped right in and then needed some space."

Grey stopped in front of her as they reached the living room and she turned on the TV. "But it's harder for you, right, because of whatever is wrong with you?"

She closed her eyes. She was so tired. Why did he have to grill her now? When she opened them, he stood with his arms crossed, mouth tight. She reached for him, but he twisted so her hand hit empty space.

"Grey," she said. "I know I'm not an easy person to live with and I'm sorry you have to deal with me. I have issues. I'm not normal. I admit it, okay? I'm working on it. I don't know what else you want me to say."

His gaze pinned her. "I just want you to say you'll fix whatever is wrong, so you won't drive Lucas away again and so we can have normal."

How wonderful his version of life sounded. If only it were that easy. "I'm going to try, Grey, but you have to let me do this my way."

"Your way isn't working, Mom." With that he stalked to his room and slammed the door.

She clicked on the TV and cranked the volume before beginning her circuit of the windows and doors. Somehow, she'd find a way to fix this, but she'd do it on her own.

LUCAS HESITATED AT Claire's door. He still had the keys she'd given him, but he hadn't been by in almost a week. Shaking his head, he pulled out his key ring and made quick work of the locks.

I miss you.

His throat tightened at the memory of her call. Didn't she know how hard it was for him to stay away? But it was harder for him to stay. He'd wanted to tell Grey he and Claire could pick out the headstone on their own, but he hadn't wanted to disappoint the boy.

Maybe he could try to talk to Claire again. If she wouldn't get help for herself, maybe he could convince her to do it for Grey. Then perhaps they could find a balance they could all live with.

He pushed through the door, tilting his head to filter through the regular racket to see if he could tell where in the house Claire and Grey might be. He glanced at his watch. It was early yet; they might still be getting dressed.

He padded down the hall to Claire's room, the room he'd shared with her when he'd stayed here.

The door stood ajar. Again, he hesitated. Was he still welcome?

He tapped on the door. "Claire?"

She didn't answer, probably because she hadn't heard. He stepped into the room and called a little louder. "Claire?"

He moved past the bed, which was already made with her neat hospital corners and covered with the fluffy white comforter that held so many memories that now brought only pain and longing. A movement in the bathroom caught his eye.

"Good morning," he called.

She stood before the mirror, applying mascara to her already dark lashes. Claire was stunning with or without makeup. Yearning filled him as he stepped into the bathroom.

He moved behind her. She jumped, dropping her mascara, her hands splayed and eyes wide. He froze as she pressed her hands to her chest and sucked in deep lungfuls of air.

Damn. In his first moments back here, he'd managed to scare the bejeezus out of her and possibly triggered another anxiety attack.

He spread his hands, wanting to hold her in his arms to soothe her, but mindful that he'd ended things with her for a reason. "I'm so sorry, Claire. I knocked and called out several times. I didn't mean to sneak up on you."

She turned, bracing herself against the counter.

She nodded and shook out her hands, clenching and unclenching them. "I know. It's okay."

He exhaled, his arms still spread. All she had to do was step into them. He ached to hold her. She leaned in, and he thought for a moment she might let him, but she merely retrieved her mascara from the floor.

"Maybe we should start over," he said. "Good morning."

She glanced at him in the mirror, her mouth a tight smile. "Good morning, Lucas. I'm almost ready. Could you please check to see if Grey is out of the shower?"

"Sure." He shook his head as he moved down the hall. Claire seemed more withdrawn than ever. It was as though she hadn't called him last night.

The bathroom door stood ajar, but the room was empty. The steam and a bunched towel on the floor were pretty good evidence the boy had at least showered. Lucas hung up the towel, then continued to Grey's room. At least Grey would be happy to see him.

Grey's room was also empty, though the open drawers and the rumpled pajamas at the foot of the bed meant Grey was likely dressed. Since he hadn't been in the living room when Lucas had entered, that left only the kitchen.

A light in Claire's home office caught Lucas's attention as he passed. Grey sat at the desk in front of

Claire's laptop. He glanced up as Lucas approached, but quickly returned his attention to the screen.

"Hey." Lucas pulled up a chair beside his young friend.

"Hey." Grey didn't look at him.

Lucas stemmed his disappointment at the lukewarm greeting. Was Grey upset that he hadn't been around? Had he and Claire had a fight?

Lucas turned his attention to the monitor. "What are you doing?"

"Looking at headstones for Lady. There are tons online." Grey glanced at Lucas. "I suggested to Mom we hang out here and find one online. Maybe have breakfast. Then you could finally fix the garbage disposal and I could help. Kind of like before."

"I take it your mom wasn't too fond of the idea."

"It would mean staying home." He made a general sweep of his arms. "I don't get why she hates it here. This is a great house. She was in such a hurry to move in, like she really wanted to be here, so what's the problem?" He pinned Lucas with a direct look. "What *is* her problem? Why won't anyone but Marty talk to me about it?"

"When did you move here?"

Grey shrugged. "I don't know, maybe like a year ago?"

Lucas nodded. Did the move have anything to do with Claire's trauma? Was that when it happened?

"Marty, as in the kid from the park?" Lucas asked.

"Yes, he was with me when we found Lady."

"What did Marty say?"

Grey shook his head. "He spent the night and, you know, she's worse at night. And, well, he noticed. When he left he told me he was sorry things are so screwed up here. It was humiliating."

"Grey," Lucas said. "I know it's tough for you, but you shouldn't be humiliated." Someone needed to explain things to the boy, but was that his place? "Your mom is a wonderful person, but she has issues she has to deal with. She's trying, though."

"Trying?" Grey nearly snorted. "Trying to do what? Drive me nuts with her?"

"No, of course not."

"Hey, are you two ready to roll?" Claire asked from the doorway.

Lucas patted Grey's shoulder. "Come on, you can have shotgun."

As they headed to the car, Claire touched Grey's arm and he pulled away. Lucas slipped his hand in hers and squeezed. He shouldn't, but her sobs when she'd called last night and the way she'd looked so hurt by Grey's rejection weakened his resistance.

She squeezed back and he almost smiled for the first time that morning. He'd at least found one small way to help. He had to get her to talk to Grey about her PTSD. And maybe, just maybe, talking to her son would prompt her to get help.

And if she did that, then there was still hope for them.

CHAPTER TWENTY-FOUR

ACUTELY AWARE OF Claire's presence as he'd been all morning, Lucas brushed the dirt from Lady's headstone. Grey had come up with the inscription. He smiled at the boy as he stood. "What do you think, Grey? Do you like it?"

"It's awesome," Grey said. "'Our beloved Lady. Her time with us was short, but filled with love.'"

"Short and simple, but it says it all." Lucas glanced at Claire. She met his gaze and for a moment the old connection sparked between them.

Grey wrapped his arms around Lucas's waist, drawing his attention away from Claire. Sadness cloaked Grey's features. He hugged Lucas close, burying his face in his T-shirt. Lucas's throat tightened as he glanced again at Claire. She'd kept her distance all morning, when all he'd wanted was to hold her close like this.

He patted the boy's back. "She's in a better place, buddy."

Grey nodded against his shirt. His shoulders shook and his silent tears made Lucas ache. Lady's death was like a catalyst, bringing up all the other grief in the boy's life, the abandonment by his father, his worry over his mother and his perpetual exhaustion. He couldn't keep this up much longer.

Tears glistened in Claire's eyes. She turned and moved up the trail, away from the sight of her son seeking comfort from Lucas. Lucas swallowed, pressing his lips together to keep from calling to her, wishing he could scoop her into his embrace with Grey. She was only respecting his wishes by keeping her distance.

A cold breeze cut through the yard, but Lucas held fast to Grey, letting the boy take as long as he needed to purge his grief. Heaven knew he had a load of it and there was no end in sight if Claire continued as she was. At long last Grey straightened and dropped his hold on Lucas.

He scrubbed his hands over his eyes, which were red and puffy. "I'm sorry," he said.

"No need to apologize, Grey," Lucas assured him. "I promised you I'd be here for you whenever you need me and that's true no matter what happens between me and your mom. Okay?"

Grey nodded, sniffing as the last shudders of grief hit him. "Are you two going to work things out?"

"I hope so. I really want to and I think she does, too." He glanced down the path Claire had taken. "It's just really complicated."

"I know she doesn't make anything easy, but

please promise you'll try. Just because you couldn't fix Lady, that doesn't mean you can't still fix Mom. She says she's doing it her way, but her way isn't working because she's too broken to fix herself, so she needs your help, even if she acts like she doesn't."

Lucas took Grey by his arms. How to make the boy understand? "It all depends on your mom. I had a friend who went through something like this and I don't think I can go through it again. I can't make her get help. Do you understand? It's up to her."

Grey nodded, his gaze downcast. He looked so dejected, Lucas felt it in the pit of his stomach. He'd thought he understood Grey's plight because of his experience with Toby, but he'd never had to deal with a mother with PTSD.

"Let's find your mom," he said.

Grey ran ahead along the trail. They found Claire in the gazebo, leaning against the railing. She startled as her son pounded up the steps, but she recovered quickly and managed a smile for him, though it fell short of her eyes. She spread her arms in welcome, but Grey stopped short, halting at arm's length.

Disappointment flickered across her face, but her smile faltered only briefly. Her gaze touched Lucas's, as though she needed the reassurance he was there.

"Are you ready for rock climbing?" she asked Grey. "Amanda wants to try the next level today."

Grey nodded and neither one commented on the other's puffy eyes. This had been a hard morning all around. Without a word, Grey turned and headed toward the car.

Lucas followed behind with Claire. Again he couldn't resist taking her hand, giving her what little comfort he could. "He's hurting," he said.

She nodded. "I know."

"It isn't just about Lady."

"Yes, I know that, too." She paused and shook out her free hand. "I'm trying."

"You can't do this on your own, Claire. You have to find someone to talk to. If you can't do it for you, please do it for Grey." He reached for her other hand, but she pulled away and wrapped her arms around her waist.

"I can't talk about it," she said. "Not yet, but I'm trying to get there."

"He can't take much more of this. At least tell him you have PTSD. You don't have to tell him why." He shrugged. "I don't know what happened to you, but I understand you're facing a very real disorder, one that's treatable."

She shook her head. "I don't know what to tell him."

"Tell him that. Tell him about the disorder and let him know that there's a solution. It's frightening for him because he knows something's wrong, but no one will tell him what it is. If he knows it's a treatable disorder, he'll have an easier time dealing with it."

Again, she shook her head. "I can't, Lucas. That won't be enough. I know my son. He won't stop until he knows everything and…I just can't."

"Then let me explain it to him. He can grill me all he wants. I don't know anything, but at least he'll have something."

"No." She stopped and faced him. "You can't. He'll just come to me for the rest and… I can't. Please, just leave it alone. I promise I'll deal with it."

"You're *not* dealing with it, though, Claire. It's getting worse, isn't it? The flashbacks, the headaches, the anxiety attacks. You can't take much more of this."

"I'm trying. Give me some time to work through it." She hurried toward the car. "I can handle it."

He shook his head as he followed her, a sense of impending doom descending on him. If she kept going as she was, would she end up like Toby?

He closed his eyes as the fear flooded him. He couldn't handle that, not again and not with Claire. God help him, he loved her.

"IT WAS NICE of you to let me meet you for coffee, Claire," Becca said the next week as she set down her drink, then sank into the chair beside Claire. "This is a nice place."

Claire glanced around the clean lines of the tables and chairs. Low-backed sofas circled a glass-and-steel coffee table at the center of the shop. Tinted windows darkened the entire space, while the strumming of an acoustic guitar filled the air. It wasn't The Coffee Stop, but this was where she and Grey had come before to avoid Lucas and, though she was dying to see him, she couldn't handle having Becca ask the million questions she was bound to ask.

She missed Lucas. She missed the sight of him, the sound of his voice, his quiet and reassuring presence. The outing to get the headstone for Lady had been so painful, she'd avoided his coffee shop since.

He'd been right to leave her. They couldn't keep going the way they had been.

"I thought you and Grey were all about that other coffee shop," Becca said. "You know, the one with that guy—what's his name…Lucas?—I've been hearing so much about from your son."

"It was time for a change," Claire said, pasting on a smile.

The last thing she'd wanted this morning was to face her perfect sister, but Becca rarely called and asked to see her like this. With the exception of their Sunday rock-climbing sessions, where they were focused on Grey and Amanda, they normally saw each other only in passing when they dropped off and picked up kids. They rarely took the time for just the two of them to sit down together.

"So, how is everything going? Grey's been behaving, hasn't he?" Claire asked.

Becca's eyes widened. "Oh, Grey has been great. He always is. You have an awesome kid there."

"I know. I'm very lucky."

Becca fidgeted with her cup, rolling it between her hands. "He's just seemed upset lately." Her gaze locked with Claire's. "Is everything okay at home?"

Claire's stomach tightened. "Everything's fine. We're keeping busy, as always."

"But, Claire, he's exhausted and frankly I don't understand why you have to drag him to kingdom come and back. It's a real issue for him."

Claire gritted her teeth. She should have known this wasn't a social call. "Becca, look, I know you mean well, but everything is fine."

"I talked to Kyle about this and I don't think I'm overreacting. This thing has been building for a long time."

"What thing? What did you talk to Kyle about?" Claire's heart thudded.

"About you. About this talk I had with Grey," Becca said.

"What *about* me? What talk with Grey? Quit beating around the bush, Becca. Obviously you wanted to meet today so you could tell me something or ask me something, so out with it."

"Grey asked me what's wrong with you. He asked why you get spooked in your own home, why you constantly check all the locks and behind the doors, why you sometimes hide yourself away in your room and don't answer, even when he pounds on the door. He asked me why you're not normal. He asked me to fix you, because Lucas couldn't anymore."

The tingling spread from Claire's fingertips and up her arms. She gasped, but managed to draw a steadying breath. She had no idea Grey had noticed all of these things. Had he pounded on her door when she'd been in the midst of a panic attack and she hadn't heard him? Why hadn't he talked to her about it? And the fact that he had talked to both Becca and Lucas sent humiliation spiraling through her.

Becca leaned over the table. "Claire, talk to me. What's going on? Do you need help?"

How had she let herself get blindsided like this? Claire pasted on a smile. "I'm fine, Becca. I appreciate your concern. I'll talk to Grey, I promise. Listen, I have to get going. I've got three new clients I'm developing proposals for and I promised one of them a cost analysis by this afternoon."

"Wait, Claire, don't go yet. Can we finish talking about this? I'm concerned about you."

Claire waved her hand as though sweeping away the conversation. "There's nothing more to talk about. I'll handle it."

Heat bloomed in her cheeks as she strode to her car. She'd pull herself together. If she focused on Grey and work, surely she could beat this thing. If

Grey needed normal, she was going to do her best to give him normal. Her son deserved that.

ADELE CROONED FROM the speakers on Gram's desktop as Grey scraped leftover spaghetti noodles into a plastic container and Gram loaded the dishwasher. It had been a satisfying evening. Gram had made good on her promise to teach him to cook. He'd made his first meatballs, cooked his first noodles and heated the sauce, while she made a salad and toasted garlic bread.

"That was a great meal," he said. "I'm stuffed."

"Me, too," she said, rubbing her stomach. "We're on our way to making you a top chef. Those meatballs were superb."

Grey nodded. "And it was fun. Can we make tacos next time?"

"Tacos would be good," she said. "And you should learn to roast a chicken. It's easy and you can do so much with the leftovers. We can shred the chicken to make barbeque, then there's soup to be made from the bones. I'd need you for at least a week to show you all that."

"A week?" What would it be like to spend an entire week at his grandmother's? "That would be like a vacation."

She laughed. "Oh, no, not a vacation. I'd make you work for your supper."

"I like to work," he said. "Especially if that means

cooking. I can do other chores, too, like wash the dishes and take out the trash. I'd be a big help."

She straightened away from the dishwasher and looked at him. "Grey, do you want to stay here with me for an extended time like that, like for a week?"

Grey could hardly contain his excitement. "I would love that. Is it a possibility? You'd have to take me to school and pick me up. I don't think the bus comes out this way."

Gram frowned. "I'd have to talk to your mom, of course, but getting you to and from school wouldn't be a problem."

"You'd do that?" he asked. "You'd let me stay?"

"Honey, Aunt Becca says you're not happy at home. Is that why you want to stay here?"

The knot he always had in his stomach at home twisted again. "Things are okay."

"Are you sure? Because it's okay of you want to talk about it. Your aunt told me a little about what you told her."

He shrugged. "I think maybe it wouldn't hurt if Mom and I had a little break from each other."

"She'll be here soon. I'm going to talk to her when she arrives, okay?"

"Okay," he said.

The sick feeling mushroomed inside him. Mom wasn't going to like this, but if he could get caught up on some sleep at least, maybe it would be easier to handle all the craziness after that.

The tight feeling in his gut intensified when her car pulled up in the driveway a short while later. Gram glanced his way as she opened the door. Mom hurried in, her hair again in the sweaty ponytail, her cheeks flushed.

"I covered a class for one of the night kickboxing teachers," she said by way of explanation.

Gram wasted no time. She gestured to the living room where Grey sat. "Come sit for a minute," she said. "I have something I want to ask you."

Mom tried to catch Grey's eye, but he looked away, feeling nauseous. She sat on the sofa beside him, her back straight and not touching the cushion.

"What's up?" she asked.

Gram settled in the chair near them. "I want you to think about this before you answer. Take the time you need. You can let me know in a day or two."

"This sounds serious." Again, Mom glanced at him, but he couldn't look her in the eye. "What's this about?" she asked.

Gram leaned forward. "I'd like to keep Grey with me for a while, for at least a week, maybe more. I think it would do you both good. I'd love it and so would he—"

"You've already talked about this?" She faced Grey. "Grey, is this something you want?"

He shrugged. "We haven't been getting along. Maybe a break would be a good idea."

She shook her head. "This is unbelievable." Turning back to Gram, she said, "You've been talking to Becca, haven't you?"

"Becca mentioned Grey was unhappy and that she'd discussed it with you. Apparently you said you had it under control." She gestured toward Grey. "Your son wants a break and this would give you an opportunity to do…whatever it is you need to do to get things under control over there. I think Grey is right. A break would do you both a lot of good."

Mom stood and pulled Grey up with her. "I appreciate the offer, really I do, Mother, but I don't need to think about it. If the offer to keep him after Becca's on Mondays, Wednesdays and Fridays is still open, we'd like to continue with that. But we'll pass on anything beyond that. Grey, get your jacket. We've got to go."

Grey felt a deep disappointment as he pulled on his jacket. He shouldn't have gotten his hopes up. He was trapped at home and there wasn't anything he could do about it.

LUCAS GLARED AT the crackling fire. November had blown into Atlanta on a frigid wind and it hadn't let up over the past weeks. The skies had been dark and overcast to match his mood.

"Hey, boss, here's something to warm you." Ken took the seat to his right, placing a steaming mug on the table between them.

Lucas frowned at him, confused. "Ken, why are you here? I thought you worked this morning."

"I did," the older gentleman said. "I'm off the clock."

"So, why are you here this evening?"

"I thought you could use a friendly ear. Besides, everyone else is afraid to come talk to you."

"What?" Lucas glanced at the counter, where Ramsey and Stephanie suddenly appeared to be intent on cleaning.

"You're making everyone miserable. You've been biting off heads left and right. Something's bugging you and you need to get it off your chest, so we can get back to business."

The thought of his staff talking behind his back made Lucas's temper flare. "Did you all draw straws and you came up short?"

"I volunteered," Ken said. "I do this job because I like it, not because I need it. If you can me it'll be a big disappointment, but I'll live."

Lucas scowled at the fire. He *had* been biting off heads. The situation with Claire was intolerable. He couldn't be with her, but he was in a living hell without her. Evidently, he'd made sure his staff had joined him in that hell.

"You're right. Something is bugging me," he said.

Ken nodded toward the steaming mug as he cupped one of his own. "That's Irish coffee, in case you're interested, heavy on the Irish."

"Thanks." Lucas took a tentative sip, then stared at the frothy drink. "I'm sorry I've made everyone miserable."

Ken waved his hand. "It hasn't bothered me and the rest of them like you enough they'll get over it. So, it's the pretty brunette, the little one with the son? That's what's got you all twisted up?"

"Yes, Claire Murphy and her son is Grey."

"Well, we all like them, too. So, how can we fix this so you're not tearing through here like an angry bear and we get that nice lady and her son back as customers?"

Lucas would have smiled if he weren't so miserable. "That's the million-dollar question." He took another sip of the coffee. "Let me ask you something, Ken. Do I strike you as a guy who wants to save everyone?"

In answer, Ken chuckled softly. "I'm sorry, Lucas, I don't mean any disrespect. It's just a funny question."

"Why?" His anger surged again. "My situation is very serious. There's nothing funny about it." He shuddered at the thought of losing Claire in a permanent way, the way he'd lost Toby.

"Again, I apologize, but don't you see the answer to your question?" He gestured toward the coffee counter, where Ramsey and Stephanie were trying hard to pretend they weren't intently following the exchange.

"Haven't you saved each of us in some way?" Ken asked. "Ramsey is the most obvious, of course, but look at Stephanie. You knew she was on food stamps, living out of her car with her mother when you hired her. I know you didn't think anyone else knew about that, but word gets around."

"I didn't save *you,*" Lucas said. "You've never needed saving a day in your life."

"No?" Ken said, his bushy white eyebrows arching. "I was a grumpy old man, alone and feeling sorry for myself. You saved me from the worst fate of all, a life sentence in my own company."

"That's a stretch," Lucas said.

"Maybe," Ken said. "But I don't think so. Why do you ask, anyway?"

Lucas shook his head. "My mother said something to me. She said I always tried to save everyone, because I felt responsible."

"That's interesting. Is it true?"

"No," Lucas said. "Why would I feel responsible for anyone else?"

"Because you love them?"

The fire crackled as Lucas considered that. "Does loving someone make you automatically feel responsible for them? We can't control anyone's actions but our own, so how can we feel responsible?"

"You're looking for a logical explanation, but the human heart doesn't work that way."

"Mine certainly doesn't," Lucas said. His heart still wanted Claire, even though she was self-destructing and bound to take everyone who loved her with her.

Did she think she was responsible for whatever

had happened to her? Was that why it was so hard for her to face?

Lucas turned to Ken. "What do you do with a heart that won't see logic?"

Ken pursed his lips. "I guess you have to tell it to let go."

CHAPTER TWENTY-FIVE

THE NIGHT WAS dark as Claire closed the door to the kickboxing studio and tried to slide the key into the dead bolt. She managed to insert the key, but it refused to turn. As if her day hadn't been frustrating enough already. At last the bolt slid into place.

Sighing, she grabbed her purse and gym bag. She was going to be late picking up Grey again.

There was a sudden movement from the jumble of cars in the parking lot. Claire's adrenaline surged as a man approached her. She had a flash of the drunk at the car crash, but Lucas wasn't here now to step in for her.

She shouldered her bags and hurried toward her car, fumbling with her key fob when she got close enough.

The numbness spread through her fingers as the man drew closer and she continued trying to unlock the door. The pad of his footsteps echoed through her ears, the sound distorting in her fear.

At last the lock clicked and she grabbed at the door handle, but her fingers had gone completely numb. She cringed, bracing herself as the man moved alongside her.

He passed her without a word, continuing up the parking lot to a car parked a few spaces away. She stood gripping her door handle as he got into his car, then left.

Claire exhaled as she finally opened her door and slipped into her car. As she headed out of the parking lot, she tried to calm her racing heart. She made it to the first light before the tingling in her hands erupted into a shaking so violent she had to clutch the wheel to keep them still.

"WHAT TIME IS IT?" Grey asked Gram as they sat watching a game show.

Gram frowned. "Five minutes later than the last time you asked. She'll be here. Relax."

Relax? How was he supposed to do that? Tensions between his mother and his grandmother had always been high, but they'd been near the breaking point since the other night. His nerves couldn't take another bout.

Headlights flashed across the curtains behind Gram. Grey popped up and grabbed his jacket and book bag. "Good night, Gram. Thanks for having me. See you Friday."

With that he ran out the door. He scooted into the passenger seat before Mom had a chance to exit the vehicle. She didn't acknowledge his presence, but she backed out of the driveway and headed toward home.

Grey settled in for the trip to their house. He stared at the stereo volume control. Should he turn the music down? It seemed louder than normal. He shook his head, deciding against it. What difference would it really make? Besides, he was too tired to argue with his mom tonight.

He stole a glance in her direction. She seemed almost sunken into herself, with her shoulders hunched forward and her knuckles white against the steering wheel. Tears streamed unchecked down her cheeks, though she didn't make a sound.

This was even worse than normal. "Mom, are you okay?"

She drove through a light as it changed from yellow to red and didn't answer. She just kept driving, through a green light, past a bunch of stores and then a sharp left turn.

Grey held on to the seat as the centrifugal force pulled him toward the door. "Mom?"

She shook her head in reply, her eyebrows drawn together and her face creased as though she were in pain, but she remained silent.

"Mom, you're scaring me. Please can we stop?" he asked.

She drove past a gas station and a church. The traffic light before them turned red. Grey closed his eyes tight and braced himself as his pulse pounded in his ears. The car swerved and came to an abrupt stop.

Breathing hard, Grey opened his eyes. She'd pulled into the parking lot of an office building. Mom's arms were now wrapped around her middle as she sat, silently crying and rocking herself.

"Mom, please talk to me. What's wrong?" Grey asked.

She seemed to curl further into herself, silent and shaking. Grey forced himself to unbuckle his seat belt and reach for her purse on the floorboard.

"Who do you want me to call, Mom? Do you want Aunt Becca or Lucas?" Gram was obviously out of the question. "I'm going to use your phone to call Lucas, okay?"

She continued her rocking as though she hadn't heard him. Although his hands were shaking, Grey managed to unlock her phone and call Lucas. It seemed to take hours before Lucas answered.

"Claire?"

"Lucas, it's Grey." Grey's voice trembled and he made himself slow down. He had to stay calm. One person freaking out right now was enough.

"Grey? Is everything okay, buddy?"

"N-no." He swallowed. He couldn't stutter like a baby. "Mom's freaking out. We're in the car, on the way home from Gram's. She won't talk. I don't know what's wrong with her. Can you please come?"

"I'm on my way," Lucas said. "Do you know what street you're on?"

Grey shook his head, and then realized Lucas couldn't see him. "I don't know. We passed the grocery store." He glanced along the street. "There's a church. It's—" he strained to read the sign "—St. Anthony's. We're in the parking lot next door with a bunch of offices."

"That's good. I think I know where you are," Lucas said. "Hang tight. I'm on my way. I'm going to take care of your mom, all right, Grey?"

"All right." He glanced again at his mom. "She doesn't look so good. Is she going to be okay?"

"I'm going to do everything I can to make her okay," Lucas said. "Do you want me to stay on the phone with you?"

Grey's throat burned and it was all he could do not to start bawling right then, but he didn't want Lucas to think he was a baby. "I'll be fine, but please hurry."

He disconnected the call and burst into tears.

THE CONCERN THAT had filled Lucas since Grey's call fifteen minutes earlier lessened slightly when he pulled into the parking lot near the church. Claire's car sat under a light and he could see both of them clearly in the front seats.

At least they were safe.

He hurried to the passenger side, where Grey quickly unlocked the door for him. "Hey, buddy," he said, "how are you doing?"

"I'm okay," Grey said, distress etching lines into his young face. "Can you please help my mom? I can't get her to talk to me."

Lucas glanced at Claire and his concern mounted. She sat with her arms wrapped around herself, rocking. The memory of her curled into herself on her knees at the foot of the basement stairs flashed through his mind. That this had happened again while she was driving with Grey in the car terrified him.

He turned back to Grey. "I'm going to take care of her. Do you think I can drop you off at your aunt's or your grandmother's?"

"I want to stay with you and my mom." Fresh tears streaked down the boy's cheeks. "What's wrong with her?"

"I know you want to be with your mom." Lucas bit his lip. He didn't want to upset Grey more than he already was, but he was also certain Claire wouldn't want her son to see her like this. And in order to get him to agree to leave her, Lucas needed to help him understand what was happening. He'd deal with any backlash from Claire later.

"Do you know what post-traumatic stress disorder is?" Lucas asked.

Grey shook his head. "No, but does my mom have it? Is that what's wrong with her?"

"I think so. She needs to see a therapist, so she can get better," Lucas said.

"But she won't go," Grey insisted. "She keeps saying she wants to handle it her own way."

"Well, maybe after tonight that will change. At

least, I hope so. All I know is she needs to acknowledge whatever happened to make her this way. And I might have a better chance of getting her to talk to me if we're alone. Do you understand?"

Grey shook his head. "No, not really. I don't get what this thing is, but you mean she can tell you stuff she can't tell me?"

"Yes."

"But what does she need to tell you?" Grey asked.

Claire wasn't going to be happy he'd explained any of this to Grey, but her son was as much a victim of Claire's disorder as she was. He had a right to know.

"PTSD is something some people get when they've been through trauma," Lucas said. "I'm going to try to get your mother to tell me about the bad thing or things that happened to her. If she can do that, I hope she'll be able to talk to someone who can really help her."

"Something bad happened to my mom?" Grey's voice broke on the question.

"I'm afraid so," Lucas said.

"And she doesn't want me to know about it?"

"I don't think she wants you to worry about her or be upset. I'm sorry, but I'm going to do everything I can to help her. I know this is hard for you."

Grey nodded. "It's okay. I just want my mom to get better. I'll do whatever she needs me to."

"Right now she needs you to go to your aunt's or your grandmother's," Lucas said.

"We just left Gram's. It isn't that far. I'll call her." Grey picked up Claire's phone, which had been lying in his lap.

"Let me get the keys while you do that." Lucas leaned across the boy to turn off the ignition.

Claire still sat silently rocking, her eyes closed, tears flowing down her cheeks. Even though his own gut twisted with apprehension, Lucas gave Grey a reassuring smile as the boy got his grandmother on the phone. Lucas held out his hand for the phone, arching his brows in question.

Grey gave his grandmother a brief explanation, then handed him the phone.

"Hello," Lucas said, "This is Lucas Williams."

"Hello, Lucas. I've heard plenty about you from my grandson. I'm Jan Bradington. I'm sorry to meet you under these circumstances. I don't understand what Grey was trying to tell me. What's going on with Claire?"

"She's…" Lucas glanced at Grey. "She's having an anxiety attack. She's probably hit a trigger of some kind and is in the middle of a bad flashback."

"An anxiety attack?" she asked. "What are you talking about? Put her on the phone. I want to speak to her."

"I'm sorry, she's not able to talk at the moment," Lucas said. "Are you familiar with PTSD?"

"Isn't that something war veterans get? I can't imagine what this has to do with my daughter."

"I don't know what caused it in this instance, but

any extreme trauma can cause PTSD." Lucas gritted his teeth. They didn't have time for all these explanations.

"Please, can I drop Grey off with you?" he asked. "Can you look after him, while I see what I can do for Claire?"

"Of course you can bring him by, but you tell that daughter of mine this is not at all amusing."

"I assure you she's in no condition to find anything amusing."

"Just tell her to snap out of it. She's always been one to overdramatize everything," Jan said.

Lucas scrubbed his hand through his hair. No wonder Claire didn't get along with her mother. "Thank you for agreeing to take Grey. Could you please tell me where you are?" He pulled out his phone and added her address to his contacts.

He thanked her, then disconnected and handed the phone to Grey. "You take this. That way you'll be able to call me directly if you have any questions while you're with your grandmother."

"Okay, as long as my mom won't need it."

"If she needs a phone when she feels better, she can use mine," Lucas said.

"Okay," Grey said. "Thanks, Lucas, for helping my mom."

"You bet. I'm going to get her into my car, and then we'll drop you at your grandmother's."

Again, Grey nodded. "Lucas?"

"Yes, Grey?"

"I'm glad my mom has you to help her."

Warmth filled Lucas. Hopefully he'd be some help to Claire. "Me, too, Grey."

CHAPTER TWENTY-SIX

LIGHTS FLASHED IN the darkness. Claire kept her eyes closed against the pain tearing at her skull. Where was she and how had she gotten here? The seat rocked gently. She was in a moving vehicle, and something warm cushioned her left side. The strumming beats of Coldplay filled the air.

"We're almost there." Lucas's voice, so familiar, calmed the rapid thudding of her heart. "I'm taking you to my house, if that's okay."

She was safe. She was with Lucas. She tried to nod, but the effort overwhelmed her. The car hit a bump and her pulse accelerated again. She clenched her fists. She couldn't go back to that time, that place of quiet and terror, of the awful weight bearing down on her.

"Hold on to me," Lucas said as he threaded her arm through his.

She gripped his arm, anchoring herself to the feel of him, the notes of the song on the radio. Lucas was the cushion beside her. She relaxed a little against him, breathing in his scent, eradicating that of the other that had seemed so real just moments ago.

"I'm here with you, sweetheart. Right here and I'm not going anywhere. Can you hear me?"

She tried to nod, but pain surged through her head. Her entire body ached.... She inhaled again, and then let the breath out slowly, as she'd learned to do to help manage the pain. She'd had another flashback—though this one had been too real, too intense, more like another experience than a memory.

The car stopped, the music ending abruptly. Lucas shifted. "Just relax. I'll come around for you."

She sat slumped in the seat as his warmth left her. Then his hands were on her, gently sliding her toward him.

He lifted her into his arms. She clung to his neck and nestled against him. For a second, she drifted as though watching him hold her from above.

"Are you with me, Claire?" he asked. "You don't have to talk to me until you're ready. Just listen to my voice. We'll turn on the stereo and the TV and whatever else you want when we get inside. I just need you to be here with me now, here, where nothing can hurt you."

A breeze swept around them as he climbed his porch steps, the cool air reviving her. But then as he stepped through his door with her, she felt uneasy. She had something important to do. She'd been driving....

Oh, God. "Grey?"

"He's okay. I took him to your mother's—who, by

the way, is a real piece of work. I totally get why she hasn't won any mother-of-the-year awards."

She groaned. Besides the ache in her head, the thought of Lucas dealing with her mother sent a wave of discomfort through her. Poor Lucas. What had her mother said to him? What had he told her about why he'd brought Grey back?

He set her down on a big sofa. She sank into the cushions as he fumbled with his remote control until the television and stereo came to life. Then he sat on the coffee table facing her.

"Hey," he said, holding her gaze. "Welcome back."

She focused, willing the words from her mouth. "Grey…what…happened? I…was on my way to get him."

"You picked him up from your mother's, but didn't make it too far after that. He called me from a parking lot a few blocks away."

"I…don't…remember getting…him." She dropped her head into her hands. Had she really been driving like that—and with Grey in the car?

She could have killed him, killed them both. The reality of what she'd done hit her hard, making her eyes overflow with fresh tears.

Lucas moved beside her, taking her again into his arms. "It's okay, sweetheart. You didn't hurt anyone. Go ahead and cry."

What kind of a mess was she that she'd put her son in that situation? How would she ever explain this to him?

"How…how was he?" she asked, when she could catch her breath. She rubbed her sleeve across her face. Her eyes felt raw.

Lucas bowed his head, but then met her gaze. "He was pretty shaken up. He didn't understand what was happening to you. It scared him, but he's a tough little guy."

"What did you tell him?"

"I explained a bit about PTSD to him. I know you didn't want that, Claire, but he needed to understand. I told him I'd take care of you."

The sick feeling twisted in her gut. Poor Grey. "What did you tell him exactly?"

"Only that this can happen when people have gone through trauma. So, really, all he knows is that something bad happened to you. I'm sorry, sweetheart. I had to tell him something."

She nodded, even as she sank deeper into the sadness. How was she going to make this right? She could never tell Grey about the bad thing that had happened to her.

And he would want to know.

"Of course, you did what you had to. Thank you, Lucas. I don't know what would have happened if Grey hadn't had you to call."

She stopped as her throat tightened and even more tears threatened. "My family…they wouldn't have known how to handle any of this."

"I'm glad he called me."

"I felt like…" She searched for the right words.

"Like I was lost in this horrible place and I followed your voice back. When you talked to me the way you did... That...helped. They wouldn't have done that." She shivered and rubbed her arms. "I might still be...there."

"This isn't the first time this has happened, is it?" he asked.

She shook her head. "But it's never been this...severe. And it's never happened when I couldn't find a quiet place to lock myself away and fall apart in private."

"Do you know what triggered it?"

"It was dark when I left the studio. There was a man in the parking lot."

"Did he hurt you?"

"No." It had been so innocent, really, she was embarrassed by her extreme reaction. "He was just going to his car, but I panicked. He didn't even say boo to me and I just...fell apart. I was so...afraid." She paused, the sick feeling stirring in her stomach. Would she always be such a coward?

"I thought I'd be okay, and I went to get Grey, but I guess it affected me more than I thought."

The damn tears continued to course down her cheeks. She was a blithering mess. Her entire body shook and she collapsed again against Lucas as he held her and stroked her arm.

"It's okay. You're safe," he said.

"I know, but I'm so screwed up. Why can't I be normal like Grey wants and just handle it? Look what I've put my son through," she said, sniffling like a baby.

She hated this—hated that she was such a disaster as a human being and a failure as a mother. Grey deserved better than this.

"What am I going to do?" she asked.

"Talk to someone, Claire. I can get you the name of a good therapist."

Why was he so intent on this talking thing? Talking stirred up the memory, brought the past to life. She felt like she'd barely made it back this time. How could she relive it again?

"Please, sweetheart, you have to give it a try."

She shook her head. "I can't. You don't understand."

"It's scary. I know, but can't you see it's getting worse? You can't just ignore it. It will never go away like that. You have to face it, in a safe environment and then you can conquer it, once and for all," he said.

"I can't. I can't bear it, Lucas. I'm not as strong as you think. I'm...not brave enough."

"Then Grey will continue to suffer." He turned her to face him, disappointment in his eyes. "Sweetheart, talk to me, if you can. Try to tell me what happened to you and you'll see it's only words."

She shook her head, but he held her and wouldn't let her turn away. "Did someone hurt you?"

Closing her eyes, she nodded. "Yes, someone hurt me."

"You were alone, in the quiet. What happened,

Claire?" He gripped her hands. "Hold on to me. You're safe now. The past can't hurt you anymore."

She squeezed his hands, focusing on the feel of his fingers against hers. "I'd just gotten home. Grey was at school. It was the old house, before this one." She shook her head as though that would keep the panic at bay. "I couldn't stay there after that."

"It's okay. You can tell me more if you want to, but only if you want. Try to calm down. Breathe."

She inhaled slowly. "It was quiet in the house, peaceful, and I stood in the hall and soaked in the stillness."

She closed her eyes as her tears once more ran freely. She had to be brave, but not here. Not with Lucas. If she talked about it, she might flip out again and he'd blame himself.

"Give me the name, Lucas," she said. "I'll make an appointment. I'll see a therapist."

THE MUFFLED SOUND of the television playing in Gram's room mingled with the distant road noise as Grey pulled his mom's cell phone out from under the pillow. He unlocked the phone and blinked at the bright display. How was he supposed to sleep when he didn't know what was happening?

He'd sent Lucas a text over an hour ago, but hadn't heard back. Should he call?

Throwing back the covers, he rolled to his feet. He couldn't sleep. Maybe he should drink some milk or something.

Moving as quietly as he could, he headed along the dark hallway toward the kitchen, carrying the phone with him.

He got the milk out of the refrigerator, and then pulled Gram's step stool over to reach the glasses from the top shelf.

"Do you need some help?" Gram asked as she stepped into the kitchen.

Startled, Grey grabbed the bottom of the cabinet to steady himself. "I didn't hear you coming."

"Here." She grabbed two big mugs from a different cabinet. "Why don't I make us some hot chocolate?"

Grey nodded as he stepped down. "Sure. Can I help?"

"Can you get out a pot and pour in a splash of water?"

"How much is a splash?" he asked as he pulled out a pot.

She shrugged. "About a quarter of a cup. We're going to add milk, so we don't need much."

"And we add chocolate, too, right?" he asked, anticipation filling him.

She brought items from the pantry and set them on the table. "Yes, some cocoa powder and sugar."

"How much?" Grey asked. He had to remember this, so he could make it for his mom. Hot chocolate made everyone feel better.

"About..." She poured the sugar into a measuring cup. "This much sugar and you only need about half of that for the cocoa powder."

"So, another quarter cup for the sugar and half that would be...an eighth of a cup for the cocoa powder," Grey said as he scooped out the brown powder.

Gram stirred the mixture as he added the sugar and cocoa into the pot.

Grey watched carefully. "If I just wanted to make enough for my mom, I'd only use half of everything, right?"

Gram kept stirring. "That's right. Are you going to make this for your mom?"

"I think it will make her feel better," he said.

"Tell me again what happened tonight, Grey. I still don't understand. How did you end up with Lucas?"

He glanced at the phone he'd left on the table, but the display was still blank. "I didn't notice anything right away, but she was driving a little fast and when I asked her something she didn't answer me. It was like she couldn't hear me, but she was sitting right there. I was getting scared, but then she pulled over into that parking lot."

Again he shrugged. "Lucas said she has PT something and she was having a flashback, because something bad happened to her."

Gram shook her head. "There's nothing wrong with your mother that a good talking-to won't fix."

"I don't understand it, either, Gram, but I tried to talk to her and it didn't work. Lucas can fix her, though."

"And how is he going to do that?" she asked.

Grey didn't know what to say. It was all too confusing. "He's going to try to get her to talk to a therapist."

Gram nodded toward the milk. "Let's go ahead and pour that in."

Grey did as she asked, then took the spoon from her and stirred the chocolaty mixture. "Do you know what happened to make her like that?"

Gram sat in one of the kitchen chairs at the little wooden table. "Nothing happened to your mom, Grey. At least nothing that isn't in her head."

Grey frowned. "What do you mean?"

"She's always had an overactive imagination. I promise you nothing bad happened to her."

That sounded good, but Grey was still confused. "Do you mean she imagined something bad happening, but it didn't?"

"The mind is a very powerful thing. Maybe your mother thinks something bad happened to her, but it was really something that she built up in her mind." She got up to pour the hot chocolate into the mugs.

Grey took his mug from her as she sat beside him again. "Thanks," he said. "But how do you know something bad didn't happen to her? It could have happened when you weren't there."

She blew across her cocoa to cool it. "I just know. I'm going to get some sleep, Grey. I suggest you do the same."

He stared after her as she left. None of this made

any sense. He checked his mom's phone and was thrilled to see a new text. He touched the icon and read the message from Lucas.

Hey, my sweet boy, this is Mom. I'm sorry I freaked out on you tonight. So very sorry. I'm okay and I'm going to get help. Will see you after school tomorrow and we'll talk. I know you have questions. I love you.

He texted back. I'm glad you're okay. I love you, too.

A yawn billowed out of him. He set his empty mug in the sink, grabbed the cell phone and headed for bed. Tomorrow he'd see his mom and she'd be better. They'd have normal now. Whether Gram was right or not, Lucas would get Mom fixed and everything would be all right.

CHAPTER TWENTY-SEVEN

THE THERAPIST'S RECEPTION area was quiet and unassuming, with one potted tree warming the space with its greenery. Claire checked in, and then sat beside Lucas, her hand clasped in his. After a short wait, a side door opened and a tall brunette with caring brown eyes looked toward them. "Claire Murphy?" she asked.

Claire nodded and rose, but instead of letting go of Lucas's hand she tugged him up with her. "Come with me," she said and then turned toward the woman. "If that's okay?"

"Whatever you'd like." The woman stepped back and held the door for them.

Lucas stopped and touched Claire's cheek. "If you want me in there with you, I'll come, but are you sure?"

She held his gaze. "I don't want there to be any secrets between us. You have a right to know...everything."

"Okay." He nodded and followed her through the door.

The woman extended her hand to Claire. "I'm Nora Phillips. I'm so glad you've come."

Claire took her hand. “Thank you for seeing me on such short notice, Ms. Phillips.”

“Please call me Nora.” She turned to Lucas. “And you must be Lucas. I’ve heard so many good things about you.”

He glanced at Claire. “Nice to meet you.”

“Well then, follow me,” Nora said.

She led them down the hall to a small room furnished with plants and soft cushioned chairs. Books crammed a bookcase along one wall and spilled into a pile on the floor. Instead of a couch, a chaise longue sat in one corner and soft light from the floor-to-ceiling window filled the space.

“Please,” Nora said, gesturing to the various seating options. “Have a seat wherever you’d like.”

Her chest tightening, Claire perched in one of the chairs and Lucas took the seat beside her. “It’s very quiet here.”

Nora’s eyebrows arched. “I usually play music. It’s a good grounding device. What kind of music do you like?”

“I usually listen to anything metal.” She glanced at Lucas. “But my tastes seem to be mellowing, so I’m flexible.”

With a nod, Nora moved to a computer sitting on a side table. She clicked the mouse a couple of times. “Let’s see if this works for you.”

The strains of Breaking Benjamin floated through the air at a low volume. Claire would have liked it harder and louder, but she flexed her hands to ward off the tingling. "I can work with this."

Nora settled into a chair across from Claire. "Are you sure? You're the one in charge here, Claire."

She gritted her teeth and nodded. The tightening of her scalp signaled the start of the dreaded headache. "It's fine. So, how does this work? Do I just talk and you write lots of notes?"

Nora's smile crinkled the corners of her eyes. "I don't have the best memory, so I may jot down a few notes and we'll talk about some options for how we'll structure the sessions. But I want to stress that you call the shots here. We won't do anything that you're not ready for."

Lucas threaded his fingers through hers, but remained silent. She stared at their joined hands. The tingling had set in and they hadn't even started the session. How would she make it through this?

"Why don't we start first by you telling me what brings you here today, Claire? I know what Lucas told me on the phone, but I'd like to hear from you." Nora smiled at her encouragingly.

"I…had an…episode last night." Even saying the words made her feel ashamed.

"What do you mean by episode?"

She glanced at Lucas, as fear rippled through her. She was moving into panic mode, here in the therapist's office. Lucas rubbed her hand. She couldn't feel her fingers.

"Go on, sweetheart," he said. "It's okay."

She nodded. “I get this thing where…I get scared, really scared and my hands tingle and then go numb and my head…gets this pain like it’s in a vise and my heart races.” She closed her eyes and swallowed. “There’ve been a couple of times where I couldn’t remember what happened afterward, like it got so bad I blacked out.”

Again she glanced at Lucas and he nodded for her to continue. “It was bad last night and I…”

She closed her eyes against the fear that threatened to overwhelm her. What if she told Nora how she’d driven like that with Grey in the car? What if they declared her unfit and took away her son? She couldn’t do this. She grabbed her chest and gasped for air.

“Sweetheart—” Lucas said, turning to her.

“Claire, take a deep breath,” Nora said as she knelt in front of her.

Tears streaked down Claire’s cheeks. Why had she thought this was a good idea? “I can’t,” she said. “I’m so sorry, but I can’t do this.” She gripped Lucas’s hand. “Lucas, please…take me home.”

Disappointment flickered in his gaze, but he nodded and pulled her from her chair.

LUCAS SHUT HIS eyes for the briefest second as Claire pushed through her front door. He was so tired. He hadn’t been drained like this since those days with Toby. But he couldn’t think about that.

Not now. Not when Claire needed him.

She moved as if each step was an effort. He slipped his arm around her shoulders. "It'll be okay."

She shook her head. "How?"

"You're not in this alone," he said, concerned by her blank tone.

Dark circles ringed her eyes. Her shoulders stooped and her head hung low. A memory of Toby standing dejected, unable to cope with his life, flashed through Lucas's mind.

He couldn't let this happen again.

"I'm not going to leave you," he said, holding her close as his throat tightened. How had he ended up back in this place?

She lifted her head, tears filling her eyes. "I'll drag you down with me."

"No." He stroked her hair. "I'll be strong enough for both of us."

"That's not fair to you."

"I don't care if it's fair or not. You aren't going to get rid of me."

She straightened and pushed away from him. "But I need to, Lucas. Look at you. You're exhausted."

"I can catch up on my sleep. It's okay."

"No. It isn't." She paced away from him and a little of the old Claire surfaced in the proud angle of her head. "We're back to the same old thing again."

He frowned. "What do you mean?"

"You can't fix me."

He bowed his head. He was too tired to get into this with her. "Claire—"

"Listen to me," she said. "I have to fix this. Me, Lucas. Not you."

"Okay, that's fine, but I can help. The next time we go to see Nora, we'll start with something simple."

She stilled. Her voice dropped to almost a whisper. "I'm not going back."

"Okay," he said. "You didn't like her. That's fine. We'll find someone else."

"No, Lucas, you're not hearing me. I'm never going back. Not to Nora, not to anybody else. I can't..." She clutched her chest and grimaced as though in pain. "I can't do it."

"Sweetheart, you're getting worked up again. Just breathe and we'll talk this out."

"I don't *want* to talk it out. Therapy isn't an option. I get that now. I accept it. I'll find a way to beat this on my own."

A chill ran through Lucas. "You can't, Claire. I've seen other people with less severe PTSD manage on their own, but it was a struggle."

She couldn't really mean it. She had Grey to consider. "You've been trying on your own and it hasn't worked. You've gotten worse. I know it's scary, but therapy works."

She stood straight and tall before him. "I'm not doing therapy."

"But you have to think about Grey. He's counting on you to get better."

Her eyes flashed with anger. "You don't think I know that?"

"Then let's find someone else," he said.

"No," she said, shaking her head. "That isn't going to happen."

This was all too familiar. Lucas's throat burned. "And I have no say in the matter?"

Tears ran down her cheeks. "Not if you insist on therapy."

"Then I can't do this, Claire. I can't stand by and watch you destroy what's left of your life. I can't watch you do this to yourself. I can't watch you do it to Grey."

"I'm sorry, Lucas." She wrapped her arms around her middle.

"So am I," he said and then walked out the door.

He should never have come back. He should have gotten her through last night, then wished her luck. She had needed him and he'd rushed to the rescue. But nothing had changed.

He'd rushed to her because he *had* felt responsible. His illogical heart had sent him right back into the fray. He had only one thing left to do.

He had to let go.

CHAPTER TWENTY-EIGHT

THE CLOCK IN Grey's classroom ticked closer and closer to the final bell. Grey bounced in his seat.

Paul Cooper leaned across the aisle. "Do you need a bathroom pass?"

Grey frowned. "No."

Paul shrugged. "You're just bouncing like you have to go to the bathroom."

"I don't," Grey said. "I'm just...excited."

Today, even nosy Paul Cooper wasn't going to bother him.

I'm okay and I'm going to get help. Will see you after school tomorrow and we'll talk.

He glanced again at the clock, willing the bell to ring. Mom would be in the pickup line. That had to be what she meant, because he never saw her after school. It was always Aunt Becca and then Gram who picked him up. He never saw Mom until late, when she got him from Gram's.

And she said she was getting help, so Lucas's plan had worked and they could go back to being normal now. She must be better and ready to start working at home again. That's probably what she meant about seeing him after school.

"So what are you excited about?" Paul asked.

When was the bell going to ring? "I'm just happy to see my mom, is all. She's coming to get me today."

"Cool," Paul said.

"She's really doing great and she's seeing this guy who's super cool and they're probably going to get married," Grey said, the words tumbling from his mouth. Okay, so that last part was a bit of a stretch, but now that Lucas had fixed Mom, she wouldn't be running him off anymore. What was to stop them from getting married? It was just a matter of time.

"Awesome," Paul said as, thankfully, the bell rang.

"See you," Grey said, then shouldered his book bag and pushed out into the crowd of kids spilling into the hallway.

Excitement pumped through him as he hit the front curb and scanned the cars for the Honda. But his mom's car was nowhere in sight. Instead, Aunt Becca waved to him from her usual spot at the front of the line.

There must have been a mistake. He opened the door. "Hi, Aunt Becca, what are you doing here? Mom's coming to get me today."

Aunt Becca frowned. "I don't know about that, Grey. She didn't say anything to me."

He showed her the text, pointing out the part about after school. "See? She wouldn't have said that if she wasn't coming to get me. I think I should wait for her."

"Sweetie, I don't think she's coming. Didn't something happen last night? Gram said you stayed with her. Is everything okay?"

"Yes," Grey said. "Everything's great."

"Let's call your mom." Aunt Becca reached for her purse.

"I'll call her," he said, gesturing to the phone. "I have her phone, so we have to call Lucas."

Becca glanced at the line of cars behind her. "Grey, why don't you get in while we figure this out?"

Grey dialed, but Lucas's cell just rang and rang. Shaking his head, he settled himself in the passenger seat, leaving his seat belt unbuckled. After all, he wasn't actually going home with his aunt.

Lucas's voice mail finally kicked in. "Hi, Lucas, this is Grey. I'm at the school and Mom said she was coming to get me and she isn't here. Can you have her call me on her cell phone, please?"

"Honey, why don't you buckle up? She can come get you from our house. That text didn't say she was picking you up, just that she'd see you."

The cell phone in Grey's hand buzzed. He smiled and showed the display to his aunt. "It's her."

He answered the call. "Mom?"

"Grey, it's Lucas. I'm sorry, I forgot you had your mom's phone."

"I'm at the school and Aunt Becca came to get

me, but I told her Mom was coming. That's what she said last night when she texted me. Didn't you get my message?"

"I didn't listen to it. I saw the missed call and called back. But I just left your mom and I don't think she's coming to get you."

"But she said she'd see me after school and what else would that mean?" Grey asked as frustration swelled in him. Where was Mom?

"I don't know, Grey. She was pretty out of it last night. She probably forgot she sent you that message," Lucas said.

"But she's better, right?" Grey asked.

A horn honked behind them. Aunt Becca leaned across him and grabbed his seat belt. "I'm just going to buckle you in, so we can get moving."

Grey wanted to growl. "Wait." But his aunt had already clicked the buckle in place and was pulling from the curb.

"Grey, she's still struggling," Lucas said.

"What?" Grey asked, pressing the phone closer against his ear. He must not have heard Lucas right. "You took care of her last night and she got more help today. The text said she was getting help. So, isn't she better?"

"Oh, buddy, I'm so sorry," Lucas said. "It's never that easy, not even in the simplest of cases and your mom's case is very complicated. She tried, Grey. She went to see a therapist today."

"Good, so she just forgot to come get me like she

said." He turned to his aunt. "Is she home? Maybe I can get Aunt Becca to drop me off there."

"Grey, I don't think that's a good idea. I left your mom at your house, but she was in a bad way. And you know how she is. She's either left already or… she isn't going to want to see anyone."

Grey's stomach roiled as if he were going to be sick. "What do you mean she's in a bad way?"

"It means we're off to a rocky start on the therapy. This thing is going to take a while, Grey. She has a lot to work through and she's going to have to do it in her own way, on her own schedule."

"So you didn't fix her?"

Lucas was silent for a long moment. "No, Grey, I'm so sorry. I didn't fix her."

LUCAS'S ALREADY DARK mood worsened as he reviewed the nightly deposit report. Ken shifted beside him, squeezing his hands together.

"I should have said something sooner, Lucas. I'm sorry. I thought it would work out. He's a good kid. I thought he'd be back."

"Wait," Lucas said. "What are you saying? Where's the deposit for this past Thursday?"

"That's what I'm trying to tell you," Ken said. He shook his head. "I don't want to rat anyone out."

"Just tell me, Ken." He glanced at the schedule on his tablet. "Ramsey closed with you that night."

"Yes," Ken said.

"Are you saying Ramsey took the deposit to the

night drop box and hasn't been seen since?" He stood and began pacing.

Damn it, he needed to hit something. First Lady, then Claire, now Ramsey. What good was he? He hadn't helped a single one of them.

"I tried calling him, but he doesn't answer," Ken said. "Maybe I should check the hospitals."

"He's not in the hospital." Lucas shook his head. He'd been so tied up with Claire and Grey, he hadn't paid any attention to Ramsey. "I'm sure we have an emergency contact for him, though. We should probably check that."

"I did."

Lucas turned to Ken. "And?"

"It was his mom. I called and got her voice mail. I left a message." He shrugged. "She never called me back."

A movement near the stockroom door caught their attention. Lucas didn't know whether to be angry or relieved as Ramsey strode toward them, the night deposit bag tucked under his arm. He walked over to them and dropped the bag on the desk.

He faced Lucas, his hands spread. "Before you say anything, please hear me out."

Lucas folded his arms, but remained silent.

"I'll be out front," Ken said, and then hurried out of the stockroom.

Ramsey took a moment to collect himself, then started talking. "I screwed up. I know that. You have been nothing but good to me and I've felt awful about taking the money. I wouldn't have taken it if it weren't really important." He gestured toward the bag. "I brought back as much as I could, but I couldn't get it all."

"How much?" Lucas asked. Not that the amount mattered. The boy had stolen from him.

"How much is missing?"

"Yes, Ramsey, how much did you steal from The Coffee Stop?" Lucas couldn't keep the anger from his voice.

Ramsey stared at the floor. "About four hundred dollars. There's an IOU in the bag. I'm going to pay it back. You can take it right out of my wages."

"You think you still have a job here?"

The color drained from the boy's face. "I...please, I know I messed up. I didn't know what else to do. I just want to make it right."

Lucas shook his head. It didn't matter what the reasons were. Ramsey had proven himself untrustworthy. "You don't get how serious this is, do you?" Lucas asked. "I should file a police report. It wouldn't be juvie court this time. No closed record."

Ramsey dropped his head and nodded. "I understand. You do whatever you have to." He met Lucas's gaze. "I'll still try to make it up to you somehow and I will pay you back."

God, Lucas was tired. "I don't know if you can, Ramsey." He clenched his fist. "I won't report the theft, but you're fired, effective immediately."

"Thank you," Ramsey said. He ducked his head, turned and left.

Lucas stayed at his desk and closed his eyes. When had his life gotten so screwed up? He needed his best friend to tell him everything would be okay. But Toby was long gone and Lucas had to soldier on by himself. The loneliness swelled over him and he laid his head in his arms.

CHAPTER TWENTY-NINE

CLAIRE GLANCED AT Grey's closed bedroom door. Her son wasn't speaking to her and she didn't know how to make it better. She hurried past his room, making her rounds of the latches and locks that kept them safe in the house.

She reached the kitchen and stopped. Grey stood at the stove, stirring something in a pot. She breathed in a waft of chocolate. A trickle of hope rose in her. At least he'd come out of his room.

"Grey." She moved to the door and checked the bolt and lock as inconspicuously as possible. "What are you doing, honey?"

He didn't turn around, but remained focused on the pot. "Making hot chocolate."

She frowned and opened the pantry. "We don't have any mix."

He looked at her then, his eyebrows drawn together and his mouth stern. "You don't need a mix to make hot chocolate." He counted off on his fingers. "You just need water, sugar, cocoa powder, milk and, if you like, a little vanilla."

She peered over his shoulder into the pot. "It

smells good. Did Aunt Becca teach you how to make that?"

He shook his head. "Gram did."

Claire should have been the one to teach him. Her mother had never had the time to teach her anything like that, though she had made time for Becca.

And now Grey.

"Do you want some?" Grey asked. "I made enough for two."

Her son's consideration lifted some of her melancholy. "I'd love to have some."

He faced her. "Okay, but we have to drink it the way Gram and I drink it."

She cocked her head. "How do you and Gram drink it?"

Instead of answering, he moved into the living room and turned off the television and then the radio. He then disappeared down the hall. The strains of Iron Maiden from her bedroom stopped and silence fell over the house.

Claire stood frozen in the kitchen. "Grey?" she called.

The floorboard in the hall creaked and panic spiked through her. She inhaled to calm herself as Grey reappeared in the kitchen. He methodically pulled two mugs from the cabinet, and then poured the contents of the pot into them.

He set the mugs on the kitchen table as he slid into one of the chairs. He wrapped his hands around his mug and blew on the hot chocolate, before taking a hesitant sip.

"It's good," he said. "You should try it."

The wind roared by, shaking the trees outside. The hum of traffic sounded in the distance. The house creaked.

Claire squeezed her hands, and then shook them out. "It's too quiet, Grey."

"No, it isn't," he said. "It's nice. It's peaceful."

She closed her eyes as the pressure in her head built. "Not to me, honey. You know I don't like quiet."

He set down his mug. "Why not? What's wrong with quiet?" He frowned. "Does it have something to do with the bad thing that happened to you?"

Claire should have been prepared for this. Somehow she'd avoided his questions in the days since her horrible episode and the visit to the therapist's.

"Did you get your homework finished?" she asked as she stepped toward the living room. She had to turn everything back on.

"Don't," Grey said with such force she stopped.

"Don't what?" she asked, turning to face him.

"Don't avoid talking to me, because you think I can't handle it. I'm not a baby. And don't turn everything back on, because *I* like the quiet. I don't like the noise and the chaos, Mom. I can't take much more of it. You said you were going to get help."

She frowned. "When did I say that?"

"You texted it to me the night I stayed at Gram's

and had your phone. The night you freaked out." His voice rose with emotion.

Claire's throat burned. The quiet pressed in around her. "I'm sorry, honey. I don't remember much about that night, but I'm really, really sorry. I know that was scary for you."

Tears rolled down his cheeks. "So are you going to get help or is it going to happen again?"

"I'm trying. I've been reading online about…what I have, and I'm working on it."

"But you said you'd get help. Are you going to see another therapist? Lucas said you should."

"It's complicated, Grey. I can't see a therapist. They can't help me, but I'm going to figure this out."

"When?" He stood, pushing back his chair with enough force that it banged into the cabinet behind it.

"Is that why Lucas hasn't been around this week?" he asked. "Did you drive him away again? Did he try to get you to see the therapist again and you wouldn't go?"

"I went," she said as the room blurred. "I went, Grey. I tried. I promise I tried."

"Well, try again." His voice broke and he stood by the table, crying.

She leaned against the wall as the wind rumbled around the house. The tightening of her chest made it difficult to draw breath. How could she make him understand? She shook her head. "I can't."

"I want to stay with Gram," Grey said.

"What?" She wiped her eyes and stared at him. "You'll see her tomorrow afternoon when she gets you from Aunt Becca's."

"I want to stay with her, like she asked you before. For a long stay. She said I could stay as long as I wanted. She said I could live with her if I wanted to."

"What?" She couldn't be hearing him right. "You asked Gram if you could live with her?"

"She offered. I was really upset when you didn't pick me up from school that day, because I thought you were better. I thought we'd have normal. But you're not and we're just going to keep on..." He gestured with a broad sweep of his arm.

She took a step toward him. "Grey, do you want to live with Gram?"

"Yes!" he yelled, shuddering with the force of his tears. "I hate it here."

With that he ran from the room. His bedroom door slammed as Claire sank to the floor in the silence of her house.

THE BUZZING ALARM clock woke Grey in the early morning darkness. He fumbled for the switch as he threw back the covers and shivered. The house vibrated with the familiar rhythm of Mom's morning mix.

He shook his head, still exhausted. He dropped his head into his hands, but he didn't have any more tears left after last night. After the past week, really, though he still couldn't shake the sadness. He didn't want to make his mom cry, but he just couldn't take it anymore.

There was a soft knock on his door. He stepped across the throw rug, past the bookcase Lucas had fixed for him, past the bag of trucks and cars he'd torn the bow off for Mom's birthday present and never put away, to the door. He straightened and took a deep breath before he opened it.

Mom stood in the hall, already dressed. Her eyes were red and puffy. He looked away, at his tae-kwon-do bag. His stomach hurt.

"Can I come in?" she asked.

He nodded. He should tell her he was sorry about last night, but he wasn't sorry he'd told her he hated it here. He did hate it here. And it was so nice at Gram's house.

She moved toward his closet. She pulled out his rolling suitcase and set it on his bed. "I can pack for you, but I thought you might want to choose some of your favorite things to take to Gram's."

His heart thumped. "Am I going to stay with her?"

She nodded. "I called her last night. We'll start with a week and see how it goes. Okay?"

Relief and sadness jumbled up inside him. He threw himself against her, wrapping his arms around her waist. "Thanks, Mom." He pushed back to look at her. "Gram thinks a little break will help us both. Maybe she's right. Maybe it will be easier for you if I'm not here."

Her eyes widened and she covered her mouth with

her fingertips. Then she hugged him close against her again. "Don't you worry about me, little man—oh, honey, I'm sorry. I forgot."

"It's okay," he said.

"I'll be fine."

He wanted to say he knew she would be fine, but he wasn't sure she'd ever be fine. "And I can come back when I want to, right?"

"Of course, honey." She pushed his hair off his forehead. "This is still your home. You can come anytime you want. All you have to do is call me and I'll come and get you. Maybe we should get you one of those prepaid phones."

Anticipation washed out some of his sadness. "My own phone?"

She nodded. "I'm going to miss you. I'm going to want to talk to you every day."

"I'd like that," he said. "I'm going to miss you, too. You'll have to make a list of meals you want me to make for you when I come back and I'll ask Gram to teach me how."

"That sounds great," she said. "But remember, this is temporary, Grey. It's just until I'm feeling a little better, okay?"

"Of course. Until we can have a more normal life, right?" he asked. Surely it wouldn't take her that long. She'd want to have him back and so she'd work on getting better.

"Why don't you pack what you want and then I'll look through it and add anything else I think you might need. I'll drop this by Gram's house while you're at school. It'll be there tonight when you get there."

"Will you get me a phone today and pack it, too?" he asked. Gram was going to be so excited. He couldn't wait to see her.

"Yes, I'll do that." Mom smiled. It wasn't her fake smile, but it wasn't her happy smile, either. It was kind of sad. "Hurry, though," she said. "You still need to hop in the shower."

"Yes, ma'am," he said.

"I love you, Grey." Her voice broke and she wasn't smiling at all anymore.

Grey's stomach ached again and his throat got all tight. "I love you, too."

She smiled that unhappy smile and then slipped out of his room. He stared at the closed door and rubbed his stomach. He was getting the break he wanted. So, why did he feel so bad? And why hadn't she answered his question about them having a more normal life?

CHAPTER THIRTY

THE LIGHT BUZZ of conversation mixed with the acoustic guitar music as Claire stared at her laptop screen. What had she just read? She sighed in frustration and scrolled to the top of the contract she was reviewing. After rereading the same paragraph four times without comprehension, she gave up.

She was so tired of being tired. Her head throbbed and her eyes felt dry and rough. A young couple sat across from her, deep in conversation, leaning in toward each other.

Lucas was probably at The Coffee Stop. Even after a week of coming to this new shop every day, she had still almost pulled into his parking lot this morning. She just couldn't face him and, after their last conversation, it wasn't likely he'd want to see her.

I can't stand by and watch you destroy the rest of your life.

Why couldn't he believe in her enough to stand by her while she figured this out? She'd downloaded three books on PTSD and had even stopped by the bookstore and bought a guide to self-managed recovery.

She really was trying, but the depression dragged her so far down, she wasn't sure she could ever lift herself back up. Every morning she struggled more and more to get herself out of bed. Normally she couldn't get up fast enough, but what good would it do for her to leave, when it seemed the anxiety followed her these days?

And it was worse to be in public with a panic attack coming on.

And Grey. She couldn't even let herself think about Grey. She missed him so much it hurt. Every day he called her and he sounded so…happy. She should be thrilled he was doing so well, but it just made her feel worse.

"Miss Murphy, can I get you anything?"

She startled, nearly knocking her laptop to the floor. Ramsey Carter, the young man who worked for Lucas, stood beside her. She stared at him in confusion.

"Ramsey? What are you doing here?" she asked.

Pink tinged his cheeks. "I work here."

"Do you mean you're working two jobs? Aren't you going to school?"

His flush deepened and he looked away. "No, ma'am, I don't work at The Coffee Stop anymore."

"I don't understand. You left Lucas's shop to come here to work? I can't believe Lucas is happy about that."

He met her gaze. “I came here after he let me go.”

“Why would he do that?” Lucas had been so supportive of the young man. What could have happened?

“I…did something stupid,” he said.

“It’s okay. You don’t have to tell me. It’s your business. I’m just surprised.”

“Thank you, ma’am.” He shifted uncomfortably. “Are you all right? I mean, it isn’t any of my business, but you…don’t look…your usual spry self. Is there anything I can get you or do for you?”

It was Claire’s turn to be embarrassed. Was her misery so obvious? “I’m fine, Ramsey,” she said. “Thank you.”

He nodded and started to leave, but turned back. “So, why are *you* here? I thought you and the boss man were…”

She bit her lip and the damn sadness welled up inside her again. She shook her head. “No, we’re not. Not anymore.”

“I’m sorry,” he said.

“Me, too.”

“Well, I should get back to work. Please let me know if you need anything.”

“Ramsey?”

“Yes, ma’am?”

“When did you leave The Coffee Stop?”

“About a week ago,” he said. “Why?”

She shrugged. “I just… How was Lucas?”

“He was in a dark mood. Granted, that was probably because I messed up so bad, but…I don't know, he just didn't seem right." He gestured toward her. "I guess you being here would explain that."

"Thank you," she said and he nodded again, and then left.

Sunlight drifted through the nearby window. She should have felt its warmth, but hearing Lucas wasn't okay only made her more miserable. Whatever Ramsey had done must have been really bad for Lucas to let him go. It must have been difficult for him to deal with that situation on the heels of the fiasco Claire had put him through.

She'd made Lucas unhappy and she'd driven away her son. She closed her eyes as the back of her head tightened yet again. Lucas had been right. Her symptoms were getting worse. She couldn't stay here any longer, in case this turned out to be another full-blown attack. She had to leave now.

RAIN POURED DOWN in sheets across Aunt Becca's front window. The sound of the TV was lost amid the onslaught on the glass and roof. Grey turned to Amanda, who leaned over the back of the sofa with him, staring out of the window.

"Do you think Gram will wait to come get me?" he asked.

The gloom of the day had settled on him. He felt…heavy. He pulled his phone out of his pocket to check the display. Mom hadn't called him back.

In fact, for the past few days she had texted instead of phoning, but she hadn't even done that today.

Had she forgotten about him?

His cousin shrugged. "I don't know. Why?"

"She might not want to drive in this," he said as the drumming of the rain on the roof intensified.

Amanda tilted her head back to look at the ceiling. "It's loud." She turned to Grey. "Will my daddy not want to drive in this?"

Grey shook his head. "He might be okay, but I wouldn't drive in this."

"You can't drive," Amanda said with a giggle.

"*If* I could drive." Grey shook his head. Amanda could be silly at times.

"Will you play dolls with me?" she asked.

"No."

"But you're done with your homework."

"I don't want to play dolls. Do you want to make something in the kitchen?" he asked.

Her eyes widened. "You mean like cook something? Mommy doesn't let me do that."

"Gram is teaching me to cook. I can make peanut butter cookies," he said. "Almost as good as your mom's."

Amanda smiled. "I like peanut butter cookies. We have to ask Mommy, though."

Grey found Aunt Becca in the laundry room. Amanda trailed along behind him. He asked, "Can we make peanut butter cookies?"

Aunt Becca's eyebrows arched. "I don't know,

Grey. I need to get the laundry finished before Kyle gets home."

"Is Daddy going to drive home in the rain?" Amanda asked.

Aunt Becca peered out the small laundry room window. "It *is* coming down pretty hard. He might be late."

"So we have time to make cookies," Grey said.

"I'm sorry, Grey. I can't right now. I have a ton of other stuff I need to do," Aunt Becca said.

"But all I need is a recipe. Or I can call Gram and she can tell me. I can do it by myself. I did it at her house before."

"I wouldn't be comfortable with you using the oven without me there to supervise you."

"But Gram lets me do it all the time. I'll come get you before I turn the oven on and when I'm going to put the cookies in and stuff," Grey said.

Why was Aunt Becca making this so hard? Why hadn't his mom returned his call? Was *she* out driving in this? Was she okay?

"Why don't you play with Amanda? I'm sure you two can find something else to do," Aunt Becca said.

Amanda bounced on her toes. "Yes, play dolls with me."

"No." Grey was getting really frustrated now. "I don't want to play dolls. Why can't I make cookies? Call Gram. She'll tell you I do a good job. I don't make a big mess and I clean up after myself."

"No cookies, Grey." Aunt Becca moved clothes

from the washing machine into the dryer. “I’m not calling Gram and I don’t want you to, either. She might be on the road in this. I don’t want to distract her.

“If you don’t want to play with Amanda, go watch TV. I’ll bet there’s something good on the History Channel.” She grabbed the empty hamper and headed out of the room.

Amanda hurried after her and Grey stared out of the window, where the rain pelted the glass so hard everything outside was a big blur. He felt like his life was a big blur.

THE STORM BATTERED the house as Claire sat on the living room floor with her back against the wall. Rain pounded the roof and wind roared through the treetops. She pulled her knees close and bowed her head as the pain in her head intensified. Her hands had long since gone numb and her chest constricted as though a band tightened around it with each breath....

The scent of musk drifted in the air. The floorboard creaked behind her as the cold blade of the knife pressed to her neck and her assailant grabbed her from behind.

“No,” she said, clawing at the hand holding the knife.

He spoke low in her ear, his breath hot against her skin. “Don’t fight. I don’t want to hurt you if I don't have to. We're just going to have a little fun. You'll like it. You'll see."

"No. Please don't," she said through her panic. She twisted, trying to see him, but he'd covered his face with a stocking.

She continued to struggle, while he dragged her to her bedroom. He pushed her facedown on the bed and climbed on top of her. She cried and kicked to no avail.

"You know you want it, the way you flaunt that body of yours," he said. His voice was rough, as if he was trying to disguise it, but something in his inflection tugged at her memory. Did she know him?

With a huge effort she bucked up, slamming her head backward into his. He yelled out in pain and swayed to the side. She grabbed the stocking and pulled it off.

Phil Adams, a neighbor of her mother's. Claire gasped, shaking her head. Before she could utter a sound he backhanded her across her face.

He slammed her onto the bed again, this time with his hand at the back of her head. She gasped for air as he pressed her face into the mattress and settled himself between her legs....

The storm raged on outside. Claire curled into fetal position, caught in the never-ending nightmare of her past.

CHAPTER THIRTY-ONE

NOVEMBERS DOOM PLAYED at a subdued volume from the overhead speakers as Lucas surveyed the morning's customers. He shook his head at the irony of how his staff had started playing metal bands now that Claire had stopped coming by. He ached with missing her and Grey. And Toby. He kept hoping Grey would call to give him an update, but he'd not heard from either of them in almost two weeks.

He passed by the Granbys, saying good morning. Mr. Granby stopped him. "Lucas, our Lucy will be back this weekend. We'll be sure to bring her by to see you."

The last thing Lucas wanted was to be set up with anyone else. He pinned on a smile. "I'm sure you'll be happy to have her home."

"Oh, look," Mrs. Granby said as she turned her tablet to show them a picture of a pile of furry kittens. "Poor abandoned babies—they were left at the animal shelter. Don't you want one? I could just cuddle one up. They were found in a Dumpster, but all they need is a little TLC to make them right as rain."

"Not for me," Lucas said.

He'd learned his lesson about fixing everyone. He was done trying. What had it gotten him but failure and disappointment?

The bell on the door tinkled and Ramsey Carter hurried inside, looking a little worse for wear. He glanced around, biting his lip. He found Lucas and strode toward him.

Lucas sighed. Maybe the boy had come to pay his debt and prove he wasn't a complete loss. Not that Lucas had thought that about him, but the kid had sorely disappointed him.

He held out his hand to the young man. "Ramsey."

Ramsey shook his hand, glanced around and then motioned Lucas to a seating area away from the other customers.

"What's up, Ramsey?" Lucas asked when they were alone. The kid looked nervous, but being here for the first time since Lucas had let him go might explain that.

"I wasn't sure if I should come." He raised his hand, palm out. "Before you ask, I'm working on the money to pay you back. I don't have it all yet, but I will soon. I'm working up the street at The Bean Brew now. I've been there for a few weeks."

"Good for you." Lucas glanced at his watch. The delivery truck would be arriving soon. He should head to the stockroom to make sure he didn't miss them.

"I thought you should know…"

"What should I know? Out with it. I have things to do," Lucas said.

"That lady—you know, the one whose house I brought breakfast to that morning? Claire Murphy."

Lucas's pulse quickened. "Yes. What about her?"

"She's been hanging out over there, at The Brew," he said. "Kind of like she used to hang out here, working and stuff." He rubbed his hands along his pants. "I guess the two of you aren't seeing each other anymore."

"No, we're not," he said. "Is that what you wanted to tell me? Just that's she working from the coffee shop up the street? It really doesn't concern me, Ramsey."

"Well, no, actually, I wanted to tell you she isn't hanging out there anymore." He shrugged. "I know she's probably just gone somewhere else, probably because she saw me there and maybe that made her uncomfortable somehow. I don't know, but first she was there all the time, like clockwork, and then there was that last time when she just didn't seem right. Now she's not there anymore."

"What do you mean, she didn't seem right?" Lucas asked with sudden concern.

"My mom, she gets depressed, like majorly depressed. She's been hospitalized for it and she…" He exhaled in a noisy rush before continuing. "She swallowed a bunch of pills and I had to call an ambulance and they put her in the hospital. You know, the one for mental health patients."

Lucas stared at him. "Ramsey, that's why you took the money?"

He ducked his head. "Yes," he said. "She doesn't have health insurance. They wouldn't even pump her stomach without a down payment. I'm sorry, Lucas. I didn't know what else to do."

Okay, universe, so the lesson here is that I'm a heartless moron?

"But that isn't what I came here to tell you," Ramsey said. "Miss Murphy, she reminded me of my mom, the way she was acting. She looked exhausted and she couldn't seem to focus. And she was really down, down like I've seen my mom. I talked to her, but she insisted she was fine." He met Lucas's gaze. "She wasn't, though. I could tell. She was anything but okay. So, when she didn't show up the other day I started to get worried."

Lucas grabbed the boy's shoulder as he tried to control his panic. What was wrong with him? So he'd felt responsible for Claire and had walked away for his own self-preservation. But he didn't have to feel responsible to help her. All he had to do was love her. Wasn't that enough?

LUCAS'S HEART THUDDED as he pounded on Claire's door twenty minutes later. How had he let this happen again? The recent storms had blown debris all over her yard and porch. He tossed a large branch from across her door. She would have moved that if she'd come in or out that way.

He banged again. "Claire, it's Lucas. Please open up."

His phone vibrated in his pocket and he withdrew it to see if it was her. He'd left three voice mails on his way over, hoping she'd pick up. It wasn't her, so he shoved it back in his pocket and kept banging.

"Come on, Claire, please just let me know you're okay," he called.

Silence. That on its own was enough to scare him. If she were home and functioning, the house would be vibrating with her music and television. He couldn't contemplate what state she'd be in if she were alone in that silence.

He moved to the window and peered in, but he saw no trace of her. He checked each window, circling the house and calling out to her at intervals. He was going to feel like an idiot if she'd left town or was out shopping, but the churning in his gut propelled him.

What good had running for his own self-preservation done? If she'd come to any harm he'd be just as devastated. He never should have left her.

The wind and rain had driven a pile of branches and leaves against the sliding glass doors at the back of the house. He kicked the debris aside and then looked through the glass. Claire lay on her side, curled into a ball against the wall on the far side of the room.

Lucas knocked on the glass and called to her again, but she didn't move. He pulled on the door, but it was locked. With adrenaline pumping through him he scanned the yard for a rock as he raced to the toolshed.

A moment later he emerged with a rag and a hammer. He ran to a side window and smashed the glass without hesitation. He quickly used the rag to clean out the broken glass, and then undid the latch. He scrambled inside and rushed to where Claire lay unmoving.

His hands shook as he rolled her toward him and took her into his arms. "I'm here, sweetheart. Talk to me," he said.

She was warm and breathing, though apparently in the midst of a flashback. Her body was locked up tight, her breathing fast. He could kill whoever had done this to her.

"You're safe," he said. "Listen to my voice. Follow it back to me." He ran his hand across her hair as tears pricked his eyes. How long had she been like this?

"I'm going to take care of you and I'm never going to leave you again, Claire. Do you hear me? I need you. Grey needs you. Whatever happened to you is over. You survived. You're safe and I'm going to keep you that way."

His throat burned and tears spilled down his

cheeks. "I'm sorry I went away," he said. "If you can't do traditional therapy, then we'll find another way." He glanced at the book on the floor next to her. "We'll do whatever this book says for self-guided healing. I'm in. Whatever you need from me, sweetheart, you've got it. I promise, Claire. Please, please come back to me."

He glanced around the room, his mind racing through the checklist of techniques he'd learned for dealing with PTSD. He needed to ground her in the present somehow. "Hold on. I'll be right back."

Gently, he set her down, and then rummaged on the coffee table for the remote. He finally found it between the sofa cushions. He focused on his own breathing to calm himself as he pressed the buttons to turn on the television and stereo. Then he dug through the side table drawer until he found matches. It took several tries because his fingers were shaking so badly, but he lit the vanilla-scented candle on the table and brought it closer to Claire.

He scooped her into his arms again, cradling and rocking her. "Okay, the History Channel is doing a program on gadgets that changed the world," he said as he sat back. "And I have no idea what this band is, but it has lots of squealing electric guitar and screaming the way you like it. So, I need you to listen to what's here and now. To the TV and the stereo and my voice. Oh, and I lit that candle you like, the vanilla one. Can you smell it?"

Continuing to rock her, he stroked her arm. "Can

you feel me, Claire? I'm holding you and stroking your arm," he said and touched her cheek and the lines of her face seemed to ease slightly.

A buzzing sounded from nearby. He scanned the coffee table again and her phone vibrated beneath a stack of papers. He stretched to reach it. "Grey's calling you," he said, checking the display. "I didn't know he had a phone. Oh, it looks like you have several missed calls from him. I'll call him for you in a minute, okay? But first, open your eyes and let me know you hear me and that you're here with me."

He stroked her cheek and the tension had definitely left her features. She opened her eyes and he'd never seen a more beautiful sight. His throat swelled with relief and he let the tears fall as he hugged her close.

"That's my girl. Welcome back, sweetheart," he said.

She touched his cheek, frowning. "Lucas?"

"I'm sorry. I broke your window. Ramsey said he saw you and I was worried," he said.

She glanced around. "I don't..."

"It's okay. You had another episode."

She hugged herself and shook with grief. He held her close and let her cry. She was going to be okay. He wouldn't let her be anything else.

"I thought...I'd lost you," she said when she could catch her breath. "You and Grey."

"No, you haven't lost us."

"I'm sorry."

"For what? You haven't done anything wrong. I'm the one who's sorry. I don't know if you heard any of my mindless rambling, but I'm here with you and I'm never going to leave you again."

"I'm…sorry…I'm not…stronger," she said.

He wiped the tears from her cheek. "You're as strong as you need to be and you're not in this alone. I'm going to help you however you want. No therapists," he said and nodded toward the book. "I see you've been working on self-help and I'm all for that. I'm going to read that and anything else you want me to and we're going to memorize every technique. I think I'm getting better at this grounding-you-in-the-moment thing, huh?"

She nodded, smiled and cried all at the same time and he hugged her close again. "Just don't ever scare me like that again, okay?"

More tears soaked the front of his shirt. "I'll…try."

"One more thing," he said and she pulled back to look at him. "And I have to say this whether you agree to let me stick around or not, because I should have said this before. I love you, Claire. Please love me back and let me be with you and Grey. I love him, too, like he was my own."

She wrapped her arms around his neck. "You have to…stop making me cry."

"I'm sorry," he said, his heart thudding. "So, is that a yes or a no? She loves me, she loves me not?"

This time her smile reached her eyes. “She loves you.”

He took her mouth with one swift movement, capturing her lips and sealing the promise in her eyes with a kiss.

CHAPTER THIRTY-TWO

GREY COULDN'T CONTAIN his excitement as he stuffed his spaceman pajamas into his suitcase. He grabbed his History Channel game from the shelf and crammed it in, as well. Gram frowned at him from the doorway of the guestroom where he'd been staying.

"You're mixing your clean clothes with your dirty ones," she said.

Grey made a swiping motion with his hand. "I'll sort it out when I get home. I have to hurry. She's on the way."

"Don't forget your toothbrush," she said.

He straightened. "I thought I could leave it here. I have another one at home and I'll be back during the week, right? You promised me you'd teach me how to do a roast. We haven't done any beef recipes yet."

Smiling, Gram unfolded her arms. "Of course, and we haven't started on pies yet, either. We haven't nearly scratched the surface on your super chef lessons."

His anticipation bubbled up. "Can we do banana cream pie and pumpkin pie and apple pie and—"

"Yes, yes. Make me a list. Oh, wait, did you get your recipes and shopping list for your Very Special Meal?" she asked.

He dug in the front pocket of his book bag. "I have it all here. See?" He pointed to the writing at the top of the page. "Very Special Meal."

"You call me if you get into any trouble with that," she said. "Remember to stir the Alfredo sauce so it doesn't clump."

"I got it," he said, then paused as they heard the front door open and close. "She's here."

Shouldering his book bag, he zipped up his suitcase, and yanked it off the bed. He dragged the suitcase as fast as he could through the hallway. "Mom!" he called.

"I'm here, honey," Mom said from the living room.

Lucas stood beside her. Happiness burst through Grey. He dropped his bags and threw himself at his mom. She caught him and lifted him up, holding him close.

"I missed you so much, li—Grey," she said, laughing.

He pushed back to look at her. "It's okay if you want to call me little man. I was just angry that day. It doesn't bother me so much."

She planted a kiss on his cheek, and then put him down. "What has Gram been feeding you? You weigh a ton."

"You'll see. I'm going to make you a Very Special Meal, all by myself and you can't peek, because it's a surprise."

She glanced at Lucas, then back at Grey. "I guess I'm going to have to trust you on this."

"Don't worry," he said. "We can totally take it to go, though honestly it makes for a better sit-down meal. Or we can blast your music if you want to try to have dinner at home, but I can't make it until we go to the grocery store and get everything first."

"Why don't we play that by ear? I'll think about trying another proper dinner. I owe Lucas one. He really helped me out the other day," she said.

"He did? What did he do?"

She glanced again at Lucas and then stooped to meet Grey's gaze. "I had an episode, like the one I had with you in the car, only this one was even worse."

The ache in Grey's stomach returned. "Worse than in the car?"

She nodded and took his hand. "Why don't you come out on the porch with me for a little bit, while Lucas loads your things in the car? I want to talk to you about what happened to me and why I acted that way. Would that be okay?"

"Yes, of course. You can talk to me about anything. Does this mean you're going to get better?" he asked, glancing from his mom to Lucas.

Lucas smiled. "It means we're working together to fix it, but we may need your help, too."

A bit of hope began to sneak back into Grey's mood. He grabbed his mom's hand. "Yes, I want to help. Come tell me everything."

Claire glanced at Gram. "Would you like to join us, Mother?"

"I don't think you need me," she said. "It looks like you've got all the help you need."

Mom frowned, but let Grey pull her out to the porch. He scooted two of Gram's rockers closer together. "Here you go."

She took her time and explained a lot to him, all about what was wrong with her and how a bad man had hurt her, but she was working on a self-recovery program and also going to therapy. Bottom line was she was doing everything she could to get better.

"All of the loud music and running from place to place, I realize these are ways I've been avoiding coping with these issues I have. I know it makes you crazy." She laughed a kind of sad laugh. "I guess it makes me a little crazy, too. So, I'm going to try to wean myself off all the craziness and find healthy ways to cope."

Lucas had come back partway through her story, and now grinned. "I'll be happy to stick around and help in anyway I can." He leaned over and kissed Mom on the lips this time.

A giggle burst out of Grey. "I guess you two are officially back together."

Mom nodded. "I'm not letting him get away this time."

Another giggle escaped. Grey plopped himself in Lucas's lap. "I'll help with that one, too. I'll sit on him and not let him escape."

SUNDAY MORNING, A few weeks later, dawned sunny, but cold. Claire woke before her television-radio duo alarm sounded. She rolled over to the warm man in the bed beside her.

His beautiful smile greeted her. "Good morning."

"Good morning," she said and managed to not pull away, in spite of her morning breath, when he kissed her quite thoroughly.

She wriggled against him, loving the feel of him flush against her as he held her close and rested his hand on her bare bottom. "I slept."

"I see that. You're all rested and sparkly this morning."

"Sparkly?" she asked.

"Yes." He gestured with his free hand. "In your eyes."

"I see." She ran her finger down his chest. "I like sleeping with you."

"I like sleeping with you, too." He kissed her nose. "I'd love to make it a permanent arrangement."

"Soon," she said.

"Promise?"

"Yes."

"Say it again," he said. "I like to hear it, even if it's kind of a future yes and you're not actually saying yes to *the* question."

"Yes," she said again and giggled. "But you still have to officially ask *the* question when it's time."

"You let me know when you're ready and I'll sweep you off your feet with the asking part."

"I'm going to hold you to that," she said, smiling, because she couldn't seem to stop doing that this morning.

Her cell phone vibrated on the nightstand. She grabbed it and laughed. "It's Grey. He wants to know if Operation Best Breakfast Ever is a go."

Lucas's green eyes turned serious on her. "Sweetheart, that's completely your call. We do have Plan B. We can make this party mobile if you need to."

"Listen," she said.

Lucas paused with his head cocked. "What am I listening for? I don't hear anything."

"Exactly."

He glanced at the TV and stereo. "They didn't go off."

"I'm setting them later and later to see if I can go longer with—" she gestured "—the quiet."

"Good job."

"I've made Grey wait to make us the Best Breakfast Ever, because I wanted to be sure." They'd enjoyed a Very Special Meal prepared by Grey shortly after they'd brought him home from her mother's.

She texted Grey. Op BBE a go. J

"Coffee," she said.

His grin broadened. "I'm on it."

The beats of Evanescence drifted to them from the kitchen as they rolled out of bed. Lucas pulled on his jeans and nodded.

"Your son likes to cook to music," he said.

She listened for a minute. "I can totally live with that."

Ten minutes and several stolen kisses later, they strolled into the kitchen. Grey was whipping something in a bowl. He bobbed his head to the music.

"Good morning," he said.

"Good morning, little man," Claire said and hugged him.

Lucas rubbed his hands together. "How are we on the espresso? Do you need any last-minute tips or reminders?"

"It's under control," Grey said. "Mom gets the first cup. It's all set for you, Mom. Just flip the top switch."

Claire smiled as she moved to the area on the counter where they'd set up the espresso machine. A small mug sat beneath the nozzles and the indicator light shone. She flipped the switch. The machine hummed and Grey cheered.

He turned to her. "I have everything ready for Plan B. We can activate it at any time."

Claire's gaze swept from Grey to Lucas, then back. How fortunate was she to have such amazing love and support in her life? "That's really great," she said and stopped to turn off the machine and retrieve her coffee. "But I'd like us to have the Best Breakfast Ever right here at home."

"All right," Grey said. "You two have a seat and I'll have it up in no time."

"Don't you want some help, buddy?" Lucas asked.

Grey eyed him with trepidation. "Can you handle the toast?"

Lucas pressed his hand to his chest. "Yes, I can handle the toast."

"Okay, you can do that," Grey said.

"Me, too," Claire said. "I need a job."

Grey waved with his spatula. "There's a cantaloupe and some blueberries in the refrigerator."

"I'm on it," she said.

"Gram says presentation is everything."

She laughed. "Okay, I'll make it pretty."

Fifteen minutes and a cup or two of espresso later Claire sat at the table with her two favorite guys. Grey insisted on serving everything on pretty plates with the food arranged just so.

"Nice presentation," she said as he set her plate before her.

"Thanks, Grey," Lucas said. "This looks incredible."

Grey nodded as he took his seat. "I wanted to make it really good, so Mom would want to do this again."

She smiled and said, "I think we should maybe make this a regular thing."

"Yes!" Grey pumped his fist.

"I'm in," Lucas said. "But if we do this during the week can we bump it a little earlier? I have some classes starting next week."

"What classes?" Claire asked.

"Medical recertification," Lucas said as he ate a bite of his scrambled eggs.

"Aren't you going to keep The Coffee Stop?" Grey asked, his eyes wide.

Lucas shrugged. "Ramsey and Ken can run the place blindfolded. I'll still be around, but they don't really need me." He glanced at Claire and said, "I just thought I might look into doing the EMT thing again."

"Lucas, that's great," Claire said.

The TV and radio down the hall came on. A news broadcast and Ashes of Soma fought for airwaves with the sultry tones of Norah Jones emanating from the music center Grey had set up in the kitchen. Lucas and Grey continued eating as though nothing had changed.

"Excuse me a minute," Claire said as she pushed back her chair.

Lucas gave her a questioning look.

"I'll be right back," she said.

She padded down the hall to her bedroom. She switched off both the radio and the television set. She padded back to the kitchen, her guys, Norah's crooning and the Best Breakfast Ever. It was a small step, but she was satisfied that, for her, everything had changed.

* * * * *